Canvas

Jamaican Java Juice hissed and spit and dripped into the mug Tanya had given me ("World's Greatest Boss") with a satisfying final cough. I grabbed it and shuffled my poor, tired old middle-aged body into what passed as a home office. My leather-bound journal sat on the faux wood desk. I opened it to today's date and scribbled—a ritual, along with my coffee, before I dressed in the mornings or whenever the urge struck me.

Today was the end of my tenure as mayor, and maybe time to retire. I don't know. I had enjoyed a successful run in the city as a lawyer, a City Council member, a director on countless boards, and two terms as mayor, quickly drawing to a close. I used the journals to muse on upcoming events for that day and then made my sometimes-accurate predictions. Most of the time my scribbles were snarky. Anyone who had the temerity to pilfer the journal and compare the words with my actual doings would think I was schizophrenic. Thank God no one had ever even known they existed.

Suicidal and schizophrenic. Good name for a rock band.

I was out of a job and soon might be back on the political treadmill. I was considering a run for senate; it felt like a natural next step. What else was I going to do? I'm a fifty-eight-year-old spinster with no prospects, few friends but too many acquaintances, and a small retirement fund who just needs to keep busy.

HERITAGE
ART PARK SERIES

BOOK 2

Canvas

A NOVEL

KATHY WEYER

Chapter One

JEN CONRAD SLID INTO THE PEW NEXT TO ME AND PATTED MY ARM. "DID you see them?" She whispered and looked over her shoulder with a grin.

I had in fact noticed the cadre of over-the-top GQ-type young men that surrounded the white hearse, hands clasped in front of them like presidential secret service men, complete with wraparound sunglasses, bulging triceps visible through the expensive wool of their gray suits, and grim expressions. Despite my grief, that should have been my first tipoff.

Before Jen slipped in, I had been thinking about Iris's life, and about mine. How do you start another chapter after one slams shut? Iris's death meant the end of an era. Jen did it after Arthur died; where she had belonged she no longer fit. Iris had several chapters to her life as well, as we were about to learn. A chapter was to imminently close in my own life and I wasn't sure how I felt about it.

It's not as easy as turning a page, clearly. Once a huge part of your life is closed, what do you do, and where do you belong? The sheer number of people honoring Iris made me think about my own reputation. Who would care?

Jen adjusted herself and faced forward. Quietly, she said, "Renee, I can't believe she's gone."

"I hear ya," I said. "It's like somebody turned out the lights."

Jen sang under her breath: "The party's over . . ."

Iris Anderson had been an extraordinary influence on me. She was my people-whisperer and imparted wise advice: how to respond, how to approach people for a favor, and even how to say no without insulting some-one. I often failed in that, but Iris would then go behind me quietly and politely and clean things up. She was my mentor, my friend, and my guiding

1

star. I'm not sure I'd be where I am if it weren't for Iris's influence. My term as mayor was up soon, and I had not yet talked to her about my plans, or lack of them; I had been too busy. Damn.

Every pew was full, standing room only, admirers and mourners and lookie-loos waiting to pay their respects to the woman who had kept Old Society alive, the philanthropist who gave more than had been publicized, and who had been a very large part of our lives for the past decade. What the rest of the world didn't know was what kind of mischief she would gleefully get into and then bat her eyelashes when the shit hit the fan.

A high-pitched screech from the back of the church, a continuing teeth-jarring blast that bounced off the concrete walls and made my ass lift off the wooden pew by a good two inches, blasted into the quiet, sacrosanct, Catholic church. Jen jumped beside me. Eight men clad in tartan kilts marched up the aisle with screeching bagpipes, a signal that this was not your ordinary adieu. "Oooh, look, the tassels on their socks are swinging in time with the music," a woman behind us whispered loudly.

"Wonder what else is swinging," I whispered to Jen.

Her shoulders shook and I snorted. I remembered her father's funeral just six months earlier when we almost lost our composure attempting to stifle our laughter through the ceremony that had to have been unbearable for her.

This is how we handle pain. We've done it for over fifty years.

The pipes faded into a low, sad moan. Eight pair of highly polished shoes marched up the aisle in perfect cadence, their steps echoing off the stone walls in otherwise respectful silence, as Iris came down the aisle for the last time in a gleaming white coffin covered with blue Irises. The sexy pallbearers held Iris's coffin on their broad shoulders. Their white collars and Windsor-knotted tartan ties showed under their vests and cut-off shirts, which rose to show off eight sets of tanned, hairless, impressive abs.

Jen lowered her head and put her hand over her eyes. I stared, grinning at the gorgeous men with grim faces bearing our friend to meet her maker. My nethers were stirred, which was exactly what Iris intended.

Leave it to Iris to have Chippendales escort her to the pearly gates.

During the hour-long service, strangers from as far away as Paris and Munich spoke about Iris. We learned things about her that would have shocked us if we didn't appreciate Iris in full. She looked like Miss Marple, but she was a Bond Girl at heart.

A lone trumpet began with *Summertime,* played slowly and painfully in the quiet of the packed stone church; it had its intent. Jen and I knew better than to expect more of the sob stuff. Iris thought there was a time for sadness, but it was limited. This was it. We both knew the switch could be flipped any second.

We sat through the usual stern and somber words, the rituals, and the blessings, a few stories, a few laughs. Just when we thought the priest would excuse us, a Dixieland band appeared from behind the organ and began to march to *Happy Days are Here Again* New Orleans style. "There it is . . ." Jen muttered. "I wondered if she had thought about *Ding Dong the Witch is Dead* . . . ." We laughed out loud as the loud, happy little New Orleans band, complete with colored beads, makeup, and big hats, danced by us, knees high, playing with gusto.

She conducted our behavior from the grave, from appropriately sad to joyfulness.

Go forth and have fun. You've mourned me. Now go.

We were the first to arrive at Heritage Park for the Celebration of Life. Jade Robinson, Iris's young, and definitely weird, companion for the past year, arrived with us. The three of us marched up the cobblestone path that led to the six Victorian houses and the greenbelt behind them. Plenty of room for a party.

"Was it all right?" Jade asked quietly.

Jen and I looked at each other, our breathing somewhat labored as our middle-aged bodies tried to keep up with the twenty-something on some-what of an incline. "Was it all right?" I breathed. "It was perfect! Iris would have loved it. Boffo."

"I didn't do it. Iris left the details to the funeral home. She left instructions about a celebration here at the park and the party at her house after. All I did was call the caterers. They did it all to Iris's wishes." Her red eyes and sniffles belied her tough-chick persona. I admired the jade bracelet on her arm that Iris had given her for Christmas a few weeks ago, and I took notice of the missing piercing in her eyebrow and the puce green hair. The sleeves on her jacket covered the tats.

"Really? How do you suppose *that* conversation went?" I asked Jen, breathing a bit too hard.

Jen's voice warbled into a high-pitched, highly exaggerated old lady voice. "Helloooo? I'd like to arrange my funeral . . . it must be *outrageous*. I'd like you to hire Chippendale dancers, dress them in exquisite gray wool suits and matching tartan ties. They must wear wraparound sunglasses and appear to be secret service boys."

"Oh, and bagpipes, with men wearing kilts the *traditional* way," I added, and turned to Jade. " . . . then Iris gave them that look, you know, the one Iris gave you when you complained about something she had asked you to do."

Jade cracked a shy smile—unusual for her.

"What did you make of the old guy's eulogy? What was his name?" Jen asked.

I shrugged. "It sounded like they worked together in the resistance during the war. Was she involved?"

Jen laughed, a sort of rumble that ran through her body. "I wouldn't be surprised." She stopped for a moment. "While we're waiting for things to start, I think I'll just pop into the shop for a moment and check on things. I'll catch up with you." She headed toward Stitches, the first shop in this art park, a few yards away.

While Jade checked with the caterers and did her thing, I walked around the complex, admiring our work. My legacy.

What had been a historical village of six houses from the early years of San Diego—the living quarters of the major players in early city development—had fallen into disrepair over the past five years. They had been used as bed and breakfasts but finally closed; old and used up. They sat, boarded up and tired, on the beautiful property for years. I could hear them groan in disappointment at the end of their glorious era.

I could relate.

As mayor, I had fought like a Marine to keep the structures, repair them, and turn the entire complex into an art park for local artisans—something we sorely missed in this town. Thanks to Iris's money and that of other cultural philanthropists, we could accumulate the funds needed to repair and renovate all six houses back to their former glory.

It. Was. Glorious.

We used old photographs and tasked students at the university to research architectural and decorative histories. The landscapers planted shrubs, hanging gardens, and airy ferns between the bricked-in walkways, using historical horticulturists to advise and support their efforts. The century-old coral tree stood at the peak of the horseshoe and provided shade for the benches surrounding it.

Jen had taken the first house, turned it into a shop for needlework enthusiasts, and called it Stitches. So far hers was the only shop open, but we were vetting more applicants. I had said two years ago that I would sponsor an artist myself to take a shop, and the time was closing in to fulfill that commitment.

I came out of my reverie when I noticed hordes of mourners began to lumber up the inclined pathway. I scooted back behind Stitches to the large green grassy area and stopped, gobsmacked.

Large white tents covered the greenbelt; each tent overflowed with fresh flowers. Minions had transported the arrangements from the church, but the size and sheer number was heart-stopping in the utter devotion displayed for Iris. It looked like a scene out of a 1920-era English countryside cricket/tea party *plein aire*, maybe a Downton Abbey cricket match.

Silver trays held elegant canapes and bite-sized cakes. Matching buckets held bottles of champagne on tables draped in light blue (Iris blue?) tablecloths, ready for a professional photographer for *Architectural Digest* or *Home and Garden*. The secret service-types stood ready to refresh an empty flute or add a bit to a bone china plate. The bagpipers, still in their kilts and tams, worked their way through the crowd with trays of canapes. No paper or plastic for Iris. Iris wanted a blast of a goodbye party. What Iris wanted Iris got.

And this is exactly what I had envisioned for the park: elegance under a Southern California sun. A happy place. A peaceful place. A creative place.

I wonder how much these guys are being paid. They all look so happy. Wonder if there is a position open for a middle-aged, burned out old politician.

"God, what a production!" Jen said from behind me. "Isn't it fabulous?" I turned to find Jen with her niece Tricia and a stranger.

"Trish!" I said and gave her a hug. I had known her since she was a baby. She beamed. "Meet my husband, Adam Pechek." She turned to him with complete adoration.

It took everything I had not to gasp. Tricia had just graduated from Harvard—she was in her late twenties. He looked to be older than even I, no spring chicken at 58. Tall, very thin, he wore white linen pants and an overshirt with no collar made of very thin white gauze, a thin leather rope around his brown but wrinkled neck, and sandals; he looked like a male model for the Baby Boomer set. His long white hair, brushed straight back and gathered into a leather strap at the back, came just past his shoulders. His full beard and moustache rounded out the old-world, casual European look. His bright blue eyes made me think of the Mediterranean. I wonder what Tricia's mother's reaction had been when she first laid eyes on her son-in-law. Egads.

He bowed a little and said, "Your Honor."

"Please, it's Renee, and I'm happy to meet you. I've not heard a word about you," I teased, and winked at Tricia.

He smiled. "I'm best kept under wraps." He held my hand in both of his, warm and welcoming. His voice reminded me of cafe au lait, creamy and comforting, a European background, no doubt, and his manners came straight out of what I assumed to be a formal boarding school.

"Adam is an artist," Tricia said. "I thought you two should talk."

"Oh! Do you know about the art park?" I asked.

"Yes, we were married right over there." He pointed his nose over my shoulder and finally smiled, showing yellowing teeth. Tricia grinned at his side like a lovestruck teenager.

"Ah, yes, my invitation must have gotten lost in the mail," I said with not a small degree of sarcasm. Jen guffawed.

"Oh?" He looked over at Tricia, his eyebrows raised in question.

"Mom." Tricia said, with a what-can-you-do shrug.

"Aha." He turned back to me. "A missed opportunity." He smiled.

Oh, a charmer. *Danger Will Robinson.*

The fact that he was probably older than his mother-in-law made me happy. Jen's sister Maggie was a world-class bitch, and Adam could tell her to go screw herself without it immediately registering.

I had not been invited to her daughter's wedding; clearly I was not considered upper crust. I may have been acceptable as mayor, but socially I was on the bottom rung, which was fine with me. Maggie wasn't in my orbit, either.

As more and more mourners came to the party, I slipped into my familiar schmoozing routine, hopping from group to group. Because it was relatively new, I happily talked about the art park and its future. I wanted it to succeed. Badly. But then I reigned myself in. This was about Iris. And no one knew about my running for senate—yet.

Chapter Two

JAMAICAN JAVA JUICE HISSED AND SPIT AND DRIPPED INTO THE MUG TANYA had given me ("World's Greatest Boss") with a satisfying final cough. I grabbed it and shuffled my poor and tired old middle-aged body into what passed as a home office. My leather-bound journal sat on the faux wood desk. I opened it to today's date and scribbled; a ritual, along with my coffee, before I dressed in the mornings or whenever the urge struck me. It seemed to help clear my brain, although to read the words you would think I was ready to commit hari-kari.

Today was the end of my tenure as Mayor, and maybe time to retire. I don't know. I had enjoyed a successful run in the city as a lawyer, a city council member, a director on countless boards, and two terms as mayor, quickly drawing to a close. I used the journals to house my thoughts, concerns, subterfuge and suspicions, running down what I had done the day before and my reactions—my real reactions, no matter how I conducted myself in front of the cameras. I mused on upcoming events for that day—what I called Big Deals—and then I made my sometimes-accurate predictions. Most of the time my scribbles were snarky. Anyone who had the temerity to pilfer the journal and compare the words with my actual doings would think I was schizophrenic. Thank God no one had ever even known they existed.

Suicidal and schizophrenic. Good name for a rock band.

I was out of a job and soon might be back on the political treadmill. I was considering a run for senate; it felt like a natural next step. What else was I going to do? A fifty-eight-year-old spinster with no prospects, few friends but too many acquaintances, and a small retirement fund just needed to keep busy.

Iris's funeral had put me in a reflective mood. The ceremony, while loosely following social and religious conventions, was Iris's last production. Iris had been beloved, a visible patron of the arts, the downtrodden, and the community in general. At ninety-something, she died in her bed surrounded by her books and her music. Not too bad a deal. Her funeral was huge and filled with tributes and constant signs of grief and loss balanced by some laughter and interesting, sometimes shocking, stories.

Because I was the mayor, I was recognizable, but I'd bet everything I had that my send-off would be nothing like what I just witnessed. I took a deep breath, a draw from the mug, picked up my green pen, and printed in big, screaming block letters:

WHAT DOES IT TAKE TO KNOW SOMEONE?

WHAT DOES IT TAKE FOR SOMEONE TO KNOW ME?

WHAT WILL THEY SAY ABOUT ME AT MY FUNERAL?

WHO WOULD CARE?

"Gah . . ." I said as I closed the book. "Sorry loser."

My cell trilled with a text message:

Back straight, chin up, boobs out.

Jen Conrad, my oldest friend, delivered the message her mother repeatedly gave us as adolescents so we would carry ourselves with comportment. I suspect the woman whom I called Mother Superior had us programmed as debutante material.

Didn't turn out that way.

Instead of the word boobs, of course, she said chest, but we had changed it years ago with our first Playtex lift-and-separate bras. I laughed out loud. Ron Walker, who was taking my place as mayor, sauntered into the office and sidled into the leather visitor's chair across from me. "What's so funny?"

"Hard to explain," I said. "Just a friend wishing me well. Jen," I explained, looking up. He smiled and produced a sexy dimple.

Stop it.

My desk was clean for the first time in eight years. Not one single solitary thing sat on the glittering, polished desktop except the industrial phone, with every red light blinking. My usual chaos and messy desktop—gone. It made me want to bite my fingernails again.

The inauguration ceremony was not for three hours yet. I had come in as usual at 8:00 even though there was not much to do. The sage green walls held no notes or posters, just original artwork that had hung in the office from various administrations. The oak bookcases were naked, having been stripped of personal awards and knickknacks that had accrued over the years, sent home earlier by a professional mover. Your tax dollars at work.

The bonsai tree received from the mayor of our sister city in Japan sat on top of a cardboard box on the credenza, along with the few personal possessions from desk drawers, all neatly packed by Tanya.

I would have killed that tree within a week; I killed living things. Tanya had been the mother to it, the caretaker, the attention giver. And now it was mine.

Don't let the door hit you on the way out . . .

"What are you going to do now, Renee?" Ron asked, with his hands clasped in his lap. I noticed his newly trimmed, tinged-with-a-hint-of-gray hair and mustache. His blue eyes matched the blue in his tie and gave him an athletic, healthy visage, and I allowed myself a hint of, what . . . attraction? Notice?

Stop it, you old ass.

"I am opening up an art store at Heritage Art Park." I said, though he should already have known this. The art park had been my focus over the past three years. I saw no need to advertise my plans to run for senate; sort of like announcing your engagement at someone else's wedding. This was his day. I can be sensitive like that.

He nodded. "Right. Do you have someone in mind to be the artist-in-residence?" He cocked his head a bit, a habit he had as a former cop, I'm guessing to get away from the two-way radio that had always perched on his shoulder.

What, you don't think I could do it myself?

Before I could answer, the City Attorney came in with reams of paperwork. We got to work making the formal transition recorded for history, then left for the ceremony and a celebratory lunch for city employees and guests.

It all happened too fast. Ron took the oath of office, we posed for pictures, made a few speeches, and had lunch. *Whoosh.* Once the reporters departed, we were once again left in the office. This time Ron was behind the desk and I was the visitor. I forced my shoulders to drop a few inches, trying to drop the sense of responsibility that stuck to me like second skin. I handed over my keys, security codes, cell phone, gas cards, and other paraphernalia that belonged to the city. I bought the city car originally issued to me eight years ago; the city had issued Ron a new car with all the bells and whistles. I got the leftovers.

Et voilà—things change. I was in the twilight zone at this point.

We reviewed projects, some big, some small, and some confidential. I handed over the last of the files and notes and discussed the various positions of the city council members and donors. He knew how I felt on most issues and agreed with me, committing to carry on as programmed. It was all very businesslike, very official.

I sat back. "So . . . how do you feel?" I asked him with a smile.

"Ready to fill some big shoes." He smiled back. "I'm wondering if you'd like to be on a special taskforce I'm forming." He leaned back in the fat leather chair that had been mine, put his left elbow on the arm and his index finger over his mustache. His eyes narrowed.

"Taskforce?"

He nodded. "The problem of the homeless. I'm starting a task force to find ways to deal with it, the mentally challenged, and the drug addicted, and get them off the streets."

"Isn't jail good enough?" It was a joke, but that was my philosophy. Druggies and crooks (because most druggies are crooks) belong in jail.

His voice dropped. "You can't believe that."

I turned my head to the side; not sure I had heard correctly.

"Ron, people who commit crimes belong in jail."

"Not necessarily."

"You mean *rehab*? The city will pay for these people to go through *rehab*? No way." I couldn't believe we were having this discussion.

"Maybe not traditional rehab. Maybe there is another way."

"And what might that be?" I asked with more tinge in my voice than I had intended. I sounded like Jen's sister Maggie. God help me.

"I don't know yet. That's what the taskforce is for." His eyes bored into mine.

Well, shit. Giving these losers another chance to screw it up at taxpayers' expense was not the solution, but this was no longer my problem.

I stood. "I wish you luck on it."

He rose from the chair. The familiar squeak gave me a toothache. "Thank you."

And that was the end my term as mayor.

On my way out, I left the bonsai tree on the ledge in Tanya's new office. She was now Ron's chief of staff, giving an interview with a journalist in the conference room. She never saw me leave.

I plopped into the driver's seat and started up the engine of what was now my car, not the city's. What to do, what to do? I had sort of thought friends would arrange something for me this afternoon, so I had left my calendar clear. Colossal mistake.

Two workmen were standing by to paint over my name on the concrete wall in the parking structure. Jesus, the body's not even cold yet.

I went home, left the sad little box in the downstairs bedroom I used as my office, and flopped on my bed. Shit. The house was so quiet. Now what?

Need a friend? Get a dog.

Chapter Three

"HOW DOES IT FEEL?" JEN ASKED OUT OF THE BLUE. I HAD DROPPED BY at drink time out of sheer restlessness. We had already gone through our own mourning process over Iris and now we were determined to celebrate her life.

Jen popped a bottle of champagne, and we shook off our shoes and settled in. She had been at the inauguration lunch, then headed out quickly back to her shop. Ron had asked her to be his chief of staff last year; she thought about it for a sliver of time and decided it really wasn't her scene. She stuck with Stitches, so Tanya took the position, as I had hoped from the beginning. I was happy for all three of them.

Jen's puppies, Sticks and Stitches, followed us everywhere. Sticks jumped up and settled in beside me. I was not big on dogs and his closeness made me a little nervous, but what the hell. The sound of the champagne cork exploding made him jump a little. Should be used to it by now. Jen and I had shared quite a few since they had come into her life a year ago.

"What's your plan?" I knew what was on her mind, and I was in for a world of hurt. After almost fifty years of friendship, I couldn't get much past her. I gulped some fizziness.

"Why, whatever do you mean???" I bat my eyelashes.

She looked at me like I was the village idiot. "Well, let's see, Miz Renee." She held up one finger. "You are no longer the mayor after two terms, only the third female in history to do it." Second finger. "Ron Walker, the man you've been pining over for the past eight years, now has your job." Third finger. "I am sure your inbox is full of invitations, but I am also sure," she took a sip, "that your calendar is clear."

"How do you know that?" I asked, not surprised she nailed it so completely, right down to the empty calendar. My index finger ran over the raised scar, a rough ridge at the back of my right ear, a habit from years ago that reminded me where I came from.

"It's who you are. As successful as you were as mayor, you don't really like the social aspect of things, so I'm guessing you haven't accepted any invitations to speak, nor have you joined any boards, to which," she took another sip (this intrusion into her dialogue always irked me), "I know for a fact you've been invited." She skipped a beat. "Plus, your incessant whining about Ron Walker over the years has made me a little ill." She chuckled. "So, what's your next step?"

I shrugged. "Run for senate."

She cocked her head as though she may not have heard me right. "I thought you were tired of the political world."

"It's two years away, but that's enough time to start a campaign and begin making plans."

"Are you really going to run?"

I shrugged. "I guess so."

"You guess so?" She stared at me through slits, a sign she was seriously considering throttling me. "You *guess* so?" Again, the third-degree stare. She placed her flute carefully on the side table, laced her hands between her knees, leaned forward, and considered her next words. "You hate the social aspect of politics. All you really want to do is sit quietly and come up with ideas, then delegate teams to make those ideas work. Schmoozing is not your thing."

"How is Mother Superior?" I asked, more to change the subject than out of real interest.

She shrugged and leaned back. "Going downhill fast. This cancer deal is just brutal, but she's kept her independence and is conducting her final act just as you would expect." Jen's mother had been diagnosed with breast cancer for the second time, and Jen and her sister Maggie were the support system.

We sat in silence for a bit. Sticks snuggled even closer, and I inched as far into the arm of the couch as I could.

"Do you ever miss your old life?" I asked Jen. "You know, the parties, the committees, the fundraisers . . ." *The things that formed a life . . .*

Jen and I are so different—had been from the day we met; her yin to my yang. We embraced different priorities. Jen is my pseudo-sister, my confidante, my better half. My reliance on her scares me from time to time. Not a week goes by that we don't connect in one way or another. She knows about my mother, about Eddie, about everything. Almost.

But to look at us . . . well, it was obvious. Just like her mother, she was raised to be proper, well dressed, well mannered, coiffed, be-jeweled, and fashion trendy. Now she is more relaxed. Her role of socialite ended when Arthur died, and she's put on a few pounds and cut her hair spiky short. She wears caftans and Birkenstocks, for God's sake.

And me? I am just shlumpy ole me. Sort of round, I wear nothing but pantsuits, no jewelry, and my hair is a frizzy helmet. I gave up the makeup routine years ago.

Jen had had a life of her own that I was not part of: the socialite while I was the politician, the do-gooder while I slammed the brakes on various projects and ideas. We are polar opposites in politics, in our assessment of people, and in how we approach life. The Beauty and the Beast. But we've saved each other more than once.

"You mean the things you used to make fun of me for doing?" She grinned and shrugged. "It was my life. I supported Arthur, and whatever I could do in the community to help him, I did."

"But do you *miss* it?"

She thought for a moment. "I miss Arthur. He was so easygoing and so much fun. That's what I miss. The partnership." She took a sip. "I had to reinvent my life, and I'm pretty happy with it, but if I could have Arthur back . . ."

I shook my head. "Your husband was an incredible man, and you were lucky to have him. Now you have Bruce."

"Well, that's . . ."—sip. "Bruce is a really nice guy, and part of my life, but he's no Arthur."

"Maybe he doesn't have to be another Arthur."

She nodded. "He's awfully sweet and very good to me. I'll never marry again, but that doesn't mean I'm celibate for the rest of my life. But what about Ron?" she asked.

"What about Ron?" My heart flipped a little.

She stared and cocked her head.

"We have fundamental differences in the social agenda," I continued.

"Fundamental differences in the social agenda . . . what, he's gay?"

"No, he's not gay. Jesus, Jen."

"Well, what then? You've had a crush on him for a long time."

I shrugged. "Guess I didn't know him as well as I thought I did." I recalled our conversation; it made the small of my back itch. "Besides, the current mayor hooking up with the past mayor who, by the way, he used to work for, is political suicide."

"Well, since neither one of us had kids and we are alone, I guess we should make a pact to go off to the Daisy Hill Puppy Farm together when the time comes." She smiled. "With rockers on the porch."

"Consider this a pinky swear," I said, pointing my little finger out while I continued to sip.

She grumbled a little. "I guess we all have to reinvent ourselves. Iris did it, given what we heard in the church. Now that we are living longer, it's not an option anymore to just stop what we are doing and die. Even you."

I sighed. "My second act and all that. I thought I saw how it was going to go, but I was wrong."

When you are alone, you create the impossibly perfect world. I'd had a delusion of me and Ron sailing off into the sunset without any provocation. Now my vision is taking over Washington, crashing all the old white men's cliques, making policy for the nation. Katharine Hepburn in the social media age.

"Yeah, I had that same thought, too." Arthur's death had hit her hard. I watched as her face blanched for a moment and real pain showed up in her eyes. "But we move on. What's on your agenda tomorrow?"

"Meeting Tricia's husband at the park tomorrow. Time to make the art store happen. I've made the commitment. He may be the answer. What do you think of him?"

Sip . . . "A bit standoffish, but elegant, in his own way. I'd sure like to have been a fly on the wall when they met. Odd pairing." Her eyes narrowed. Tricia was Jen's niece, her sister Maggie's daughter, and Tricia seemed happier to be with Jen than with her own mother. Can't say as I blame her.

"Hmmm. What about your day tomorrow?"

"Mammogram."

"Ugh."

Chapter Four

As promised, I went to Heritage Park to meet with Adam Pechek. I lumbered up the wide, curved cobblestone pathway again and groaned inwardly as Suzanne Finch's distinctive high-pitched almost-southern voice came from behind me. She was, unfortunately, the leasing agent for the art park. Not because she was good, which admittedly she was, but because she donated some of her commission into a special fund to support artists should they need help with rent from time to time. She was exiting a blue house across the way, and I spied several people examining its exterior. I hoped they were prospective tenants—it would be huge kudos if we were to fill it up quickly.

"Yoooo-hooooo!"

Damn. She'd spotted me. Her charm bracelet made such a racket she could never sneak up on anyone. Her big blonde hair and bright red suit headed toward me, a train off its rails. I thought of her as a walking Barbie doll: makeup perfect, shoes matched bag and tiny little belt, and her hair never moved. It didn't fit that her mannerisms were not fluid but harsh and forced, as though she had taken in too much caffeine; or maybe she was a meth addict.

"Ms. Mayor, how nice to see you. Ron is really looking forward to starting this new chapter in his life." Suzanne's voice had a hint of ownership over Ron, which made me ice over. Before I could respond, she said, "Yes, just this morning at breakfast he was telling me how excited he was. He has lots of plans . . ."

"That's exactly what he should be doing," I said, with more force than I needed to.

Wait. Breakfast?

Her left hand came up and waved in front of the houses. "Which house do you like? We can sign the docs today. No references needed!"

"Suzanne . . ."

"You can have any house but the Carlisle house." She flipped her head and dazzled me with a bleached-tooth smile. That, the noise of that bracelet, and her perfume almost knocked me out.

Oh, she was good. The Carlisle was my favorite; had been since the beginning, and she knew it.

"Well, that's that, isn't it? If it were available, I'd take it in a heartbeat. Let me think about the others, but that's the one I had plans for," I said, with my f-you grin.

"Oh, too bad," she pouted. "Well, I'll certainly let you know if it becomes available."

We were both aware that no one had expressed interest in the house. She was just hooking me on the line. I'd be reeled in sooner rather than later. I would take it, find someone to run it (Adam?), and maybe get involved in the business. This was a brilliant place to come to work every day. It was near the house, an easy commute, something to occupy myself while running a campaign. I might even use the upstairs rooms for campaign headquarters.

"You do that, Suzanne." We smiled at the game we were playing, and she negotiated the cobblestones with her spiked heels as she trudged back down the walkway, that damn bracelet accenting her every step.

When she disappeared, I made my way to the Carlisle house and opened the front door with my contraband key.

I stopped into the living room; a bit stunned by what I had picked up.

Ron and Suzanne? No. It couldn't be. No.

I shook it off and toured the house once again, this time with an eye toward reality. The living room, dining room and parlor, painted white, were sizeable rooms, well lit, and open. Oak floors and sheer curtains kept the atmosphere light and airy, and the big selling point was the huge fireplace that stood on the far wall of the parlor.

The dining room held a built-in breakfront with leaded glass cupboard doors and a dozen flat drawers designed for linens and silverware, perfect for art supplies. The enormous kitchen had black-and-white flooring, black Victorian-faced modern appliances, and windows that came right out of an old advertisement from *Colliers Magazine* circa 1921.

A voice echoed from the entrance hall. "Oh, this will do very nicely." Once again, I was struck by Adam's years, and took a deep breath. We chatted a bit about lighting and space, toured the lower level and then ascended a wooden staircase that creaked like in a spooky movie scene. The second floor held four bedrooms, empty except for radiators and sheer curtains. The largest of the bedrooms was perfect for art classes; we could rent the others to individual painters as studios or for a special showing; a place to escape and be surrounded by others of similar temperament. Loners, maybe.

Does that include me?

You bet your ass it does. And, I suspect, him.

"So, what are your plans for this establishment?" Adam asked as we finished up and stood in the small, brick-paved patio area. He relaxed against the doorjamb, hands in pockets, ankles crossed.

"I have none."

One eyebrow shot toward his hairline. "So, your plan is to jump in?"

My chin went up. "No, my plan was to sponsor an artist and let *them* jump in."

"Ah, I see. A benefactor of sorts." He stared off into the wisteria that separated this house from the next. The scent of the purple blooms wafted over us in the breeze; a few coins clinked in his pocket as he mused.

"Of sorts. I started this art park. It was my idea, and I feel an obligation to contribute to it and support the cause, as they say." I waited a beat, then confessed, "I have no idea where I'm heading or what I'm doing, so if I can just sponsor it and not get involved, it's probably best."

"Not get involved? Perhaps you are distancing yourself from life itself?" His tone was teasing, but I recognized the truth when I heard it.

What has Tricia told him?

"Possibly." I stared into those blue eyes. The best defense is a good offense.

He missed a beat and lowered his voice. "I'm not interested in a partner-ship with someone who's not willing to take part."

"Now, hold on . . ."

He pushed himself away from the door and took his hands out of his pockets, raising them in supplication. "Apologies. Sometimes my mouth works faster than my manners. Let me restate." He took a deep breath and contemplated his next sentence. "What I mean is, if we are to work together, I don't want to carry the entire load."

"What do you propose?"

"I'm willing to teach classes and keep the place up in exchange for a place to use as my studio and sell my pieces. You own the place and pay the bills and manage the business. My name doesn't get associated with the shop; it's all yours."

"So, a silent partner, I suppose."

"If you so wish to categorize it." He bowed a little and looked at the brick, then his head raised. "But I will make suggestions as to improvements before we get started."

"All right. Can you guide me as to what supplies to buy and where to buy them?"

He nodded. "I'll work up an estimate for supplies and improvements and get it over to you."

I took a deep breath. "Let me understand this. You want no salary, no profit sharing, just the materials and the space to work, and you will manage the operations of the shop, correct? No rental payment or salary?"

His eyes wandered to his left, then over my head to the right, then focused on me. "Yes, and no liability. An unpaid employee, if you will, a vol-unteer with benefits." A slight smile.

What's not to love about this proposal? I was willing to pay the rent anyway.

I took a beat, and, as he expected, made the commitment. "Then you're on. But I'll need a budget before we begin."

"Of course, dear lady." We shook on it.

As much as I hated to do it, I called Suzanne and told her I wanted the Carlisle house. She didn't even try to tell me I'd have to fight for it. She knew better.

She trundled over to the park within ten minutes of my call with the lease all filled out.

I signed it and gave her a check for the deposit, while Adam looked on.

"Ronny will be so excited," she said.

"Ronny?" Adam asked.

"Oh, yes, our new mayor." She turned to me. "He was telling me just the other day that you were meant to do this, and he hoped you'd sign a lease soon. He's in your corner, you know."

"Is he, now?" She had no idea how our relationship had worked or might work. Neither did I, for that matter.

She turned to Adam. "Well, I call him Ronny. He's kind of cute, isn't he?" She winked at me.

Adam intercepted with incredible finesse: "Well, he wouldn't appeal to me, but . . ." and smiled at us both.

"Thank you, Suzanne," I said in my dismissive voice.

"Allow me to walk you to your car," Adam said, with a dash of gallantry, extending an arm to Suzanne. They left me on the porch of my new store. The word "Canvas" flitted across my brain, and my guts told me the name fit. As I left, I took in the historic village and reveled in how well it had turned out. So far, Jen's was the only shop open, but we had a few interested people being vetted. I had made a public commitment to sponsor an artist to take a shop.

And now I was making it happen. Two down, four to go.

Time to do some housekeeping—literally. I had ignored my house for years, and if I were to spend more time at home, I needed to spiff it up and get myself organized. The downstairs bedroom had become my office, very basic with a cheap desk and thrift-store file cabinets and shelves. The desk held an old tower computer and not much else.

The second bedroom upstairs was the room where I put my art things—not that I did much, but there was an easel, drop cloth, paints, brushes, and palettes. I sometimes indulged in haphazard creative time, and if I were honest, I admitted this room was much more comfortable than my office. Unfinished artwork sat glaring at me, unprofessional and abandoned. *Amateur.* I knew I could do better, but never took the time to prove it. There was an old couch against a bare wall, and I often went in that room to read late at night when I couldn't sleep. It was comforting, the smell of paint and turpentine. I decided it was time to get my shit together and possibly decorate. I had an incredible amount of unused vacation pay that burned a hole in my checking account.

On a whim, I went to the cell phone place and got a spiffy new smartphone, along with a plan that would last forever. They offered a second phone and phone line for free, so I decided that one would be for campaign business and one for personal use.

I bought a new expensive top-of-the-line computer I had no business buying.

Why not?

I gathered paint chips, wallpaper samples, and fabrics to redecorate my office, but quickly grew overwhelmed and disinterested. Bah. The problem was I didn't have a vision. No clue. After a nap, I drove to the bank, took out my keys, signed into the safe deposit box area, and followed the manager into the vault.

Move it along, honey. We all have things to do today. Ha. Ha.

She slipped her key into one slot; I slid mine in to the other, and *voilà*, the door opened to reveal a steel box. She placed it on the table and discreetly left the room. Twenty-two leather-bound journals of the same size but varying colors popped into view, labeled with the month and year. The odor of worn leather and time smacked me in the face, and I couldn't help but grin.

My journals contained my life from the age of ten. My world was recorded entirely within those books. I held nothing back, revealing my plans, my hopes and my dreams, my hates, my fears. Everything I was thinking or fearing got scribbled into those books and dropped in this box when finished. When I became involved in politics, I rented this box and hid away the finished books. The current journal was always with me, zipped into its own secure pocket in the briefcase that never left my side. Tanya knew better than to touch the case. Since I didn't carry a purse, it was deemed just as private. When I was in my office, it was locked in the lower drawer. When I was at an event, it was either with me or locked in the trunk of my car. I valued my privacy.

A large navy canvas tote bag I had brought with me for just this purpose, folded and tucked under my arm, held them perfectly. I put all twenty-two books in it and lugged the bag back out to my car.

I drove into my garage, locked the garage door down, entered my office, and placed the notebooks on a shelf, enjoying the different colors and patinaed spines of each one as I lined them up in chronological order, smiling as I ran my fingers along the bindings of books I had worked on over the years, from when I went to live with Jen and her parents to just yesterday. My life.

There you are, my little friends. Safe and home.

Then I took the awards from the cardboard box, placed them on the shelves, decided to make more of an effort to redecorate, and then turned to my email and began to make commitments—board memberships, graduation speeches, presentations to service clubs, ribbon cuttings; whatever I was invited to, I accepted, proving to Jen I was not a wallflower.

My calendar was filling up. Why wasn't I?

Chapter Five

WHY AM I DOING THIS?

An old office building had been retrofitted into separate rooms for the homeless, built with funds donated by various charities and public offerings. When it looked like this project was finally going to be approved, I committed to supporting it. It wasn't my project, but the City Council had championed it and I supported it because, as mayor at the time, I had to, putting my personal feelings aside.

I'm there for five minutes, shake some hands, cut a ribbon, pose for some pictures, and I'm out.

I combed my short, bushy hair, at least to tame it down a little, slashed on some Chapstick and snapped my watch around my wrist. Goddamn it. Another "Let's invite the ex-mayor; that'll get the press here."

As a courtesy, I had emailed Ron to inform him of the previous commitment and advised him that if he wanted to go in my place, I would step aside.

"Fine," was the response.

What? Fine that I go, or that you go?

I wasn't sure what he meant; his terse response made me not want to ask. They were expecting me, and if he showed up, I would be gracious and share the scissors.

But that was all I heard from him. Since our last discussion about the homeless and our differing philosophies on how to handle the issue, we had both backed off. What must he think of my convictions going to bless something I'm against?

Fuck him. If he wanted to coddle the lazy people who refused to get a job or contribute to society, let him. I did my part to shield the tax-payers from that expense, but it was no longer my call. The drug dealers and child molesters need to all go away to some private island as far as I was concerned, but I knew that was not practical, nor was it terribly P.C. to have that attitude. But it's how I felt. If I can rise above, anybody can. So I went to cut the ribbon on a project I did not believe in. Welcome to my world.

Escorted through the building, I did my oohs and ahhs, asked a few questions, cut the ribbon, posed for pictures, signed the Certificate of Opening . . . and found myself off to the side as well-dressed patrons formed a line to get in and tour the building.

"Renee?" I heard from behind me. I turned to find Jen's niece approaching me.

"Trish!" I thought a second. "Are you part of this project?"

"Sort of. I'm representing a few of the potential residents."

I stopped for a moment, trying to make sense of it. "Representing?" My finger came up to the ridge behind my ear.

She nodded. "I started a new division of the law firm that helps underserved women. Domestic violence, abuse, addiction, women who have been desperate enough to commit a crime to survive."

"Desperate enough . . ."

She shook her head. "Listen, I know you and Adam have discussed the art gallery, and I'm thrilled that he has something to do." She laughed. "He's not one to sit around all day. He can't paint twelve hours a day, and God knows he's not a handyman or coin collector."

"Are you happy?" I asked. Tricia and Adam had only been married a few months, and I wondered how the marriage was faring.

Her head jerked back a fraction of an inch and her eyes wandered over my shoulder and back again. "It's good. We're finding our way. I'm so busy with the law firm. You're aware Dad left it in a mess, and I'm working on getting it all straightened out." Her father had turned over the reins to his daughter when she discovered he was cooking the books. After Tricia made quiet reparations to his clients, she insisted he leave the firm. I admired her strength.

"I'm glad, Trish. I'm so happy for you." What else was I going to say?

"What are you doing with your time now that you're retired?"

"Well, the art store, for one . . ."

"Yes, of course, but you won't really get involved, will you?"

"Why do you ask? Is Adam nervous?"

"No, nothing like that . . ."

"What, then? Trish, I've known you your whole life. Something's up. What is it?"

She sighed. "I have an ethical dilemma."

"Ah. I'm familiar with those, believe me. Want to chat?"

"What do you know about the foster system? Child Protective Services?"

"The foster system? Not much. Why?"

She shook her head. "Never mind. I'll figure it out."

The art park was on my way home; I swung by on impulse to check in on Jen and look again at the complex. A van with an internet logo was parked in the employee parking area and took up two spaces. Dumbass. Apparently somebody had taken the house in between Stitches and what was to be Canvas, and I witnessed two guys with cables and various unidentifiable tools enter through the door that had been propped open. That means three houses are spoken for. Progress.

In Stitches, Jen was at the cash counter, eyes glued to a laptop screen.

"Whatcha doin'?" I asked, like a teenager.

"Trying to reconcile the month's receipts."

"Yeah, right. You're watching porn."

Jen guffawed. "Can you believe how far we've come? No cash registers any more. It's all done on this thing." She pointed to the laptop. "It even takes credit cards."

"Good God, doesn't anyone deal with cold hard cash anymore?"

"Hardly. Let's sit for a minute."

The shop was quiet, peaceful. Just as it should be for a ladylike hobby like needlework. We turned into the parlor. She'd replicated her living room in the old manse by moving her old furniture, familiar and comfortable. She had bought a small Craftsman house closer to the art park and seemed to be happy with warehouse furniture and thrift store vintage lamps and decorations. I sunk into the overstuffed couch I had always preferred amid a number of needlepoint and crewel pillows Jen had made over the years.

"What's happening next door?"

"Remember Iris's companion, Jade? She's taken it over. It will be a haven for writers and readers—the literati." Jen picked up her knitting, a jade green something that looked fairly complicated. But, then again, all this stuff looked complicated to me.

"Excellent! The park will be full before we know it." I watched Jen manipulate the yarn through her fingers and tried to catch the intricate crossing over of needles. I couldn't keep up. "I just saw Tricia at a ribbon cutting. She looks tired."

Jen nodded. "You *should* be kicking ass at her age trying to make it work. That's why I like being the age I am. I can relax." She looked up. "But I didn't work. You did. You should be relaxed, but I don't see that yet. What's up?"

"I'm finding my feet. Keeping occupied, but it's all busy work. I don't know what to do with myself otherwise." I picked up a pillow next to me and ran my fingers over the silk tassel at the corner. "Tricia is now in family law?"

Jen nodded again while counting stitches. "Yes," she said when the count was done. "Her friend Lacey and she have formed a section of the law firm to deal with women's issues. Carl will stay on in the corporate side." Jen looked at me as I raised my eyebrows. "Carl has been with the firm forever. He and Tricia's brother were supposed to take over the firm . . . but that didn't work out." She sighed. "Tricia does a lot of pro bono work for the courts." Jen grimaced. "The firm isn't what it used to be, all brass and glass and top-tier clients." Arthur and Dave, Tricia's father, had been partners and Carl had been with them for years. "Tricia has to do it her own way. I just hope she's being smart about it. Pro bono work is usually for the well-established."

I had had some experience with both Arthur and Dave when I was mayor, getting advice about legal actions coming across the bow so I could be informed and not look like an idiot. They were smart, conservative, and extremely helpful, both of them.

"But we were talking about you." Jen looked up at me while still somehow managing to keep those fingers and needles going in the right direction. "When does Canvas open?"

"As soon as I get numbers from Adam and we work out the partnership deal."

"Partnership?"

"I will be the technical owner, but he will run the place."

"Like me and Lupe," she nodded. Lupe had been with Stitches from day one and was now the manager, giving Jen some much-needed time for herself.

"Yes, but since I know nothing about the business and very little about art, Adam has complete control. We just have to agree on what it will cost me." I curled my feet up under me and hugged the pillow I had been caressing. "What do you know about him?"

"That's something you should have asked before you decided to go into business with him, isn't it?" She laughed. "But I guess being married to Tricia is reference enough. No, from what I've seen, he can be pretty charming, funny, sarcastic, and veddy veddy proppah. I would put my complete faith in him."

"I did. After only five minutes. It could be the dumbest decision I've ever made."

"Or the best." Jen the optimist. "What else is on your plate? Washington?"

I sighed. "My priority right now is to support the shop. I have no idea how much this is going to cost."

"But the senate? Really? I thought you wanted to back off the political stage. Just because someone asked you doesn't mean to have to say yes. It's not like the prom."

Jen's mom had been apoplectic when Jen said no to a boy who asked her to the prom because she was waiting for another guy to ask her. It had caused real problems at the time. Patricia Palmer made her go back and accept his invitation. The fact that I never even got one invitation never came into discussion.

"You'll be okay. How's your sex life?" Jen grinned up at me. Her change of topic didn't faze me. I was used to it. "Renee . . .I've said it before, and I'll say it again. You deserve some happiness. I may not have agreed with how you got your jollies before, but if there is anyone who needs some companionship and affection, it's you. You deserve some happiness. Eddie was . . ."

My hand raised involuntarily. "Please don't even mention his name. You'll never understand."

"No." Jen stared at me. "I won't." Her voice turned uncharacteristically stern. Her lips slashed into a thin line. It was an age-old discussion. My twenty-plus year relationship with a married man stuck in her craw. Stuck in mine, too. But our friendship had survived that and much more.

"So why can't I ever have it?" The words were out before I could censor myself.

She put her knitting down. "Because you won't allow it."

I stared at her for a few moments, not sure where to go with this.

"Every time somebody gets within a yard of you, you back off. I've seen it for years. You only had Eddie because he was already taken. It worked for you. You didn't have to commit." She shrugged. "And when I have introduced you over the years to my friends, you've not been very interested."

"I have plenty of friends."

"Oh, yeah? Do you go to the movies, to lunch, to parties?"

"Sure."

"No, you don't. Only in an official capacity."

"I was busy and exhausted at the end of the day."

"I get that. But what about now? Is this going to be the rest of your life?"

"I don't think I would know how . . ."

Her eyes lit up. "How about a dating service? It could be fun."

"Or a complete disaster. Please." I was getting itchy.

"Seriously. Let's take a look." She pulled out a tablet and began tapping. "Here. Baby Boomer Dating Service. Perfect." She scanned a bit, grinning. "Not bad," she said and handed it over.

Pictures of handsome men stared at me from the home page. "Do you think these guys are real people or models? In any event, not interested." I handed it back. Even so, it wouldn't be appropriate running for senate.

"Coward." Jen grinned.

A dating service. Good God. What happens when I announce I'm running for a senate seat? No, I can't.

Jen sighed. "Promise me you'll try to get into life."

Get into life???

Chapter Six

*J*EN'S VOICE CAME OVER THE CELL. "I SEE YOU CALLED."

"Yeah, two days ago," I whined. "Are you okay?" I thought back to her mammogram.

"What? I'm at Mother's. It won't be long now." Jen's mother, Patricia Palmer, diagnosed with stage four cancer, had been going downhill the last few weeks.

"God, Jen, I'm so sorry. Here I am so involved in my own life I forgot to check in. Anything I can do?"

Jen wasn't listening. I heard her mumble. "It's Renee . . . really? All right." Her mouth centered back over the cell phone. "Mother would like to see you," she said in a cheery voice. The sound of her footsteps told me she was walking from her mother's bedroom into the hallway and her voice lowered. "But you better make it quick."

"On my way."

Damn. Why didn't she call me? My entire world was shifting. I drove to the cottage her mother had bought with a small inheritance from her own parents years ago, an investment tucked away for what she knew would be her years alone at the end of her life. Smart woman. Jen's father had died a few months ago after a long bout with Alzheimer's. Now Jen was losing her other parent. They had not been close, but at least she had them.

Jen's sister Maggie answered the door. She looked like she had been put through her own version of hell, and for a second I felt bad about all the horrible thoughts I'd had about her recently. Sort of. The normally coiffed hair and made-up face was gone, leaving her with flat, wiry, overly processed hair and a wrinkled, expressionless, gray, sunken face. I hardly recognized her. She opened the door wider and stepped aside.

"Hello, Maggie."

She nodded to me as I walked through. Her normal mode would be to make some kind of sarcastic comment. Our relationship had been somewhat adversarial, but neither one of us had gone so far as to declare open warfare. We were too civilized for that.

Jen came through the hallway and into the living room. She gave me a hug and rubbed my back. "Glad you're here. She's asking for you." She pointed down the hall to an open door. I followed her finger and entered a darkened bedroom.

"Hello, Mrs. Palmer." The dimly lit room smelled of lavender and illness.

"Renee. Come sit," she said in a very weak voice. She patted the bed beside her. Her hair had recently been done, and she had makeup on. It didn't help.

Perching gingerly, I wondered if I should grab her hand in comfort. No. She was not touchy-feely. I sat, back erect, and waited for her to speak.

"I did not treat you well."

I didn't know how to respond.

"No argument? I see. Well . . . perhaps you're right."

I had to say something. "You took me in. You kept me clothed and fed, and you sent me to school. I had a roof over my head and a built-in family. For that I am grateful."

"Believe me, I wish . . . we had done more." Her breathing was erratic and labored.

"I'm not sure what you mean, but I do wonder about some things."

"What things?" Even through her weariness, the sharp tone brought back memories.

"How did I come to live with you so easily? There was no adoption, no formality to it. I lived with you for three weeks before you realized I hadn't gone home."

She closed her eyes for a minute and pinched her lips together as though experiencing some pain.

"Your mother . . . was a drug addict."

"I know that. I wasn't stupid," I said, and instantly regretted my sharp tone. The visions of going to get Mom from the flophouses came back as flashbulb memories. Of course the dying woman wouldn't know that as a seven-year-old I had run around in the middle of the night rescuing my own mother. My finger found its way to the ear ridge.

Her breathing became even more labored, her voice lowered. "She went . . . to jail. Her judge set bail at $10,000. We knew . . . there was no way she could come up with that money and that you would go into the system." She pointed to a glass of water at her bedside, and I handed it to her. She took a small sip and collapsed against the pillow. I waited for her to continue.

"Jennifer would have been devastated, you would have lost your schooling, and more than likely would end up like all the other children in the system. Lost." This took forever for her to get out, but I knew it was important, and I wanted to hear it.

"And?"

"My husband drafted up a document . . . giving us custody of you. Constantine went down, posted bail, and gave her an additional five hundred dollars cash for signing it." She closed her eyes for a minute, then continued. "She put your mother on a bus and we've never heard from her again."

"That explains a lot. She was willing to sell me for her freedom."

Patricia Palmer shook her head. "She was a drug addict. They do that." She licked her lips, closed her eyes again and reached for my hand. I took it and felt the thin, soft skin and wondered, not for the first time, what was going through her mind.

"So she jumped bail?" *How could they do that to her?*

"Technically, yes. An arrest warrant was never issued. I don't know why, and I never asked. I should have told you this years ago, but I didn't want you to feel that your mother didn't love you. I know she did." I could tell she was wearing out, but I also knew this opportunity would not come up again.

"No she didn't."

She sighed. "Perhaps not the way she should have, but a mother cannot help but love the child that comes from her. It's ingrained."

Yeah, so what about Jen's baby? But this was no time to argue. "Did you call me in to tell me this?"

"Yes, and that I'm sorry you were never welcomed into the family the way you should have been. Jennifer's situation had a huge impact on the family, and I'm afraid we did not handle it well at all." She stopped and clamped her lips together. "You were not easy to get to know. I suppose I could have tried harder, but you were always so . . . distant."

Jen's situation, as she called it, was an atomic bomb that hit dead center; Jen didn't recover until last winter when she finally confronted the man who had raped and impregnated her when she was fourteen. No, her parents did not handle it well at all, but I now realized they did the best they could under the circumstances.

"I'm becoming very weary," she said. "Perhaps we should stop now."

"All right. I'll go." I thought about saying goodbye but knew better.

Jen and Maggie were having a cup of coffee at the dining room table. Maggie froze in place. Jen looked up and smiled when I entered the room. "Coffee?"

"No thanks. Do you have Constantine's phone number?"

"Constantine? Our old den mother?" She grinned. Constantine was at the Palmer house when I got there and was still there when I left, cleaning, straightening, and keeping an eye on things. "I don't, but let's see if Mother does." She went into the kitchen where her mother had her address book by an old rotary phone. "Here it is." She wrote it down and handed the paper to me.

"What's this all about?" Jen asked.

"She may know where my mother is."

"Why would you want to contact that whore?" Maggie muttered.

"Maggie, shut up." Jen said over her shoulder while she looked at me.

"Jesus, Jen. You've never spoken to her like that. What's up with you?"

"I'm just not putting up with any more bullshit."

The world where Jen Conrad was a nice, conventionally quiet yes woman had collapsed over the past year, but now this was a complete turnaround, and it shocked me. This was not my friend, the woman I had known for over fifty years.

"I'm going to find my mother and get some answers."

"Like, who your father is?"

"Yes, that, and maybe find something I've lost."

"What's that?"

"Me."

Chapter Seven

*I*ENTERED CANVAS JUST TO BE ALONE IN THE SPACE AND THINK. I HAD not heard from Adam yet and wanted to sit in it and absorb the history, the, I don't know, the feel of it I guess, before we began work transforming it into an art studio.

The place seemed darker. I remembered it as bright and breezy, but today it seemed gloomy, scary. The creaking door didn't help. I took a deep breath and just stood in the foyer, sucking in the air and history.

When I opened my eyes, I found an envelope with my name on it propped up against the mirror in the dining room. I tore it open and found a ledger sheet with neat handwriting, showing expenses projected for the business for the first six months. My eye wandered to the bottom right-hand corner for the total. I stopped breathing.

Son of a fucking bitch.

I took a deep breath and regrouped. No reason to panic, just deal with it. This would take a huge chunk of my retirement savings. What was I thinking? No way I could take that risk. My feet moved fast as I left the building, locked the door, and slid into the seat of my car. I turned the key to start the engine and sat there idling for a bit while I refocused.

No way. Absolutely no way was I going to be that irresponsible. It's simply not going to work.

But what else was I going to do?

My house was quiet, as usual. The refrigerator hummed and dropped its ice into the bin, the only noise ever to come from this house. Maybe

I need a roommate. Someone who won't judge. Someone who will be glad to see me when I come home.

I had been so careful as a single woman to put aside funds and be very systematic about money. I was in good shape and my funds should take me through age 90 if I lived that long. But this? This would put it all in jeopardy.

I exchanged my pantsuit for a track suit, poured a coffee and added some Kahlua (why not?), and approached my journals, where I listed pros and cons and fears and questions on one page. I let 'er rip for a half hour, pouring all my thoughts onto the page. As usual, it was all negative, and concluded with a definite no and a cramped hand.

There. A business decision. The project would not be going forward. But I have a signed lease. Probably did this backward. Adam had scribbled his phone number at the bottom of the page, and I dialed it.

"This is Adam Pechek," his amiable voice said. I had a vision of a fuzzy blanket covering me.

"Adam—Renee Murphy here."

"Ms. Murphy. I assume you received my estimate."

"Yes, and we should talk about it."

"Very well. Shall we meet in, let us say, an hour?"

Nothing like the present . . . "Yes, that's fine." We planned to meet at a coffee shop. I shoved the paper in my pocket and laced up my trainers, then stopped and marked the appointment on my calendar, as is my habit, to track my activity.

God this house is quiet.

I wandered down to the coffee shop on foot. I hadn't walked in some time, and it was freeing to be out in the fresh air and take some time to reflect on my path forward. I wished I had a dog to walk.

Again, Jen was right: real friends were nowhere to be found. She was more like a sister—we've been together so long she kind of has to love me.

The art shop was one way to meet people on my terms, on my territory. It would be good for me to have this project that brings a business together with a hobby. Isn't that what I had intended to do with the art park all along: encourage people to take a risk and create for the greater good of our community?

But who knew it would cost so much? My retirement fund would be at risk.

Damn it. Why did I jump on the lease before I learned what it involved? Because I'm being responsible, living up to the commitment made because I thought I should. I'm too old for this. This is something a young person would do because they had very little to lose, no experience making decisions, and I acted on impulse. But I had made the commitment early on; how was I not to honor that?

Maybe I'm just a kid at heart. I had my retirement to lose. And that is unacceptable. *WTF is wrong with me?*

Adam sat in a wooden chair with two steaming mugs on the table. I noted he was fresh out of the shower, pressed linen shirt and pants pristine, casually elegant as he perused the London Times. Of course. Here I am in old sweats, stained, and disgusting trainers that had been through some rough times. I hoped the Kahlua wasn't detectible.

Kid, you're taking retirement a little too seriously.

"Dear lady, for you," he said as he edged a mug toward me. I plopped onto the hard seat and smelled an earthy brew coming from the mug— something very pleasing, spicy, and delicious.

"Thank you." The tea was too hot to approach at the moment, and I didn't quite know what to do or say.

"You wanted to review the numbers?" He asked, an eyebrow raised.

"I do. Adam . . ."

His knock-your-socks-off, unbelievably bright piercing blue eyes locked onto my own, and I stopped. "Shall we review them one by one?" I said.

"Right-oh," he said, and reached over to the empty chair beside him. He pulled out a well-worn leather portfolio and opened it to what looked to be well-organized papers, numbered one through nine.

Oh, God.

"Forgive the handwritten format. I don't like the new computers and trust myself more than artificial intelligence. I'm old school, as they say." He sort of grinned.

"I'm more comfortable with that myself," I said.

Another raised eyebrow.

"I had help," I said in response to his unspoken question of *how the hell can the mayor of a large city not use a compute*r?

"Ah . . . here is the projection of expenses I left for you." He shoved a hand-written copy, number for number, of what he had left me. Not even a photocopy. He took the time to replicate the same sheet. Interesting. Old school is right. I pulled out my copy and we discussed the expenses: business license, electricity, signage, office supplies, advertising, and whatnot, knowing in the back of my head the basics of what it took to run a business, but he had added some things I had not considered.

"We would benefit by having more natural light in the space. I took the liberty of attaining some bids for windows on the north side and on the east side of the building, and possibly some skylights."

I shook my head. "That will not work. These are historical buildings, and we cannot alter them in any way." I said, a bit too abruptly.

"Mark that off," and he drew a straight line through the window line. "Perhaps new lighting?"

"Adam . . ."

He laid his pencil down, furrowing his brow. He folded his hands together and looked up. "Yes?"

"I'm not sure I can do this. It's too much."

He took a sip of his tea. "Why, may I ask?"

"My retirement funds. I cannot put them at risk."

"My dear lady, may I ask . . . how did you expect to pay for your store?"

My head nearly exploded with outrage. No one ever questioned me. I realized I didn't have an answer.

"The numbers are too high."

"This is not a negotiation, madam. These are firm numbers." He continued to stare at me.

"If the lighting is not right, perhaps this isn't the right house . . ."

He took another sip. "Are you sure you want to do this?"

I realized I desperately wanted to do this. I just didn't want to take the risk.

I slumped. "Yes."

"Then let's look at the other side of this particular coin and see what the income could be."

"All right."

He pulled out another sheet that showed projected income. He had thought about this all the way through. Classes, sales of art supplies, consignment art projects, and a full gallery showing twice a year, among other ideas. After some time reviewing these numbers, we estimated the shop would be in the black approximately three years after opening if a minimum number of people joined up for classes and we sold serious artwork.

Not too bad. The typical guideline was five years. But this was an aggressive plan. We finished talking and leaned back in our chairs.

"Let me say one thing to you, Ms. Murphy." He stopped and those eyes became even a brighter blue. "There are some things on which a risk is worthy. I believe this is one of them. If you don't take a risk, you don't live fully."

Right, and if I lose it all I won't live at all.

"Let me think about it."

Three years. I won't even be collecting Social Security.

The beach had always sucked me in when I needed to think about something, so I headed west and plopped myself on the sand. My arms wrapped around my legs, and I rocked back and forth.

I had two choices. Go for it, risk everything, or stay safe and warm, secure in my little house until the day I die. Alone. With nothing to do, or join the rat race and run for senate. Or sell the house, buy an RV, and roam the country. By myself.

If I opened the store, I'd have to stop contributing to all the busyness—the ribbon cuttings, the luncheons, the speeches, that I had thrown myself into. They were just something to do, and I doubt I'd be missed. What if I didn't have them? What would I do? And how would it affect a potential campaign?

But if I got a Senate seat I'd have a steady income. Can I do both?

I had fantasized more than I should have that Ron and I would end up together, literally sailing off into the distance on his boat, living together, traveling, and having fun. I envisioned laughter, drinks, sunsets, great sex, and adventures. He may have had the same visions. I don't know, we never got that far.

But that was not to be, and I had put all my eggs in that dream. So make a decision. Run for the senate seat, get a paycheck, and support the store. I had no choice. I sat up, reflected on the sun sparkling on the ocean waves, pulled out my cell, called Adam, and told him to go ahead. I was in.

God help me.

Chapter Eight

*I*T TOOK TWO WEEKS FOR ME TO FIND THE TIME TO CALL CONSTANTINE. That and some guts I had to pull up, not sure I wanted to hear the answer. I punched the phone number with a shaking index finger. The first ring sent a ping through my heart, the second a thud. On the third ring a voice answered. An ancient voice.

"H . . . hello?"

"Constantine? This is Renee Murphy."

"Miz Renee? How good to hear your voice, child. I been watching you on the box."

"Thank you. Would you consider having a visitor? I'd love to come by and catch up."

"Why, yes. I'd be honored." She gave me her address and I found it easily enough. It was an old yellow clapboard house in South City, somewhat the worse for wear, and when I knocked on the screen door it bounced back, echoing the sound of my knock. The door squeaked open and Constantine, forty years older and three inches shorter, opened the door.

Her cloudy eyes, the ones that used to catch us in spelling errors or mismatched socks, gathered me in and her wrinkled arms came out for a hug. I stepped into them and smelled the vanilla scent that I remembered as a child in the Putnam house that Constantine managed so well.

It was she who helped me get my homework done. Not by helping academically, but by setting time limits and keeping our butts glued to the chair to complete our assignments—all three of us: me, Jen, and Maggie, although Maggie was dismissed in high school to do it on her own. We tried to snivel out of it—she checked. We lost dessert when that happened.

43

We used to make fun of what we called her "Mammy" ways, talking like she came from a plantation. When we discovered her family history and learned the basics of American history, we stopped, embarrassed we had contributed to a stereotype; we loved her and could not have survived without her firm hand and kind spirit.

I walked into the living room, surprised to find three framed pictures on a table. Our school pictures. She was behind me and said, "You were my babies."

"We were?"

"Yes'm. Miz Palmer disapproved, said it was inappropriate, but I always thought of you as mine. Yes, ma'am." She nodded and used her cane to settle herself down into a large rocker with a grunt. "I guess you want to know about your mamma."

"How did you know?"

"A child needs to know." She rocked; her cane settled across her lap. I saw the deep crevices in her face reflecting decades of worry. Her Coke-bottle glasses were a shock.

"Tell me about the day you took my mom away." I didn't mean to sound accusatory. "Mrs. Palmer told me you put her on a bus."

She repeated everything that Jen's mother had told me, that she had bailed my mother out of jail, gave her five hundred dollars, and put her on a bus to Des Moines.

"Why Des Moines?"

"It was the first bus leaving. That's the only reason." She looked over my shoulder. "I gave her my phone number. Don't tell Miz Palmer that, child, she'd hit the *roof*."

"No worries. Did you hear from her?"

"Only once. That was about five years later, at Thanksgiving. She called to thank me for putting her on that bus and to tell me she was fine, that she was sober, and that she was married and happy. I told her that was real fine."

"That was, what, forty years ago."

"I 'spec' so now." She started to rock again.

"Did you get a phone number?"

"No, child, there was no reason for that. I couldn't afford the long distance if I wanted to."

"But she was still in Des Moines."

"Some little town just outside of it, Betty-somethin'. Why? You thinkin' about goin' to find her?"

"Maybe. I don't know." I paused. "You know Mrs. Palmer is dying, don't you?"

She hummed a bit before saying, "The Lord takes you when you're ready. I 'spec' she be ready now. He'll call me when it's time. You, too." She cackled. "Miz Palmer not goin' to go without a fight, though." She smiled. "Miz Jen doin' all right alone?"

"Yes, you wouldn't recognize her. She's tough."

"She always been tough, only no one ever saw it but me." She shifted in the rocker. "Listen, you go find your mamma and come back and tell me all about it."

"Yes, I will."

"But don't be too upset if she don't welcome you in. She been through hell and now she has a life. She might not want it upset."

"You always were a very wise woman."

She shook her head. "No 'm." I wondered what she meant but didn't challenge it.

Trying to do this quietly, I searched the internet for her name anywhere in Iowa. No go, but I didn't really expect anything. I did get a record of a marriage, though, and her husband's name. God bless the internet. The city was Bettendorf. God bless Constantine's memory, too. But no address or phone number.

I poured a glass of wine and tried to figure out how to get the information. *Bingo.*

My source for private intel had been a whiz kid named Jack, the son of friends who had no idea he was clandestinely providing me with information from time to time. Nothing illegal or unethical, just information that helped me to know if I could trust someone. I never used that information, but I did write it down in my journals using fake names just to ensure their privacy; sometimes I had a hard time tracking my own cryptic notes. I had written a letter and worked with our local congressman to get Jack into the Naval Academy, and it had worked. As I saw it, Jack could do a quick favor for me. He was happy to help without asking questions. He came back to me within the hour with a phone number.

Jen didn't answer her phone when I called wanting to bounce this off her. It was three o'clock in the afternoon. Probably with Mother Superior. Damn. There was no one else to talk to.

Was I wanting permission to do this? Support? Approval? What was I waiting for? I had spent my life making decisions on my own, and suddenly I'm afraid to pick up the phone to call my own mother without checking in with someone?

Well, shit. I hit the ten digits. Ring. Ring. Ring. My heart dropped with each round, and I hadn't taken a breath.

"Hello?" A man's deep voice. Older, warm.

I cleared my throat. "Yes. May I speak with Lorna, please?"

"Yes, who's calling, please?"

Her daughter?

"Renee Murphy."

"Somebody named Renee Murphy calling for you." The voice was muffled, as though he held the phone to his chest.

"What?" I heard what must have been a ring slam on the phone and heard her breathing hard.

"Hello?"

"Mom? It's Renee."

"Who?"

"Renee? Your daughter?"

"I'm sorry, you must have a wrong number. I don't know anyone by that name." I heard a man's voice in the background.

"Mom. It's me."

"I'm so sorry. I hope . . . you find her." Click.

No. It was not a wrong number. That was her voice. For one tiny speck of a moment, the world stopped spinning. I stopped breathing. My heart stopped. Everything. Just. Stopped.

Patricia Palmer was wrong. My own mother didn't care enough to remember or acknowledge me.

Chapter Nine

I HAD STOPPED BY JEN'S HOUSE TO FILL HER IN ON CONSTANTINE. LUPE was keeping Stitches open while Jen took some time with her mother.

"Hi!" Jen said as I entered her Craftsman house, a far cry from The Manse she and Arthur had lived in for the past twenty years. Small, warm, and intimate; this was a home.

"Mother Superior okay?" I asked.

She nodded. "Medication takes her away to dreamland most of the time now. Maggie's with her tonight." She adjusted a cushion to the perfect angle. Some habits never go away. "Bar's open. Tricia is coming by any minute."

"Want me to go?"

"Heavens, no." I poured myself a scotch and I just sat down when the doorbell rang, an old train whistle that never ceased to surprise me. Clearly I wasn't going to get to the Constantine news just yet.

Tricia Putnam entered the living room, along with a young man of I guessed about fourteen, who trailed behind her. His face was horizontal to the floor, hidden by long greasy hair. He wore a stretched-out black tee-shirt and dirty jeans. His shoulders hunched forward, and he stared at the rug like it was a new best friend. He was a little puffy, like he held in huge lungsful of air.

I stayed where I was, plastered to the couch. My ears tickled. I reached for the scar.

"Tricia! So good to see you!" Jen gave her niece a huge hug. I noticed that the young man quietly stepped away from them. My radar went up.

"This is Lenny," Tricia said after giving me a small wave and a smile. She stepped back. "This is highly unorthodox, but he needs a place to stay." We both gaped at her while he shifted from foot to foot, continuing to stare at the floor. "Lenny's mom is my client. I'm doing some pro bono work, and he doesn't have a place to go." She looked at him "For the moment. He *will* have to go into the system eventually, but right now I'm trying to prolong that." She looked back at us. "I'm sorry, I can't tell you more than that, but can he stay with you until her hearing? It won't be long, maybe just a few days." She looked over at a confused Jen, then said, "After that, we may not have a choice, but we can say his mother made these arrangements until then."

"Sure . . ." Jen reached over to Lenny and enveloped him in a hug.

Jen's a hugger these days.

I watched as Lenny stiffened like a soldier being inspected. His arms were at his sides and his eyes glazed as he stared blankly at the wall, and I recognized something familiar—the profile of an unloved person.

"Lenny, so nice to meet you," Jen said as she stepped away from him.

He mumbled something.

"Can I get you anything? A Coke? Milk? Cookies?"

I wanted to poke Jen in the ribs for talking to him like a small child. This kid had had to grow up fast.

Milk and cookies my ass.

His eyes flicked over to me, then back down to the floor. "I dunno." The quiet made my palms itch. Jen and I eyed each other, wondering what came next. Tricia knocked Lenny on his upper arm, blew a kiss to her aunt and stepped out, pointing to her watch.

"Feel free to talk," I said. "Nobody's going to turn you in or make you do anything. We trust your mom's lawyer. If she thinks we can help, then we need to know how." I tried a smile. No response. His arms, still at his side, had relaxed a little from Jen's hug, but now they became stiff again and I watched as his fists became pieces of granite. Michelangelo could have used him for a model: *Boy in Pain.*

"I am not going back there." I could barely hear him.

Jen jumped in. "Back where?"

"Back into the *system*." He hissed the word. "I won't do it. I'll run away and live on the streets before I'll let someone else take me in."

Oh, shit.

"Fifteen placements," he told the rug.

I held my finger up to stop Jen, who had taken a breath to say something. *Shut the hell up.*

He looked at me and I pointed to the closest chair. He sat and folded his hands together between his knees. His left foot balanced on the ball of his foot and his entire leg shook up and down like a jackhammer.

After about three minutes, I decided it was time to redirect.

"Tell me where you come from."

He shrugged. "Lots of places."

"Clearly."

Silence. His eyes were fixed on the wall behind me, his hands still clasped together between his knees. His left leg kept jackhammering. Jen got up and left the room.

Thank God. I thought she might hug him again.

I took a wild guess and started slowly, almost whispering. I had not told this story to anyone. Jen knew, of course, because she was there, but I had not relayed this information to anyone. Why I did now was anyone's guess.

I started in slowly. "My mom was a drug addict. Just left me one day. We were living in the basement of a church. She cleaned houses from time to time, but whatever she earned went into her veins or up her nose. I ate by making friends and eating dinner at their houses. I sometimes stole money so I could buy lunch at school." I ran my finger down the bumpy road of my scar, something I do often.

Silence. He started to rub his hands together between his knees, up and back, up and back. He blinked.

I continued. "I was eight the first time I went to the flophouse to go get her and bring her home."

"But she was your mom." His voice cracked.

"Yup. She was my mom."

His eyes raised to mine, and I saw green eyes with dots of brown scattered in the iris. Very unusual eyes. "Then what happened?" he asked.

I shrugged. "She boogied. I was alone in the basement of a church with some canned spaghetti and dried bread. Once that ran out, I snuck into a friend's house and never left. You know the woman who just left? It was her house."

"Really?" His eyebrows shot up. "They let you stay?"

Jen came back into the room with a big glass of soda and handed it to him, smiling. She handed him a napkin and he wiped his face with it.

"They didn't notice I was living there for quite a while. I was there so much they probably didn't even think about it."

Jen laughed. "We've been friends since we were little."

"You were lucky." He whispered.

I had always known it could have been much, much worse. "Don't I know it."

"I don't have any friends. I don't need any friends." This time his voice was stronger, angry.

As usual, I decided to be pragmatic before this became a pity party. "That's probably because you've never landed anywhere long enough to make friends, much less trust anybody." I settled back into the sofa. "Why did Tricia bring you here?"

"I'm not supposed to know her. She's a lawyer; I'm a minor on the loose." The adult sarcasm didn't escape me.

Jen laughed, piercing the tension in the room. "That's my girl. Always looking out for others, skirting the rules. We won't see her again. She can't get involved. Okay, so you need a place to stay. There's room here. I won't ask questions, I promise." She stopped for a bit. "What about school? Won't they be looking for you?"

"I haven't been in school for about a year . . ."

"So, what do you do all day?"

He shrugged. "Hang."

It was time for me to go before I got involved any further. I put my hand on Lenny's forearm and said, "You're safe here. Whatever happens, we've got your back." I stood and gathered my things.

"But you don't even know me."

"You'd be surprised how well I know you."

I left them staring at each other. Not my circus, not my monkey. Got enough to worry about.

Chapter Ten

I DON'T BELIEVE IN DEBT, BUT AFTER THINKING ABOUT IT I DECIDED TO call SCORE and see what kind of advice I could get about a business loan. They sent over reams of papers to fill out and, since I was honest and asked for a very large amount thought it might be worth a try.

I was declined. My credit rating was excellent, but the risk was too much for them. I had no experience as an artist and, according to them, they were not willing to risk a debt that high with a woman with no income and no experience in the field in an unknown art park. I could gt a second on the house, but that put both my house and my retirement fund at risk. Nope.

I called my financial advisor and made arrangements to transfer a lot of money over to my personal account. I got some pushback from him but stood firm.

"You could always get a small business loan . . ."

"I'm aware of that." I didn't tell him I had already tried.

Silence.

"If you lose it all, you can't get a loan since you won't be employed."

"I'm aware of that." *Yeah, tell me about it.*

"It's your money," he said.

"Gee, really?" The sarcasm didn't faze him. I had made up my mind. I didn't want to be left with a debt if it all went to hell. The little woman can do this. My pride got in the way of financial responsibility. A stupid decision. Stupid, stupid, stupid. But I made it. The funds were transferred into my personal account that afternoon. I then called a woman broker I knew and moved everything over to her. So there. *Boy, I sure showed you.*

God I am such a child.

Adam and I worked on getting Canvas open without much fanfare. It didn't take much other than reams of paperwork for business license, tax forms, fictitious business statement and other formalities that took some time. Adam recommended a supplier, placed some orders, and Lupe very kindly made up some flyers for classes, and she took an afternoon to show me some software that I could work with, and I think I got it right away. I duplicated what Stitches had, and Lupe offered to do a website for me.

The easels, paints, and canvases began to arrive within a few weeks, and we set to work setting things up.

I had talked to Jen's friend Bruce, the general contractor for the art park, and he said he thought he knew what we could do to get more natural light into the space during the day. Without my knowledge, he had gone to the development committee and presented a proposal that was approved, and he banged through walls and put leaded glass windows in to Adam's satisfaction. It cost twice what he estimated, even with a discount.

Once I do something, I do it. Go big or go home. While I advocated for a big blowout grand opening, Adam convinced me to have a soft opening while we figured things out.

It was nice to share the responsibility with someone who had no financial interest and just wanted the shop to succeed. Adam and I worked very well together, if somewhat formally while getting to know each other's rhythms, and I followed his lead since he was the expert.

We were going to be fully supplied in no time and were getting some interest from the community. We had a few drop-ins and a few sign-ups for classes. Word was getting around. It was a comfortable pace, but one that I would have accelerated if I had been the only one making this happen. Partnership can be a bitch. It slows you down.

Adam was quiet, going about his work like a ghost, floating in his ever-present gauziness and sandals from one room to the other, a pencil stuck behind his ear. From time to time he'd stop at an easel that displayed one of the various projects he had going, and he'd add some paint or some accent to it, stand back with a critical eye, then go into the office and place another order. It was like he needed the art to think.

Hunh.

Adam had taken on total management responsibilities: he had contacted local artists to see if they wanted to display their art in the gallery; he negotiated sale prices and restrictions. He set up classes and said, naturally, he would teach them himself. All I did was price and stock whatever came in those big brown boxes every day. I watched dollar signs fly out the window with each brush, canvas, and paint set.

Jen came out of Stiches when the sign guy came to install the sign over the porch—nothing special, just the word Canvas in painted brushstrokes to match the exterior of the house. All the signs were similar, one word for the shop with matching colors for the house, hanging from brass chains. For the first time I had a spark of excitement.

"I know exactly what you are feeling," Jen said. "It's scary. You've got it all on the line, but, believe me, you can do this."

"I'm not doing much. Adam is doing it all. I'm just the lackey," I said with a smile.

"It's your shop, remember," she muttered. "You don't have to delegate everything."

"I know, but he's the one with experience. He knows what he's doing and seems to relish it."

"So you're distancing yourself? Are you paying him now?"

"That's the weird part. No. He just wants a place to paint and sell his art. In exchange he'll manage the place. I just sign the checks." I turned to her. "And what do you mean by distancing myself?" *Didn't Adam say something similar?*

She shrugged. "I don't know. It seems to me the past eight years have been about setting up projects and delegating them out to others; I have not seen you with any passion about any project. You just did what you had to do to get things done." She paused. "This seems like just another project." She stopped while I grappled with my own response. "It's not like I've ever heard you talk about anything on a deeper level. Animals? Kids? The environment? That would help you not only in your personal life, but if you run for senate, it would focus you in one area. Maybe the arts or culture? Climate change?"

All I ever did was solve problems as they came up. Everyone else had projects; I just signed for them and managed the process. Damn. She's right.

"Think about it. You'd be a great advocate for something." A slight breeze came off the ocean and ruffled the leaves on the Ficus tree to the right of the house. Jen wrapped her hand-knit sweater around her as we watched the final winch of the signage place the placard exactly where it was meant to be.

One thing accomplished. Canvas was official. I gave her a thumbs up and she went back to her store. A weird conversation to have while my sign was going up, but that's how we rolled. I was feeling a bit to the left of my own body, something that I attributed to my subconscious wrestling with my nature. Jen had hit on something.

The truth was I was not passionate. Nothing had struck me as vital to my own survival or that of others. My two terms were fortunate in that I had not had to deal with life and death issues; all my time as mayor entailed constant lists of to-do items that needed to be ticked off and were usually somebody else's idea or germ of an idea. Smooth sailing, no catastrophes.

Jen had always had her socialite work when Arthur was alive: galas and fashion shows and luncheons to raise money for worthy projects. Hell, she even held some events for me for both campaigns. She had her knitting and her decorating, and she'd been a hell of a gourmet cook in her day. But now all that was gone; she had the shop, and she was totally invested in it because she loved the creativity. Money was not an issue for her, but in the beginning I knew it had been.

Our situations, as usual, were totally different. There was no way she could understand. Hell, I'm not sure I did.

How can one person be so shallow? I cannot get invested in anything. If it were to all go away tomorrow, I would not be sad. I'd just find something else to do with my time. Maybe read in my rocking chair by the fire all day.

Or maybe just not be in the world at all.

One morning I headed over to the store to check things out. I hadn't heard from Adam in a while and wondered exactly what was happening in the space.

The smell of fresh paint and varnish surrounded me as I took in the buttercream walls and highly polished floors. What an improvement! Bright, airy, and light. Track lights lay on the floor on drop cloths, ready, I suspect, to be hung to spotlight individual art pieces on the wall. Boxes and crates sat in the living room. Dozens and dozens of them.

This was becoming even more real. A landline had been installed; I recognized the ring. Adam was nowhere to be found, so I picked it up.

"Canvas Art Store." We hadn't come up with a logo or a tag line yet. Oops.

"Ah, Ms. Murphy. At last."

I didn't recognize the voice.

"Just a warning. If you don't back out of your political plans, there will be more rumors, and I cannot guarantee your safety."

"What do you . . ." *Click.*

What the hell?

Adam had come in from the back door and watched as I hung up the phone. "Problem?"

"Just a crank call."

"Ah, yes, whoever it is has been asking for you. Very insistent. Wants to know when you will be in."

"Just some crackpot. All politicians have them."

"Politicians?" His eyebrow went up.

I said nothing.

"My dear lady, if you have upset someone in the past, I see no reason for them to continue to hound you after you've given up the reins . . ."

"He said something about my political plans."

"Have you any plans?"

"Possibly. I haven't really decided yet."

"Did he threaten you?"

"Well . . . it was nothing." I waved my hand. "Forget it."

"I suggest you call the police. Just for the record." Those eyes were focused on me.

"Well, he sent a message and I received it. That should be the end of it." Wait. How did he know my plans? I don't even know who I'd run against yet.

"I do have some experience with this type of thing. I suggest if you are not going to call for help, then at least get a dog. A big dog."

"I'm a big girl."

"Consider, please, the store and the customers. You want to mitigate any danger, do you not?"

"We could use a mascot of sorts. Everyone likes dogs, right?" I was warming to the idea. Sticks and Stitches had added quite a lot to Jen's store. People came around just to visit with them and sneak them dog treats, some homemade.

What the hell am I thinking? Me? A dog? A store? Who am I?

Chapter Eleven

"MOTHER DIED THIS MORNING," JEN SAID, PLOPPING INTO AN OLD, worn out couch that sat in my living room. "The service is on Friday." She sounded exhausted. Losing her husband and two parents in the space of a year, no matter how distant they had been, had to be tough.

I handed her a beer, cold from the fridge. "I am so sorry. What can I do?"

"Bruce is such an angel. He's taking care of everything. I don't know what I would do without him." She took a large glug and I followed. "He even took Lenny to his house to give me some time."

"How is the kid?"

Jen just shrugged. "He's there but not there."

"Bruce seems like a great guy, Jen. You're lucky to have him. Are you sure there's nothing I can do?"

"No, I know how much you dislike the Catholic ceremonies. You really don't have to come if you don't want to."

Ouch. "I'll be there. She was the closest thing to a mother I had.".

When Jen's husband Arthur died, I literally and figuratively supported her through the days before and after the funeral. When her father died, I had been right there by her side. Now she had Bruce. I was just the person who'd sat in between Arthur and Bruce.

Patricia Palmer was laid to rest after an elaborate Catholic mass. At the reception, Jen handed me an envelope in a Conrad & Putnam envelope. "This is for you," she said. "It was among Mother's things to be distributed upon her death."

When I opened it at home later, I found a statement from an investment account with me as the Trustee. It was an accounting of every check I'd written to the Palmers to repay my college expenses. She had deposited those funds into an account that had accrued interest and dividends that more than doubled the original investment over the years.

No note, no explanation, but a complete accounting of each check I had written to them, how it had been invested, and how it had grown. It would certainly help with the store. Rather than feel as though this was a nice gesture, one to show how much Patricia Palmer cared for me, I felt as though it was a way to close the book on me, as though I had never existed. One final chore before dying to release whatever ties we had.

So much dying. First Jen's husband, then her father, then Iris, now her mother.

How does she stand it?

Canvas's labor pains—decisions on money, equipment, signs, websites, social media, vendors, licenses, the whole shebang—took weeks to get organized. Adam worked slowly, methodically. I wanted to scream in frustration. My motto had always been just do it, but he stopped me more than once. We were both losing our patience.

I ran into Jen's shop two doors down to get away. Lupe stood in the dining room with a customer going over needlepoint canvases or something. Jen's original dining room table and chairs were there, very elegant, with a fresh centerpiece of white roses, baby's breath, and maidenhair fern. I went into the parlor to find five women sitting around knitting and chatting amiably. I had forgotten today was Tuesday, Jen's knitting group's day, and started to back out of the shop, not intending to get involved with a bunch of knitters, when I heard my name mentioned.

"What is Mayor Murphy going to do now that she's out of office?" I didn't recognize the voice.

Jen's voice came back. "Oh, she's opening a store here in the art park, didn't you know?"

"Well, she's certainly not going to get romantically involved, looking the way she does." Jen's sister Maggie's voice came at me like buckshot aimed at my stomach.

"That's not fair," Jen said quietly. "She has her own style."

"Yeah, none. She needs to amp up her game." Maggie started to chortle. "Are we sure she's not a lesbian?"

"What are you wearing to the gala, Jen?" Whoever it was changed the subject quickly, and others jumped in enthusiastically.

Maggie and I had never been best friends, although when I was in office, she did condescend to speak to me from time to time when she needed something for one of her charities or a nice photo op with the mayor. Even though we went through adolescence together, we still didn't understand each other or communicate effectively.

I backed out quietly and left the park, the gray cloud descending once again around me. Why wasn't I good enough? It's true that my time as mayor didn't leave me any free time at all, and was full of carb dinners and fancy desserts, which resulted in getting my pantsuits in a size larger every year or so. My haircut was plain and easy (Jen once called it my helmet), my suits were expensive but similar, often the same suit in different colors, and I bought the same shoes in black, brown, beige and navy because they were comfortable, easy, and could go with anything.

It was boring, and that's just the way I wanted it: no comments about how I presented myself in the media that I would have to defend or apologize for. Makeup was minimal, often missing, and jewelry was the one ring I wore every day. And as for catching a man? Well, that was something I hadn't thought of for some time, with the exception of my brief flirtation with Ron; that was last year and probably fifteen pounds ago.

My relationship with Eddie started in my college years, when I cared more about how I looked, and I did put a little more effort in when I knew I was going to see him, but that was a long time ago, too. That affair lasted over twenty years. It worked for me, as I was a student and then a young professional. I was busy and the non-committal committal worked for me. It gave me companionship, caring, and love at least once a week. But it came to a natural end one day when he said he just couldn't do it anymore. I wasn't entirely devastated, but it did hurt.

That was fine, too. If he had left his wife and asked me to marry him I would have said no. Why? Because then I'd have a man willing to cheat on his wife. Ironic, I know. But I was smart enough to know that wasn't the goal, so I went on my merry way, content just to be alone and work on my career. I am fifty-eight, round and plain. I'm okay with it—why isn't anyone else?

Lenny's attitude that first day at Jen's about friendships and family was spot on, and I understood it completely. Now that Mrs. Palmer was gone, I realized I was an orphan. I had considered her a pseudo-mom, God help me.

After pouring a slug of Kahlua into my morning coffee, I scribbled again in my journal about the men in my life. I have lived my life in an open, honest way. I was aware that some people thought I was a lesbian, and I did nothing to sway their thinking. It's none of their business whether I like men or women.

For the record, I like men.

I had used my friend Joe (which is only fair, since it was mutual), who is a closeted gay man, as an escort from time to time, and he in turn had used me for events to camouflage his own orientation. We had fun together but understood that this was an arrangement for both of our benefits. Joe was a very successful man in the software industry, but his board consisted of most of the individuals on the Catholic Charities board. The woman who had originally given him the seed money for his company brought all her friends with her to the board, and he was stuck. His partner was also closeted. Everybody uses everybody else, it seems.

Ron Walker is, as far as I am concerned, the perfect man. He is handsome, smart, ambitious, and cares about his community. Why he never married is beyond me. He rides a motorcycle, has a boat, and takes long vacations to sail and fish. He is, like me, a loner at heart. He and Mrs. Palmer had had a courteous relationship, and I think he admired the woman she had been, the strong, stalwart social queen who had ordered efficiency over the chaos that was the judge's life and his social concerns.

Mrs. Palmer did not know about Eddie, who was someone to fill my time and give me some excitement in an otherwise stagnant, although busy, life. She certainly would not have approved, which may be why I did it in the first place.

Everything was his call—the timing of our meetings, where we met, where we made love, what kinds of gifts or cards were appropriate—and I was well aware of the limits of our relationship. I met him when I was a young grad student. He helped me grow into adulthood.

I adored Eddie, I still do, and I am secure in the knowledge that I will always be a big part of his life. I also was aware he had someone waiting at home for him, unaware of his wanderings with me, and I was sure I was the only one outside of his marriage. We lasted twenty-five years.

Now I no longer had Eddie or Joe and wondered if anyone out there really actually valued who I was and what I had to offer, if anything.

Lenny's mom tolerated him, like mine did me. Hindsight tells me I was in the way of her drugs and her "friends." I was on my own, just like Lenny is now.

My heart lurched a little when I thought about how lonely he must be—no school, no friends, no parents. Just a social worker who had too many cases to get in line. And his mom's attorney who just palmed him off on a stranger.

I wrote in my journal:

This will make Jen's life a bit brighter—having a child, even a grown-up child, may make her happy and add to her life. What it will do to Lenny is anybody's guess. Rage comes from strange places. I know.

I can't help a whole lot—I'm opening up a store and running for political office. I am of no use, but I will help and support any way I can.

I ended the day's writings allowing the following:

It's not my problem. I cannot get involved. I have too much on my plate.

I was painting my office, turning the walls to a soft yellow,, when my phone rang. I ignored it, thinking instead about the Moroccan print stencil that I would do in bright blue.

Maybe I have a future in interior decorating.

I had a beer up on the ladder and took a swig, then kept going. It was a small room, so it didn't take too long, but I was exhausted by the time it was done. I pulled another beer out of the fridge and checked my voice mails.

Ron. I took a deep breath and got into voice mail.

"Hi, there. Just thinking about you and hoping you are enjoying your time off. You've earned it. Give me a call when you get a chance, okay?" *What the hell?*

I waited a day to call. Tanya greeted me warmly and said Ron was tied up but would be sure to let him know I returned his call. He never called back.

Chapter Twelve

So, MY LIFE WAS PLANNED OUT. I WOULD RUN FOR SENATE, EITHER BE elected or not, and support, not run, an art store. I may not have any money if I don't get elected, but, whatever. As for a partner or a companion? Meh.

I had a drink in my hand (why not?), watching a talk show in the middle of the afternoon, when my home phone rang.

"Ms. Murphy? Dick Abraham here." He was the de facto head of the party, and the only person I had tested the waters with about a run for senate. He was encouraging at the time, and his very slight British accent didn't hurt, either. I am sure that when he became an American citizen he changed his name from Richard to Dick.

"Yes, Dick. How are you?"

He cleared his throat. "I'm just fine . . . but look . . . I wanted to chat you up about something that's come up."

"Yes?" I couldn't imagine.

"I just have to ask you straight up. Were you having an affair with the chief of police, now mayor Ron Walker?"

"Whaaat? No!"

"You have no relationship with him whatsoever?"

"We were . . . we are friends."

"Do you see each other socially?"

"We've had a drink or two together, and in the past several weeks we have spent a lot of time together getting the transition done, but no, if you are asking if we were dating or if we were romantically involved, the answer is a definitive no."

"You're sure."

"Of course I am sure. Why do you ask?"

"It has been reported to us that you had an inappropriate relationship with him while he was under your supervision."

"Who?"

"I'm not at liberty to say. May I ask you why you gave him a ten percent increase in pay while other city employees only received a two percent increase?"

"Yes. It's because he had not received an increase in five years. He had done an exceptional job, increasing training for his officers in technical skills and psychological skills, and his staff had been increased by twenty percent. There was not one officer-involved shooting while he was chief. His staff supported him and the community adores him. He made it a point to get out in the community and create a positive atmosphere with adults and children to trust the police force. He is a man of unimpeachable ethics and morals." I tripped over my words.

"That is a very strong advocate statement for one of your staff members."

"He was not a staff member. He was the chief of police, and he did a damn good job." My heart was pounding. My judgment had never been questioned before, and this raised my hackles. "I also gave a large increase to my assistant, who is now his chief of staff. Are you questioning that as well?"

I heard him sigh, then ask, "Why did he resign?"

"You'd have to ask him," I said. "I received his resignation on my desk one morning, we had a conversation and he said it was time. He wanted to pursue other avenues. I accepted his resignation."

"I see. Well, this will be cleared up shortly, I am sure. In the meantime, have you told anyone you are running? It might be a good idea to keep the kettle cold for the moment."

I seethed and said through gritted teeth, "Understood."

Click.

Who would do this to me?

Chapter Thirteen

"CAN YOU COME OVER?" JEN'S VOICE SHOOK A LITTLE. NOT GOOD.

"On my way." That's the thing about this friendship. We rarely ask for anything, so when a request is made, it's more like a command. I wondered if something had happened to her relationship with Bruce and gave myself a dope slap when I realized that would not make me unhappy.

The front door was open, and I found Jen on the couch, her legs tucked under her, with a very large glass in her hand. It could have been water, but after hearing the tone in her voice, my bet was on vodka.

"What's up, buttercup?" I asked as I plopped myself down on the chair across from her, slouched down with my feet out, and laced my hands over my tummy.

So not mayoral.

Jen's lips formed a straight line before she said, "Just got a call from my doctor. It appears my second mammogram came back as . . . he used the word concerning. He wants to do a procedure and check the cells. Major surgery. Like maybe a mastectomy. Or two." She took a drink. "Tomorrow."

"Oh shit."

"Yeah."

I looked around in the quiet hose. "Where is Lenny? And the babies?"

"I asked Bruce to take them for a walk."

I suddenly flashed back to Jen after Arthur died. She had spiraled into a deep depression, using a bottle of vodka as her bed buddy. Not this time. I stood and took the drink from her. "If you're going into surgery tomorrow, you probably will have to fast, and this is not going to make it any easier, so out it goes."

Eight dog paws scrambled on the wood floor as Sticks and Stiches bee-lined to Jen on the couch, dragging their leashes and sitting on either side of her. Bruce stood in the arched doorway, smiling. "Probably a good idea," he said, gesturing to the glass still in my hand, on my way to the sink to throw it out. Lenny slouched into the kitchen behind me.

I returned to the living room. "So, what are the instructions from the doc? When do you have to be there, and what do you have to do tonight?" I put my hands on my hips, hoping for all the world I looked like I could manage this. Inside I was melting.

What would I do without her?

"I wrote it all down. I knew I wouldn't remember anything he said." I went back to the kitchen and retrieved the notebook I knew she always kept by the phone. I ignored the sulking kid at the counter. Shaky handwriting said no food after eight tonight, check in at seven a. m., surgery at ten. Got it. Back to the living room. "I'll take the dogs tonight if that will help," Bruce said.

"No, I want them here with me. But thanks. Can you take Lenny home with you?"

Bruce's face fell. "Okay. Whatever you want."

"Renee, can you stay tonight? And get me to the hospital in the morning?"

"I'm all over it." I turned to Bruce and saw the disappointment in his eyes.

"Guess I'll go, then," he said.

"Thanks, Bruce," Jen said distractedly. "Lenny?" she said loudly.

"Yeah?" He came around the corner with a peanut butter sandwich clutched in his fist.

"Lenny, how would you like to spend the night at Bruce's?"

I saw a flash of anger in his eyes. Shoved around again. "Okay," he said, and clumped back into the kitchen. "Guess I'll pack a bag." He came down shortly thereafter with a plastic shopping bag with a few things in it. The subject of schooling had not been approached yet. Lenny left through the front door without saying goodbye to any of us. Bruce and I walked to the door. He turned around on the front stoop.

"I don't know what I'll do if anything happens to her," he said. "She won't let me in. I've been biding my time, but if we don't have much time left . . ."

"Don't even think about that," I said. "Let's just take this one step at a time. It may turn out to be nothing, or something really manageable. We just don't know yet what we're dealing with." God, I sounded so strong, so in charge.

He nodded. "Yeah. Will you call me, please? Let me know whatever happens."

"Of course." I wasn't sure what Jen wanted him to know, but we'd cross that bridge when we came to it.

Bruce lowered his head and he ambled off to his own house two blocks away, Lenny in tow. Both had their heads down.

"Why are you shutting him out?" I asked Jen before I even sat down.

"I don't know. I just couldn't have him beside me. I know what I went through with Arthur, and I just didn't want to put him through that." Jen had been Arthur's sole caregiver for a brutal four months.

"What about Maggie?"

"She can't handle this. She's still dealing with Mother dying. I don't want her knowing until we know what's what."

"Martyr."

She started to giggle and, as usual, we got rid of all the angst with a fit of laughter. Then she started to cry. "I'm so scared."

"Don't blame you. Scary shit. We'll know tomorrow what we are dealing with." I sat on my hands so she wouldn't see them shake and hoped I looked calm.

She sniffed a bit and wiped the tears away. "You know, a year ago I would have just given up. There was nothing to live for. Arthur was gone, my whole reason for being was gone, the money was gone, and the people who I thought were my friends were gone. But now . . ."

"But now what?"

"Now I see that life is . . . precarious. Jesus, that sounded trite." She blew her nose and looked at me. "I want to live."

"And I want you to live. We're supposed to have rocking chairs next to each other at Daisy Hill Puppy Farm, remember?"

"Ha! Yeah. Can Bruce come with us there?"

Again with Bruce. "Whatever you want, but I think maybe the time has come for you to stop putting him off. He needs to know how you feel." The words were out. Damn it.

She smiled. "Yeah. What the hell am I waiting for?" She put on her best Rosalind Russell in Auntie Mame. "Life is a banquet, and most poor bastards are starving to death!" Her left arm raised.

I never left. We polished off a pizza by eight. We watched movies that made us laugh and talked about Arthur and Bruce, and Ron. I fell asleep on the couch and woke up once to find Jen had gone to bed. An afghan had been draped over me.

The next morning we loaded up in my car and headed off to the hospital, checked in, and got her situated in the room in her gown and shower cap. I sat on the chair and we kept talking about innocuous things. She finally told me that she and Bruce had had a long talk over the phone. "You were right, but for now I still want you at the helm here."

The nurse kept coming in, apologizing for the doctor running late; a previous surgery had complications and he needed to wrap that up before he began Jen's. We were both starving. I just kept chattering, hoping that I could keep my body numb until she was wheeled off to surgery.

Finally, a young doctor came in, I estimated him to be about twelve, and explained that they would be opening up the right breast and looking at the "mass" that was seen there and removing it. They would check the lymph nodes and do more surgery if they found cancer cells. She signed a few documents, the nurse came in and gave her a sedative, and shortly she was wheeled off, down the hallway. She gave me a thumbs up, knowing I was watching, and I followed until they got into the elevator. I continued out to the waiting area. Tears escaped my lower lids and I angrily swept them away with the back of my hand.

Bruce stood up the second he saw me. "Is it over?"

"No, it hasn't even started yet. Let's get some coffee."

"Way ahead of you." He gestured to a thermos and a bag on the chair. I consumed the sandwich inside and poured myself a cup of coffee while he patiently waited, smiling. What a guy. Why can't I get a guy like this?

"You look way too relaxed," I said in between bites.

"Whatever happens, happens. We talked, really talked, and that's enough for now. She wants to live and be with me, can you believe it?"

I smiled. "Yes, I can." I sighed.

Surgery was only supposed to be an hour. Four hours later, a very weary doctor came into the waiting area and gave us an update. "We found the tumor to be malignant," he said as he lowered his head. "We removed the lump and surrounding tissue. There was no sign on the left side on the mammogram and no sign of it in the lymph nodes, so that is very good news."

It was hard to reconcile what was the good news. I had just been told that Jen had cancer. I had yet to catch up to the good news part.

"What does that mean?" Bruce said.

"It means that we caught and excised it, but I am recommending a series of chemotherapy to wipe out any lingering cells that may decide to invade. We took a biopsy of some cells from the other side just to see if there's anything there; we'll have the results back in a few days.

"What's the prognosis?" I asked.

"If there are no indications of malignant cells when the tests come back, I believe we can expect a full recovery; it's too early to make any promises. You can reasonably expect a healthy life, but the next six months will tell the entire story. Any other questions?"

We both numbly shook our heads. He nodded and left.

"Well, we now know what we are dealing with," I said as I fell back into my chair.

"Yes, but now we can deal with it together." He smiled.

A thought occurred to me. "What about Lenny?"

Bruce chimed in. "I called Tricia and told her the situation and asked her to find another place for him until we know what's happening."

"Where is he now?"

"I left him at the YMCA. Didn't know what else to do with him." He shrugged. "Tricia will pick him up after work."

Poor kid. Blown around like a dust bunny.

Chapter Fourteen

I DIDN'T RECOGNIZE THE NUMBER ON MY CELL BUT ANSWERED IT ANYWAY. Could be a new friend. LOL.

Tricia's voice came over the air. "Can you meet me at The Ground Bean? Real quick. I need to ask a favor." The local coffee shop was a hangout for we Baby Boomers, with a mixture of Frank Sinatra et al and some 70's music mixed in coming from the speakers, reminding us of our disco days.

Adam and I were through stocking and he was there painting so we would have something to display, and probably doing other things to the shop to get it ready for the opening. I dressed and headed to the coffee shop.

"What's up?" I asked Tricia as I poured some fabulous smelling brew from a French Press into a ceramic mug.

She sighed. "Lenny's mom is a drug addict. Long history. The one thing she asked for was for me see what I could do for him. I can only do that until he's back in the system." She shrugged. "There's not much I can do legally. She'll be in jail for a long time. I'll try to get her admitted to a rehab instead, but that has not worked the three times she's made that deal, so . . ."

My reaction was familiar—drug addicts were hopeless losers and shouldn't be allowed anywhere near polite society. "Jesus. Where's dad?"

She shook her head. "He's got a rap sheet as long as the Mississippi. Bad guy. On probation. Never married." She shifted in her seat. "Look. I have no business getting into this at all, but I'm honoring my client's wishes. I can't see Lenny getting another placement at his age and with his record." She put her hand up, palm out, like she was directing traffic. "Don't ask."

"What will happen to him?"

She shrugged. "He'll probably be in a group home unless someone wants to foster him. It's where they go if they can't get fostered out. It's not so bad, but it's not good, either." Tricia stared into my eyes for a minute.

"Well, what do you want *me* to do? Adopt him?" It was a joke.

She winced. "I was sort of hoping you could foster him. We don't know how Aunt Jen will do, and she's not in a position to devote herself to him now." She sat back, clearly exhausted. "He will soon be in the system, but I don't suppose he'll get many takers. It occurs to me you do have something in common. You understand him. I know you do." She looked over my shoulder. "My grandmother told me your story." She sipped. "I thought maybe what he needs is someone who's not going to fawn all over him, someone who's going to bring him along at his own pace and not give him any bullshit. He's had to deal with that his whole life. He doesn't know who to trust."

Welcome to my world. *Wait. I was discussed?* We sat in silence as I absorbed this. I stalled for time.

She smiled. "You can have a real impact on this kid." Then she turned serious. "Please. He doesn't have a chance anywhere else. No one will take him, and he will be a lost cause without someone to rescue him, like you were."

Ouch. "Have you *met* me?" I am definitely not mom material. But neither is his mom, and look where it got him.

She smiled. "All I ask is that you try. The last thing this kid needs is to move again. Besides, you're not without influence. Make some calls. I know from experience the system is not set up efficiently. They are doing the best they can, but kids like Lenny get lost in the shuffle and shoved around. It's not right, but bio parents have all the rights, even though they may not be the best choice for the kids. You can get into the system and see what's what and have some pull with legislators and congress to get some things changed."

"I'm about to open up an art store," I said. "Besides, Lenny stated empirically he'll run away before allowing anyone to foster him again. Where is he now?"

"At the Anderson Center, where we put kids recently removed from homes. It's an awful place and he needs to get out of there quick. You'll need to go through the foster care application process, which will take a while." She stopped. "I've been able to stall him getting into the formal system, but I can't do it much longer. He'll probably go into a group home soon."

Great. That means he'll be back in the system. There would be nowhere for him to hide. Shit.

She reached into her bag and handed over a small white envelope. "Can you at least get his stuff from where he and his mom were living? The address is in here, along with a set of keys. They are about to be evicted anyway; the sooner the better." She stood up. "Thanks for doing this."

"Do I have a choice?"

Tricia smiled. "Always. But, um . . . no?" She cocked her head and squinted. Well shit.

I followed instructions and immediately drove to a long-term motel that had seen better days. Carpets had worn through in places, cheap furniture cracked, mirrors broken. The sink dripped brown water. It was a hovel.

I walked in to find trash on the floor and a very hungry cat, who bolted out the minute I opened the door. The place smelled like cat urine, and my eyes watered. I saw what I knew were meth pipes on the floor and in the bathroom. The refrigerator was empty but for a half-gallon of milk that had solidified. Cockroaches skittered everywhere and I swear I saw a long tail disappear behind the couch. Apparently they both slept on the mattress on the floor. Along with the cat. The closet had no hangers. Clothes were everywhere, balled up and wet with cat tootsie rolls.

"Jesus. How can you do this to a kid?" I mumbled. The skin on my forearms felt like needles were trying to pop through, itching and burning with the injustice.

You have the right to screw up your own life any way you want, but you don't have the right to do it to a kid. Lenny's angry face popped into my head. No wonder—I'd be pissed, too.

There was a video game on the table, and I saw a case labelled with the same name, with cartridges and cords. I grabbed everything electronic and left the rest. Not worth it.

The smell was nauseating. Never had I wanted to shower more than at that minute. On the drive home, it occurred to me that that may have been my fortune if not for Jen and her family. Without them I may very well have been where Lenny is now. I shuddered to think how lucky I was and how easily it could have gone in the other direction.

I stopped by the hospital that night and found Bruce by Jen's bedside, and her wrapped up like a mummy from the neck down, and in the ozone.

"Drugs is good," she said when I asked. Bruce grinned.

"A little housekeeping . . ." I said as I plopped down after dropping some magazines on her rollaway dinner table.

"Yes . . .?"

Tricia slipped into the room with a bouquet of roses. "Aunt Jen, you look great," she said.

"No, I don't. Look, I don't want your mother knowing anything about this until absolutely necessary."

"Agreed," Tricia said with a sigh. "You're always protecting her, and this time I think it's a good idea. She's just not in a position right now to take on much more." We were all silent for a bit. "In fact, I'm going to highly suggest Mom goes away for a bit to relax in a therapeutic environment."

"That might be just the thing," Jen said. "It will buy me some time to get back on my feet and for her to get a grip."

"Jen!" I couldn't help it. She was normally so circumspect and respectful.

She started to shrug, winced, then rolled her eyes. "She's just not very strong when it comes to challenges. If a vacay will help her cope, I'm all for it. I certainly don't need the drama. I have enough right now to fill a movie script."

"Yes. Yes you do, and I completely understand. I'll do Mom, you do you." Where Tricia got her strength was anybody's guess, but she had it in bucketfuls. Maybe she sucked it out of her mom during the gestation period. I don't know, but she was my hero at that moment.

We made arrangements for the foreseeable future about dogs, food, mail, and her shop. Everything was doled out to the three of us, with Bruce taking the brunt of it. Jen collapsed back onto her pillow with a satisfied sigh. "I'll be out of here and recuperating in no time, and back to my life."

We all nodded enthusiastically, like a bobble heads in the back windows of cars.

Chapter Fifteen

I WENT TO HEALTH AND HUMAN SERVICES DOWNTOWN TO MEET WITH the Executive Director, an old friend, to get some info about the system and how I might be able to work it. I needed an education.

The uniformed receptionist behind the glass wall didn't seem impressed that I had asked for the head of the department. She picked up the phone, asked if Ms. Rigby had time to see . . . "What is your name?" she asked over the mouthpiece.

"Renee Murphy."

"Renee Munday." How soon they forget.

While I waited to be announced, I sat on a plastic chair that leaned with my weight and watched as several children ran rampant through the waiting room, screaming and holding crayons like knives, barefoot, dirty clothes, smelly diapers. Babies squirmed on defeated mothers' arms, grim faces looked at each other with compassion and understanding. Fathers sporting torn tee-shirts and tattoos stood around with their arms crossed, angry they had to report in. The security guard who signed people in just looked bored when he told me I was allowed to go upstairs to the administrative offices. He handed me a filthy visitor's badge which I dutifully clipped onto my lapel.

"You haven't changed your name, I see." The words Eleanor Rigby, on a plastic black plaque on her door, never ceased to grab my attention. The poor woman was born with that name and had suffered her entire life. Honestly, what parent does that?

"Ha. Ha. What can I do for you? How's retirement? Keeping busy?" She stood up from her chair and came around for a hug. I looked over her shoulder to find at least three dozen files piled on the desk in disarray, covering the entire desk. Papers were stacked up neatly in a box on the corner, and she had red markers and highlighters strewn everywhere.

Ellie's personality was perfect for this job, which she'd had for close to a decade. Single, focused, but with a very large helping of humor, she dealt with the lowest of the low in my book: those people who abused, neglected or abandoned their children. As head of Health and Human Services, she was the perfect fit.

"I need some advice, off the record."

"O . . . kay." We sat.

"I know of a kid in the system, about fourteen . . ." and I tried to be non-specific so she wouldn't know who I was talking about, just in case. "What would happen if I just took him in and got him out of the system?"

She sighed. "Do you know how many kids fit that description? I know you're trying to dodge or mislead me, but, honestly," she waved at the mayhem on her desk, "I don't have time to follow up on every case. That's why God made social workers, God love 'em, overworked and underpaid as they are."

She leaned forward, arms folded on her desk. "Look, Renee. Let me give you some general, very broad advice. Keep him in the system. Remember, bio parents have all the rights, and you can't do anything unless you are in the system and begin to make some changes in that kid's life. It's a hassle, it's tough, and you're going to be asked to jump through hoops you won't believe, but it's the system. You can't even get health insurance for him without some kind of documentation that you are taking care of him. You probably can't get him enrolled in school, and believe me, if he's like most of the kids his age that are unclaimed in the system, his record alone is something you can't even begin to approach. I'm not discouraging you from taking him. I'm only telling you like it is. You have an uphill battle, but if you know this kid and have the inclination, it will be well worth it."

"Does the fact that I am the former mayor have any impact on this?"

She shook her curly head. "No. No one gets through the system without meeting all requirements. No one."

"The bio parents have the rights? What if they are in jail?"

"They still call the shots."

"What???"

"True dat."

"Ellie, the mom's in jail and the dad apparently has a rap sheet that reads like the Declaration of Independence. Are you telling me that in the state's better judgement, these losers have control over this kid's life?"

"They are the parents, yes. Until the court says otherwise."

"Ellie . . ."

Her voice lowered. "Renee, do you know that the story you just told me is about ninety-nine percent of my cases? How else would these kids come into the system? Drugs, domestic violence, general under-education about how to care for a child, and basic neglect. That's what I see every single day. My job would be so much easier if someone were to get in there and change the laws, but for now, that's all I have to offer."

"Shit."

"Not the first time I've heard that, not going to be the last." She leaned back in her chair and crossed her fingers together over her tummy.

I thought about Lenny and how he was being treated. We all had the best of intentions for him, but for God's sake, could we just land him somewhere permanent? The hearing would be in fairly soon, and we had no real rights. So far, he was just existing because his mother had given permission to his attorney to find suitable housing for him until the trial.

My electrical system went into overdrive. I felt the familiar tingling all through my limbs and the needles popping through my skin when I thought about how it could have turned out for me. The Palmers had taken me in; without them I probably would have been in fifteen placements myself, or in jail, and I had taken it for granted. Where was he going next?

My head popped up and the words came out without thinking. "Tell me about becoming a foster parent."

———◁|

Congresswoman Barbara Morse and I met for lunch, having put her off several times, and I noticed right away she was not her normal, relaxed, casual self. Her face was pale and the light had gone out of her eyes. Plus my inner gut check was vibrating. She was incredibly sad. Worn out. It felt like grief.

"Is there something wrong?" I asked after we had had our normal chit chat about the state of the union, as it were.

She lowered her eyes and dabbed at her mouth with her napkin. "I'm in a bit of a pickle."

"Oh?"

She leaned back in her chair. "Politics has not been my entire life. My family supported me in my career, but they have always been front and center, even above the State of California."

"As it should be." My reaction was rote. I'm not sure I would have had the same priority.

"I just won re-election and I have no doubt that I will be the Congressperson for this district for the foreseeable future. I've done a good job and I like what I do. My children are grown and I can get more in depth and devote more time to my pet causes."

"But . . ."

Her eyes hardened. "My husband has been diagnosed with Alzheimer's. I need to be home."

The implication astounded me. "You want to give up your seat?"

"I have to. He's my priority, and I think it's also a good message to send; we do have priorities and we need to take care of those we love, above our duties to our state and our country. Both women and men." She took a deep breath. "You don't have a family, so it might be hard for you to understand." Her head came up quickly. "I didn't mean that the way it came out. I've lost my filters. I didn't mean to imply . . ."

"I know what you meant," I said, even though I felt a quick pang. "You're right. I don't have a family, or a significant other, so I don't know, but I suspect what you are doing is right for you." What else was I going to say? I have no idea what the right thing would be.

"I wanted to talk to you first to see if you would be interested in taking my spot. It won't be immediate; I have some things to work out first, and of course there would have to be a special election, but I know you are dedicated to politics and this would be a great opportunity for you if you were interested. I am not about to broadcast this yet, but wanted you to think about it for a while before anything happens."

"Oh, I don't know . . ." Of course I would jump at it, but that's not the way this game is played.

"Just think about it."

"I will."

She took a bite of her salad. "So, what else is going on?"

"I'm worried about a kid in the system."

The astonishment on her face should have surprised me, but it didn't.

"Really."

I smiled. "A young man has come to my attention who is in the system . . ."

She grimaced. "One of my projects. I hate the foster system. Tell me about him."

I told her what I knew. "How would you handle it?"

She sighed. "The problem is once you've become a foster parent, you're in the system, too, with reports, social workers all over the place, and people inspecting your house and your history. Nothing is sacred. I don't blame him for not wanting to go to a foster home again."

"So do you think someone can keep him without becoming part of the system?"

She shook her head. "No. At some point you'll have to show guardianship—school, college applications, medical insurance, and all that. Don't forget the bio parents have all the rights until the court takes those rights away. It takes a long time for that to happen—too long—and in the meantime everyone's in limbo. It's not fair to anyone, but that's the system. As much as I hate to say it, if you are really interested in helping this kid, you have to be registered as a foster parent and go by the book. Otherwise you may lose him, and God knows where he will go. Do you love this kid?"

Love? "I just met him, but I feel an obligation to help." I smelled cat urine again and shuddered. No way was I going to let this kid slip back into that.

"Well, if you do take him, please don't even consider running for my seat. You'll need all the energy you can get, believe me. How old is he?"

"I'm guessing fourteen, fifteen . . ."

"Yikes." She made the sign of the cross in front of me. "God be with you should you decide to do this."

I laughed. "Probably not. It's just something to think about, along with your proposition. I'm also sponsoring an art shop at Heritage Park."

"You'll figure it out," she said. "I suspect becoming a mom is not something you ever considered but believe me when I tell you it will change your life."

Becoming a mom? Yeah. I'm mom material.

Chapter Sixteen

I HAD NOT BEEN SLEEPING WELL. NO HORRIBLE THOUGHTS RAN THROUGH my brain, no nightmares, no worries, just an emptiness that wouldn't go away. I tried to read, but nothing caught my attention. I tried to paint, but globs appeared. All I wanted to do was stay in bed. It took a monumental effort to get out of it; sometimes I waited until late afternoon.

I sat down with my spiked coffee to start another boring day. I swear, this retirement thing stinks. Where is the structure? The busy phone? The people I dreaded seeing because they always either a) wanted something, or b) complained a lot. I missed them.

My phone trilled. Oh, goodie. Just a number.

"Hello?"

"Mrs. Murphy?"

"Ms. Murphy, yes. Who's calling?"

"This is Officer Dan Wheeler from the IRS."

"Yes?"

"I'm calling to tell you that we have identified some non-reported income on your tax return and am calling to collect those funds. Something niggled at the back of my brain.

"How much?"

"Seventeen thousand, four hundred sixty-three dollars and seventy-two cents."

"I don't owe that."

"Yes, ma'am, you do, and if I cannot collect today I will have to send the police out to your house to arrest you."

A light bulb went on. This scam was on TV last night. The IRS doesn't call you, and if there is a problem, they don't send the police. They sue you. But I decided to play along and waste his time just for my own amusement. I was bored and cranky and this served my purposes easily.

A half-hour later, when he thought he had me good and cornered and I was about to give him my account number, my PIN, and the authority to go get it out of my account, I turned on him and gave him every expletive in the book. I had been so sweet, so old-ladyish, so scared and compliant, he was shocked and listened to every word. I then hung up on him and called back the number incessantly so he had to pick it up and listen to very loud hip hop music. I laughed out loud while I blocked his number from my own phone and carried this on for another hour. In my final call, I said, "See how it feels to have your time wasted?" and hung up.

I sure showed him. *Jesus, I'm reduced to playing childish games.*

My phone trilled again. "I told you I don't want to waste any more time!" *Wait. Didn't I block him?*

Nothing. Then finally, "Renee?" It was Ron's voice. Oops. I tried to laugh, but it came out a sort of sob. "I'm being harassed by a horrible scam. What can I do for you?" My professional voice was back.

"Um. Nothing, really. I just heard about Jen and wanted to check in and see how you were doing."

"So far we don't have much news; we are hoping for the best."

"Okay . . . so, how are you?"

"I'm okay. Bored, but okay." Don't know why I said that.

"Bored? You?" He laughed. "Want to meet for lunch?"

My gut—or something—clenched. Shit. I already said I was bored, so he knows I have time.

"Sure," I said, trying to sound cheerful. Is this a date? Nah.

"Good. I want to support you. I know you and Jen are close."

Oh.

We met at a burger joint. He ordered iced tea and I had a cold beer. We talked about city business a bit, a little more about Jen, and laughed at some old history of crazy people we had run across. I began to relax and enjoy his company once again. But I was so tired.

Once the plates were cleared, he ordered coffee and I had another beer. His eyebrows rose just a hint (I was watching), but he said nothing.

"I hear you have a lease on the Carlisle house at the art park."

Ah. His new girlfriend has been filling him in.

I nodded and put down my beer. "Yes, and it's being put together as we speak." I filled him in on Adam and our projected opening date, noting that another lease had been signed. He nodded.

I decided to jump in. "Ron, has anyone from the party contacted you?"

"The party? You mean Ambrose?"

"Uh-huh. Ambrose. He's asking questions."

"About what?"

"About us."

"Us?" The look on his face told me that thought was preposterous. "You mean *us* us?"

I nodded. "Apparently they think something was going on with us and that's why I gave you that ten percent raise."

"We have nothing to hide." He held his hands up. "If asked, I'll tell the truth, just as I know you have."

"So he hasn't called you."

He nodded. "There was a message this morning, but I haven't returned the call."

"Please call him back this afternoon and put this to rest."

"Will do. Is there anything I can do for you and Jen? You look exhausted" *Gee thanks.*

"Thank you, no. If I know Jen, and I think I do, she'll want to handle this quietly and without much fanfare. But thanks."

We stood and he put a hand on my shoulder, like an older brother. "Just call if you need anything."

"I will." *Say hi to Suzanne for me. Gag.*

What the hell was I doing? Only what my old, withered, beaten up heart told me to do. This kid needed me.

God help him. Ellie had fast tracked it for me, and a team of social workers showed up right at three o'clock and went through my house. If this was a normal house inspection, I'd eat my sombrero.

They took five minutes and asked few questions. They noted there were no animals, no toxins, no booze or trash evident. My bed was made and there was the room I had used for storage and art supplies that Lenny could have, with its own bathroom. I had always planned on making it a real art studio. It ended up being a catch-all.

They looked in my cupboards, my refrigerator, and my closets. For about two seconds. Two of the social workers left and the third stayed behind. "I am so sorry, but we do need these forms filled out, and you'll have to go get a background check done for the record. After that, we will do another inspection and you will be cleared. Then you go to a series of classes and you can have a foster child placed with you." Her name was Camille, with long bangs and huge eyes; she looked like a Holly Hobby girl from my childhood. She was tiny but professional and, I could tell, strong. I guess she had to be in this business.

"But . . .I was the mayor. There is nothing the public doesn't know about me." Not quite true, but at least I'm not on a sex offender registry.

"Yes, ma'am, but we have to run our own. I'm so sorry." She cocked her head. "If it were up to me . . ."

"Of course," I said.

"You know," she said, a bit shyly, I thought, and put her hand on my arm, "what you are doing is wonderful. We need more like you. There are too many kids out there, and not nearly enough fosters." She handed me a stack of papers about three inches thick to fill out, along with instructions on how to get the background check, including fingerprinting and a drug test. She said good-bye and left. I had just collapsed onto my thrift store couch when my phone buzzed, a text from Bruce:

911. Come to downtown police station.

Chapter Seventeen

"I DON'T CARE WHAT THE SITUATION IS, HE'S A KID IN THE SYSTEM WITH A record and he's stolen something. I had to bring him here." The young cop was harsh, unemotional. I wondered what he actually looked like under all that Kevlar and padding.

"May I talk to him?" I asked. The cop, Officer Brandt, clearly and unhappily recognized me.

"He's being processed right now, so no." *There's one vote I didn't get.*

"So what do we do?"

"You wait. His social worker will be in touch."

"But . . ."

He held his hand up. "Not my problem." And walked away. He must see these kids all the time. I tamped down my anger, knowing I was tired and out of place. I pushed the double doors to get outside to call Bruce. I had my phone in hand when he came out of the building behind me. "Whew."

"What happened?"

"Tricia called and asked me to take him shopping. The little snot decided to not pay for the underwear he picked out. He wouldn't let me, so he stuffed it under his shirt and left the store before I could convince him not to. They got him at the scanner and had him arrested. Since he has a record, they wasted no time, and since I was not a relative or a guardian, I had no power. They did, however, let me sit with him because he said he wouldn't talk without someone there."

"Oh, Bruce, thank you."

"That is one scared kid."

"Want him?" The words were out of my mouth before I could sensor them.

"What? No. I'm too old, but if you were to take him I'd help out." He fished in his pocket for his keys. "I have to go get Jen from the hospital. You'll have to take him." He turned and walked back to his car.

"Jesus." I turned around and went back into Juvenile Hall and confronted my BFF Officer Brandt. "Where do I go to get a background check?" I knew I was going to have to get one if I was going to have a kid in my house. Might as well do it now, and the police station was one place on the list.

"We do them here, but not for the public."

"I'm not the public. I'm a public servant." My stare didn't faze him.

"Ms. Murphy?" Another officer came down the hall. I recognized him as one of Ron's recruits. "The mayor just called and said to help you any way we can. Come this way, please, and we can process that background check right now." Thank God. Jen must have called in a favor and reached out to Ron for help.

"Thank you." I wanted to stick my tongue out at Brandt but thought better of it. I am, after all, a public servant.

After I filled out the form they took my fingerprints and picture, then I asked to be allowed to see Lenny. "Of course. This way to the visitors' room."

I waited. And waited. Lenny came through, his hands shackled.

"Is that really necessary?" I asked his companion.

"Yes, ma'am."

"It's okay. I'm a criminal." Lenny's voice was almost a whisper.

"No, you're not. You're a scared kid who is too proud and too lonely to know what's up and what's down."

His head whipped up. "I'm not a kid." `

"Oh, yes you are. You're, what, fourteen? That's not an adult. You have some learning and growing to do before you can honestly say you're not a kid."

"I'm fifteen."

"Fifteen. Big whup."

The rage on his face frightened me. "I have seen more in my life that you ever have, lady, and I know more about this world that you ever will." His voice was that of a man. A very pissed-off man.

"Don't bet on it, my friend, but this is not a competition."

"I am not your friend."

"No, you are not. You have to earn the right to be my friend." The staring contest continued.

"I fucked up," he said, lowering his head.

Ha. Don't mess with Mayor Me. "Yes, you certainly did. What are you going to do about it?"

"Whatever they want me to do, I guess."

"Don't you want to be in charge of your own life?"

"Yes, but like you said, I'm just a kid." His thin, white lips told me he was still fighting. I can't win.

"You can't have it both ways, Lenny. Either you take charge, or you let everyone else tell you how it's going to be. What's your choice? Make it now. Because, yes, they are in charge in this situation, but your input and your attitude will have a huge influence on the power they hold over you right now."

He hung his head. After a few minutes he whispered, "You know how some kids want a car, new clothes, expensive shoes?"

"Yeah."

"All I want is someone to love me."

The punch to my gut made me sit up straight and fight back tears. I stood up and walked around the table to get my composure back. "Okay, then. I don't know anything about love myself, to be honest. But I do know that there are three people right now who want to help you. Me, Jen, and Bruce. You can live with any one of us, but I'm sorry, it has to be through the system. I've already had a house inspection and my application is pending. You've been with Jen and you know Bruce, but Jen is sick right now. All three of us will work on this together, but you have to live with just one of us. Who's it going to be?"

"That's easy. You."

"Why me?"

His face came up and our eyes locked. "Because we are the same."

Maybe he wasn't such a kid after all.

Lennie was going to be in juvvie for a while.

I called the head of the K-9 unit for the Police Department, a woman I had worked with to expand the program. There was a pup who had washed out. I was welcome to adopt him. His name was Gunnar. He would be an answer to my quiet house, someone would be there to greet me, and now I realized a boy needs a dog, too. It might help break the ice. Every kid likes dogs, right?

Gunnar turned out to be a German Shepherd, full grown but clearly too sweet for the job. Less than a year old, he was fully trained, but his records reflected that he lacked the killer instinct to be a reliable K-9 cop. He just wanted to be buddies. Make love, not war.

He looked scary to me, but I relaxed when he placed his chin on my knee as I signed the papers and he turned his gray eyes up to my face. Some killer. He came with a canine backpack; I watched as they packed some food and treats, along with instructions on how to assimilate him into the house. I smiled when I remembered the political adage: Want a friend? Get a dog.

We ran around town together, Gunnar in the back seat, and gathered supplies for him—a bed, food, toys, and bowls. He hung over my shoulder and watched through the windshield, his hot breath breezing past my cheek. We went into the pet store together and he never left my side. I unloaded the car and started to set things up.

"Where are we going to put you, boy?" I asked as he sniffed every inch of the house. I put his huge bed in a corner of the kitchen and set out bowls and found homes for his food and toys. When I opened his pack, I found his badge with a red stripe across it, indicating he was no longer in service. When I turned around he was gone. I found him sound asleep on my bed, so I curled up next to him.

I had a new bestie.

The store was ready. I stopped in to chat with Adam about the opening. Boxes had been neatly broken down, supplies had been put away, and I had a pile of invoices sitting on the desk in what had clearly been the cleaning closet.

I was impressed with the progress made: easels had been set up in the parlor, stools in front, and a table had been set against the wall for still-life demonstrations. Cubbies were built, like those in kindergarten, for stowing personal effects while the students were in front of their easels, out of the way and out of paint drippings. Nice touch. One room upstairs had four long tables arranged in a square for a sketch, watercolor, or mosaic class. It could also be used as a conference room. Another room had a bit of a stage set up for models and demonstrations.

Lighting had been added to spotlight works of art that had already started to come in from local artists. Some had price tags on them, some not, but each had a label behind a plate of acrylic with the name of the piece and the artist. There were a few compositions as well, made from newspaper and magazine pages, that formed impressive pictures with texture and paint on canvas: a different form of art—collage.

When we got down to specifics, I was surprised to find that Adam had arranged for a soft opening day. He had made arrangements for some local artists to hang pieces in the studio for that day and to be available to talk about the process of painting and perhaps give demonstrations for the afternoon. His vision was to have the store look like a normal studio day, artists at easels, a class in session, and a display of paints and tools for sale. Very easy, very relaxed.

He had placed flyers about the opening, offering a free class for the day, noting who the visiting artists were, and in general talking about the shop.

"But what about PR? We need to get people in here."

"Have faith, dear lady. They will come." I took that to mean that this would bring people in on a small scale and it would grow, and that he knew what he was doing. Maybe a soft opening was best. Find out what people wanted, get feedback on the shop, and be able to speak one-on-one with prospective members and students.

I let it go. Perhaps he was right. Interested parties were those who would either want to sell their art on the gallery side or learn how to make art on the studio side, and those people, I assumed from Adam's comments, would not appreciate a huge blowout.

I stopped in to check up on Jen. We had been in touch over the phone, but I had not seen her. I was aware she had started her treatments and knew she was not well. Chemo is a bitch. Bruce opened the door and ushered me in with a falsely cheerful voice. I found Jen on the living room couch, covered in a blanket. My heart stopped.

She was gray, wrinkled, and old-looking. She also had lost quite a lot of weight. *In ten days???*

"I think I'll take the dogs out for a nice, long walk," said Bruce, "while you two catch up." He leaned down and kissed Jen on the forehead, then left with the dogs.

I tried some humor. "You look like the dog's dinner."

"Gee, thanks."

"I'm serious. What's going on?" I needed details.

Jen's eyes bored into mine. "The lab report came back with more bad cells and I had my first chemo yesterday."

I plopped down on the couch next to her.

"Close your mouth," she said, and closed her eyes.

"What . . ."

"They are doing everything they can, Renee. The chemo is grueling, but they say it might save my life. Radiation starts soon, too."

"The full Monty, huh?"

"The full Monty." Her face spasmed and she grabbed a bowl from the side table and wretched into it. "Nothing left," she gasped.

"Oh, God, Jen."

"Now I know what my mother was going through. How's the shop coming?"

"I think I told you opening day is in two weeks. Adam has arranged for a soft opening, just a few artists and people who are wanna-be artists." I shrugged.

"I take it you don't agree."

"I had visions of the entire town showing up, but maybe this is best."

"Then why did I put the word out? Oops," she said quietly while she wretched again. "I told everyone I know." The doorbell rang. "Oh thank God. Get that, will you?"

I opened the door to find a young man wearing an auto mechanic's shirt that said, "Matthew" on it. He looked a little confused. "Is Mrs. Conrad home?"

"Jen? It's someone named Matthew."

"Hallelujah. Have him come in."

Matthew found his way to the living room. "What, first your husband, then your mother, now you?"

"Afraid so. Got the stuff?"

He smiled. "Natch."

He handed her a zipped bag full of what I recognized from my high school days. He also pulled out a few hand-rolled joints from his shirt pocket. "Here."

"I've never smoked it before. I just put it in brownies." *What? Goody two-shoes Jen???*

"This is more instant. It's now legal medically, you know. You don't have to call me."

Jen smiled. "Then when would I see your smiling face? Renee, meet my drug dealer. I met him last year; he introduced me to this stuff that helped Mother get through her illness. She never knew it, but I suppose she suspected because she kept asking for the 'special' brownies." Jen smiled. "Matt bought Arthur's car."

"Big Bessie?"

"Yes, ma'am. She's my pride and joy now." He turned to Jen. "Call me if you need anything else." Jen reached for her purse. "No ma'am, this round is on me."

"Thank you, Matthew." He left and she lit up a joint. "Big Bessie now has bright yellow and orange flames going down her sides." She rolled her eyes. "I can't decide if Arthur would be pleased or not."

"What are you *doing*?" My world view was being shattered. The prim socialite, the perfectly coiffed and manicured grown-up pseudo-debutante, smoked pot.

"I'm taking care of myself. Want some?"

By the time Bruce came back we were giggling the way we used to in her room at the Putnam mansion.

"I'm sorry if you disapprove," Jen said to Bruce. "I probably should have told you I was doing this."

Bruce smiled. "I was going to suggest it myself but wasn't sure where to get it. I see you have your own source." He looked directly at me.

"It's not me," I shouted. Then laughed. "I'm starving. I'm leaving."

"You might want to wait a bit," Bruce said. "Let's go outside and get some fresh air and let Jen take a nap." So we did. He caught me up on the medical end of things, and I understood how serious this was. They weren't sure they got everything, contrary to what the surgeon told us in the waiting room.

It was going to be a long haul, and I was glad to be a little high. Otherwise I might just fall apart.

Chapter Eighteen

ODAY WAS LENNY'S MOVE-IN DAY; I HAD FINISHED MY PARENTING CLASSES weeks ago. I was just home from a visit with Jen when I saw social worker Camille's car pull up and watched as she and Lenny sat for a minute talking. It looked like Camille was lecturing him.

Gunnar, killer guard dog that he is, met them at the door, wagging his tail and piddling on the floor.

"You have a dog." Lenny said. Camille looked surprised. Gunnar was not here on the inspection and I wondered if this would be a problem.

"Yeah, I just got him. He was supposed to be a police dog, but he washed out. Didn't have the killer instinct, so he came here. He's trained, but unreliable."

"I don't like dogs." Okay, then.

Camille stayed with us while we inspected the house. Lenny stood in the middle of what had been marked for my studio but was now his room, furnished quickly with warehouse dorm-type furnishings. He held a plastic grocery bag that Gunnar nudged and sniffed. I didn't know what was inside but assumed it held personal items from his stint.

"This room is for me?"

"Well . . . yeah."

He walked into the bathroom. "And this is mine? I don't have to share it?"

"All yours, Dude." I felt like an ass. I'd never used that word before.

"Wow." He picked up a gift card that I had laid on the desk. "What's this?"

"I thought you might need stuff for school, some clothes and supplies. I had no idea what you would want, so I just got that."

"Oh . . . okay."

"Well . . .I guess I'll leave you to sort things out." The bag of things I'd retrieved from the cat place sat under the desk, and I saw him eye it as I left the room. Gunnar elected to stay with him. I heard his door close softly as I went down the stairs.

Camille left without saying a thing about Gunnar. She nodded to me, gave me yet another card, turned around, and left. I could see her metaphorically wiping her hands of this mess.

"We have to talk about school . . ."

"Shit." Lenny's face faced the floor. "I don't want to."

"What, talk, or go to school?" I fumbled around the kitchen. Lenny had had his bowl of Cocoa Puffs (was that OK?) and began to fling his knee up and down like the nervous kid he was.

Do I correct the language, or be cool?

"I'm pretty far behind. My grades weren't that good." He sniffed. "Do I smell grass?"

"No . . . okay, yes. Jen had some for her chemo treatment." I didn't admit to partaking.

He smiled. "Cool."

"No, it's not. It's medically legal, and if it helps my friend feel better I'm all for it. Now, what are we going to do about school?" I was still waiting for his school records to come through the system, so I didn't know where he stood, but I knew that Camille was going to be getting on me soon to get some schooling down his throat.

"I don't know. I'm not going."

"Let me see what Camille says." Better to take the bull by the horns, but God I hated to start that process. I texted Camille, asking what our next step was. I got one back in a few minutes saying she was setting an appointment for testing to see if he was "age appropriate" for his education.

Age appropriate? What the hell does that even mean? Lenny saw my frown.

"Let's do our own testing, shall we?" I suggested.

"Taking control?"

"Yup. Let's see where you are and see if we can get some tutoring before you have to take that test." I saw the look on his face and knew I might be heading into a brick wall. "Really. It can only help. You don't want them to put you back in third grade, do you?" I smiled, hoping he got the joke.

He didn't. "I'm smarter than a third-grader." His voice rose and my backbone braced.

"I know. It was a joke."

"It sucked."

"I'm sorry. Lenny, I don't know how to do this. You didn't come with an instruction manual."

"If I did, it would say to replace all parts."

Chills ran down my arms, raising goose bumps. I took a deep breath. "Maybe just a tune-up and lube job."

"Now *that* was a joke." Interesting. No smile, but an attempt at a connection.

We went to the big bookstore and picked up ten small books of self-testing intelligence tests. He could pick and choose which ones he wanted to take. I was sort of interested in taking some of the tests myself. We stopped for some fried chicken to go and went home. Gunnar had made a huge accident in the kitchen.

"Argghhh . . .I didn't think about letting him out before we left. I should have thought about that. Damn it!" I exploded. *What am I doing with a kid if I can't even take care of a dog's basic needs?* I let Gunnar out and cleaned up the mess while Lenny went upstairs.

I called Bruce. "How's Jen?"

"She's got a needle in her arm and earphones in. This process is . . . basically just wait while they pump poison into you."

"Are you hiring a nurse to stay with her?" Silence. "Bruce?"

"I don't know yet. I'm sure we'll work it out."

"Let me know if you need anything."

"You've got enough on your plate. How's Lenny?"

"Enigmous. Is that even a word?"

"You'll work it out. I have to go now; the doctor is here." Click.

Oh, God.

The next morning, Lenny came downstairs with the bag of books. Shit. He's not going to take them. I knew it. Now what do I do? He plopped the bag on the table. "Can I have some cereal?"

"You don't have to ask. This is your house. Get whatever you want."

He stood and grabbed the box of cereal, then opened the door to the fridge. "Out of milk."

"How can we be out of milk? I just got a gallon."

He shrugged. "I had some last night while I worked on those." He pointed to the bag.

"Oh?" My heart sped up. "How do you think you did? Not that it means anything," I added quickly.

He shrugged again. "I did okay, I think. They weren't hard." Teen bravado or confidence? Silence for a bit as he chomped on dry cereal. "I'm going out."

"Where?"

"I don't know. Just out." Probably wants to be rid of me. Can't say as I blame him. He put his bowl in the sink and turned to leave. "See you later."

Do I put a time frame on him? What do I do? "When do you think you'll be . . . back?"

He shrugged. "I don't know."

We stared at each other a while, then I started to laugh. "Okay, Lenny. Just be back by five or I'll worry." He nodded and left.

I hoped that was okay. It's all right to let a fifteen-year-old walk alone, right?

The mail had arrived, and I found my first check from HHS. Apparently, you get paid to raise somebody else's kid.

I realized that he needed a phone and I happened to have an extra one, the one that I planned to use for business. Why not have him use it? I grabbed it and threw it in my purse.

"Want to go to the park, boy?" Gunnar threw himself into a tizzy and I finally got him leashed and into the car. Off we went to the dog park to play with other dogs. Gunnar wore himself out and we headed out to do our business.

What else? Lenny will need some pocket money. How much? I got $100 in small bills and decided to figure it out later. Maybe it's too much. Maybe it's not enough. Kids need stuff. Like supplies at the art store.

What the hell am I doing?

I found myself at Canvas. Gunnar dragged me up the stairs, where he exploded through the door and right into Adam, who was carrying a series of canvases. They dropped to the floor, and Adam turned pale. "Well, I see you have a bodyguard," he said, his voice somewhat rough. He had plastered himself against the wall. "I don't particularly like big dogs."

"I'm so sorry . . . wasn't this your idea?" Adam remained glued to the wall. I think he wanted to disappear into it and come out the other side.

"It's quite all right," he said as he took out a handkerchief and wiped his brow. "Just an old childhood phobia."

"Gunnar. Here." I heard Lenny's voice come from the kitchen, then he came out into the foyer. "Are you checking up on me?" Gunnar happily sat at Lenny's side, drool dripping on the floor, eyes adoringly pointed at his face. *Impressive.*

"No . . . no. I had no idea you were here, but I do have something for you." I handed him the phone.

"Whoa. For me?"

"Yes, so you can call me. My number's already in there."

"Thanks." He tried to be nonchalant, but I could tell he was really pleased. He shoved the phone into his back pocket.

"Counting pennies?" I said, as I took in all the change on the counter.

"Having a lesson in percentages." Adam turned to Lenny. "It helps if you break it down into a language one can understand. Money seems to do it," Adam whispered as he continued to shove the coins around. "So what percentage is this?"

"Seventy, eighty-four cents . . . eighty-four percent of a dollar."

"And if I wanted to know the percentage of two dollars?"

"Half of that? Forty-two percent?"

"Excellent, my boy. Now," he looked at his watch, "go set up the easels for this afternoon's class." Adam turned to me. "I've hired him. His payment is all the art supplies he can use." He grinned. "Plus some sage advice from time to time." I sighed. An ally. Thank God.

Chapter Nineteen

I WAS AT THE SHOP ON OPENING DAY AT EIGHT A. M. THE OFFICIAL opening was 3:00 that afternoon, but I wanted to make sure everything was ready. Plus I needed to tell Adam this was not going to be the quiet opening he had envisioned. I had run a major city but was a bit anxious about this.

Who am I?

Knowing that Jen had contacted everyone she knew, I had arranged for a caterer to come in with wine and appetizers. The social set would expect this at the very least, and I thought an art gallery opening warranted some whiz-bang action. I also suspected that these people broadcast to everyone else they knew, and the crowd would be much larger than Adam was expecting.

Flower arrangements started to arrive, and Adam looked a little annoyed.

"What's wrong?" I asked after the third basket arrived.

"Nothing, my dear lady. I was hoping to do this under the radar, as they say."

"Why? I was the mayor, you know, and people are going to support this."

"Ma'am? Where would you like us to set up?" Oh, God. The caterers. I turned to point to the back patio and saw that Adam had disappeared.

The first person to arrive was Jen, looking rosier than the last time I saw her, wearing a turban *a la* Gloria Swanson and floating inside a watercolor-y chiffon caftan. Bruce supported her by the elbow, and I could tell she was irked. I started to give her a hug, but Bruce intervened. "Remember, she's just had surgery," he said.

Jen's eyes rolled and she placed her hand on his arm. For the first time I realized she did not have a manicure. How her world has changed. "Bruce, please don't hover."

"What do you want me to do?"

"Well, for starters, how about a glass of wine?"

"But your medication . . ."

"Bruce, please. Just a glass of white wine."

"As you wish . . ."

"Jesus, what I would give for a moment alone," she said quietly as she watched Bruce's back disappear into the kitchen.

"Ah, let yourself be pampered for a bit," I said lightly.

"Renee, I've been pampered my whole life and I'm sick of it."

I stood, stunned. "You can't think this treatment is pampering you."

"You have a point there. But I am in this alone. Nobody can help. It's up to me and science, maybe God. I'm alone. Having someone hovering who can't help is just embarrassing."

"Well . . . is there anything I can do?" I began to laugh, and Jen snorted. "Just keep him occupied. I need some time."

"Will do." I saluted smartly and walked away.

I had brought Gunnar and tied him to a tree outside, thinking he would be a draw. He was far enough away to not bother anyone who didn't like dogs, but close enough for people to approach if they wanted to. He was kept busy with a rawhide bone and several toys, but I could tell he was on alert. I was getting to know him and his moods, and he did have moods.

Adam had put Lenny to work moving tables and chairs and generally cleaning up. They both disappeared the minute visitors arrived. I was more than irritated to do this alone; I felt like a wife whose husband had deserted his hosting duties.

A caricature artist came in and took his spot in what had been the dining room, ready with a sketchpad, and began to get to work, hunched over on a stool. He had long blonde hair and a serious expression. Before I knew it, sketches of me, Adam, and Jen were displayed on the table. They were good likenesses in black pen, with one particular feature done in colored pencil. Jen's picture featured her turban, bright pink, and he had added a diamond to the center of it. Adam's blue eyes were startlingly accurate, the exact color and shape. If I had seen only the eyes I would have known it was Adam. Mine was my hair—he had not colored it but drawn in light yellow and white strands through the dark curls. Very unflattering, I thought. Jen loved it. "He got you!"

He sure did. Old.

"Where is everybody?" Jen asked. "I thought you'd be inundated by now." She had seen the baskets of flowers and recognized the names of friends of hers. "How nice. They never come to these things, but it was nice of them to acknowledge your opening." She deliberately pulled the notes and handed them to me with a sly look. God, Jen is prompting me to write thank you's. Some things never change. I stomped into the office to deposit them on my desk to write them later and found Adam there, fidgeting with envelopes and invoices. "Be there in a mo!" he said with forced cheer.

"Where is Lenny?" I asked. I had a minor in my possession, and I didn't know where he was. Adam shrugged, focused on an invoice.

Great.

I headed back out to find about twenty people wandering around quietly, glass in hand. Waitstaff stood with trays of appetizers; clearly they had already made the rounds and had no takers. They looked bored. A clipboard had been on the table next to the sketched caricatures with sign-ups for his class. No one had signed up yet. I scribbled my own name.

Maybe portrait sketching wasn't their thing. I wandered into the parlor where one artist stood at an easel and two people watched him recreate the wax fruits in a gold bowl on the table. They were quiet, as though they were in the gallery of a golf tournament and the pro was about to tee off. I glanced at the sign-up sheet and saw one person had signed up. I was getting down at the response and the lack of enthusiasm, and so I added a pseudonym just to see if I could start something.

I heard her before I saw her. That damn bracelet. In the entryway stood Suzanne, with a death grip on Ron's arm. "Idn't it cute?" she exclaimed.

This just gets better and better.

I greeted them and pointed them to the wine. Suzanne started in that direction, but Ron stayed with me. I saw her hesitate, then, mercifully, Jen's voice called out to her in recognition, and she had no choice but to leave her date with me.

"I like it," he said. "Very nice." He turned back to me. "I understand the place next to you is leased as well. This art park is going to be a hit, thanks to you."

"From yoah mouth to Gawd's eah," I said. He laughed, and Suzanne was there in two seconds, carrying one glass of white and one of red. "Here you go. I know you prefer red," she said to him. I could have told her he really preferred a beer, but whatever.

"Come on, let's check it all out," she said to him, grabbing his sleeve. I left them to do what they would.

Bitch. Why did this bother me so much?

Maggie Putnam, all dressed up, freshly coiffed and manicured, stood in the entryway with Tricia, Jen and Bruce. I could tell Maggie was tight as a tick, uncomfortable in this casual environment, and unhappy that Bruce was hovering. Jen had told me Maggie referred to Bruce as nothing but a construction guy, as though he were not worthy of her sister. Jen did not correct her, nor was Maggie aware that Bruce came from a well-known, very successful architectural dynasty that he had been expected to carry on. He chose not to follow in his father's footsteps, but rather went the creative, building side of the business. He had, in fact, been a very successful architect, had designed some very well-known structures, and had made a fortune doing what he hated. What he wanted was to design and produce small pieces as art, not production buildings.

Bruce's past was none of Maggie's business, and I admired the fact that neither one of them took enough interest to correct her. Snob.

"Mind if I wander?" said Tricia. "I've heard so much about Canvas, but Adam wouldn't let me come until it was finished." She followed me into the parlor, where we were alone.

"I haven't seen Adam since we opened the door. I have no idea where he is," I said.

"Oh, I can see him at home," she said after a brief hesitation and wandered off.

Jen waved to me as she and Bruce left a few minutes later. Maggie was nowhere to be seen. I wandered into the dining area and checked out the portraitist. Suzanne had been depicted very nicely, all curves and perfection, but her bracelet received the star treatment. He had used a glittering silver pencil and oversized the charms.

But Maggie! Maggie had been illustrated with her large expensive conspicuous-consumer bag hanging from both hands at the center of her skirt, feet planted shoulder-width, with a forlorn look on her face. The bag had been colored in green, although I could have sworn it was brown in real life. The artist saw me looking at it. He pointed. "That one has a lot of baggage, and most of it is green." I grinned. He just made up for the insult he had hurled at me with my portrait. I turned around to find the caterers cleaning up.

It was over. So disappointing.

Chapter Twenty

*O*UR FIRST CLASS, A STILL-LIFE IN OILS, HAD TWO PEOPLE SIGNED UP AT the opening. I decided to join them. I asked Lenny to come with me, but he declined and stayed in his room. I wanted to do the same. My energy level was so low, but I had to show up; it was my shop.

Adam had created various beginner kits to be sold, the price of which astounded me. If everyone bought just the kit, we'd be making our lease payment in no time.

I carried my painter's kit into Canvas to find that Adam had set up a workshop. What was once the parlor had been turned into a classroom with easels pointed toward the front. A bowl of fruit sat on a table to be duplicated in oils. I became immediately intimidated.

There were only four people in this first class, all beginners, I hoped. I had run a city of approximately one-and-a-half million people, and here four strangers intimidated me. The woman on my right was a bleached blonde, sort of puffy woman who wore too much makeup and smelled of baby powder. Her fingernails were bright red, clearly acrylic. She wore a loose black-and-white zebra-print top with black pants and black patent leather flats.

One of our classmates was a woman approaching middle age who looked like a librarian: cashmere twinset over plaid skirt, cat eyeglasses hung from a rhinestone chain around her neck, and tight curls on her head that once had been brown but was now fading into a dim, washed-out auburn with white streaks. She introduced herself as Marjorie Butterworth (dear God, what a name), and I recognized her as a well-known, highly respected psychiatrist who was in great demand. She had written several books and was a graduate of Harvard Medical School.

Next to her was a buttoned-up young man introduced as Dan. He wore a green V-neck sweater over a starched white oxford shirt. He dusted his easel with a pristine hankie. I had watched him pull out an anti-bacterial wipe and sterilize his seat before he planted himself delicately. I immediately dubbed him Fancy Dan.

And then . . . Suzanne showed up, all bounces and smiles. I found myself hoping that her red dress got splotched with paint.

Bad Renee.

She giggled as she set up her station and made a huge production of putting her things away and hanging a pristine white apron around her neck, tying it in back, that damn bracelet clanging.

After introductions, Adam said as he pointed to the table, "By the end of six weeks, you will have this still life finished and framed. You are all at the beginning of this journey, so feel free to talk and share your apprehensions and your fears." He smiled and turned away, throwing over his shoulder, "Then discard them and have fun."

"I don't have a creative bone in my body." I turned to the Marge-In-Charge to my right. "Sally, right?"

"Yes, I'm Sally. Me, neither. I'm an economics professor. How's that for creative . . . and you were the mayor?" She sounded like she couldn't quite believe it.

I nodded. "What brought you here?"

"My husband made me. Said I was no fun anymore since I stopped drinking. Apparently, I'm boring when I'm sober. Hopefully I'll find a new addiction."

"Ah, I see." I had known many alcoholics in recovery in my time.

"Does that make you uncomfortable?" she asked.

"A little. Does my last job make you uncomfortable?"

"A little." She giggled.

"Well . . . good," I said, and we laughed.

"Class clowns," Adam said, and nodded to us. The rest of the group smiled indulgently.

The class, while I was very rusty, was fun and allowed the other side of my brain to work, and Sally and I chatted while we painted. She understood my sense of humor, and I let it free for once. There was no one to judge me.

I came home from unboxing even more supplies and moving furniture to find Camille and Lenny in the living room. They were talking about going back to school. I had a headache and my back was screaming. I just wanted to escape the real world.

"I'm afraid you didn't do too well on those tests," she said to Lenny. "But that doesn't mean we can't get you up to speed." He hung his head. My heart raced. This was not his fault. None of this was his fault.

"What do we do?" I asked. "Tutoring? Special Ed?"

Lenny's head jerked up. "Special Ed?"

Camille quietly said, "That is the wrong phrase. Special Ed means he has special needs, like he is developmentally delayed. He is not. He is educationally delayed."

"I'm sorry." I looked at Lenny. "I don't know the lingo yet." I smiled, but he didn't smile back. He leaned back and crossed his arms over his chest. The jackhammer was going again in his knee. Uh-oh.

"You'll be entering halfway through the school year," Camille said. "But you will be considerably behind. I have a list here of approved and recommended tutors and educators that can help." She handed a many-times-over Xeroxed list of names. I could hardly read some of them. Lenny put his head down.

"You have to go to school, Lenny," she said.

"Any chance to homeschool?" I asked.

"No. Not unless you go through some really advanced training and get approved by the state to do it. It's better if he goes to school with people his own age."

"I'm right here." His voice was so soft it hurt me. "You don't have to talk about me when I'm right in front of you," he said, a look of defiance on this face.

"He's right," I said, pointing at Lenny. "Talk to him. It's his life."

"But you are in charge of his life. You're responsible."

"Yes, I'm aware of that." Total silence as we stared each other down. This was not going to be easy, but I was used to people stonewalling me.

"We'll talk it out and get back to you," I said, and stood.

Camille grabbed her notebook and stood as well. "I don't think you understand how this works . . ."

"I do, and I'm telling you we want to talk this over before any commitment is made."

"You may not have a choice."

"Be that as it may, we still want to have a quiet discussion between the two of us."

"Fine. Call me tomorrow and we'll make arrangements to get him into school." She left.

"She's a ballbuster," he mumbled. Progress. More than one word.

"I know her type. She's by-the-book, and probably right. We may not have a choice in this. But tell me what you are thinking."

"Really?"

"Yeah. It's your life."

"Guess I'll go."

"Okay, then. That's settled. We'll tell Camille tomorrow that's the decision."

"Won't she be surprised," he said, and clomped up to his room.

I wondered how he would do. Academically, I suspected he would catch up just fine. It was the horrible social aspect of high school I was worried about. I poured a drink and sat in front of the boob tube. I really just wanted to curl up and disappear.

"What?" I screamed into my phone. Well, it wasn't a scream, more of an outraged question. "Are you telling me I have to take Lenny to see his mother *in jail?*"

I could hear Camille take a deep breath. "Yes. That is her right, and she is exercising it. I will take him. It's my job."

"What the hell?" It was out before I could stop myself. "Excuse me. This is a shock. He's getting ready to go to school tomorrow. I'm not sure I want to spring this on him."

"Well, I can if it's better for you, but I have to have him there soon. Visiting days are Wednesdays."

"But we don't even know what will happen at school. What if he has to do something?"

"This takes priority." Her voice was firm, strong. Like what I had to say didn't matter.

"What if he doesn't want to?"

"It's his mother's right." She didn't answer the question.

I sighed. "All right. I'll tell him."

"I'll text you with all the info." Suddenly she was cheerful, like I had answered correctly.

Great. As I hung up, I realized Wednesday night would be a painting class at Canvas, and Adam would need Lenny's help getting set up.

No time like the present.

I offered to take Lenny, but Camille said it was her job and she had to check in on Mom anyway and wanted to watch their interaction. She showed up right on time on Wednesday, and Lenny silently got in her car, fists clutched at his sides.

My office space was still in flux—I had given up the decorating, procrastinating a bit out of sheer disinterest. I poured a drink after Lenny left with Camille and worked on the journal, after tripping on the drop cloth and knocking into the ladder. Really should finish this up. The phone rang.

"Ms. Murphy?"

"Yes."

"Dick Ambrose here. Look, I'm afraid this is turning into something of a hornet's nest."

"How do you mean?"

"There are other allegations. Whispers. Accusations . . ."

"I have been warned." I was referring to the phone call, but however he took that was on him.

He waited for me to finish. "Nothing is substantiated, but I'm afraid if you announce your candidacy, you will be hit with all sorts of salacious allegations, and we cannot help you."

"What do you mean? The party will desert me?" I was shocked. As far as I knew, my record was spotless and I was the party's golden girl.

A pause. "There is a tsunami awaiting you."

"Yes." After that weird phone call I'd received, I was reluctant to make any announcements one way or the other. Apparently, they knew I didn't take the threat seriously and knew that I'd get wind of more serious accusations.

"I cannot speak any further about this. Just be assured that there is very strong opposition to your running, and it will get, ah, complicated. There are forces here with which we have had a tough time dealing." I knew immediately what he meant. There was a faction in our party that if they didn't want you, you weren't getting in. They'd manufacture things to taint your reputation. I had watched someone else get creamed by them, and I had stood up for him. Now it was retribution.

"Understood. Thank you for the call."

"Let me know what you decide. I'm afraid you're on your own in this one."

Well, shit. I will fight this. I have nothing to hide. My knee-jerk fight before flight reaction kicked in, but once I thought about it I wondered if I really cared enough.

———◀┨

Lenny was quiet when he came back from his visit with Mom in prison. He headed into the kitchen, grabbed a donut and leaned against the counter, cramming almost all of it into his face.

"Can I ask how it went?"

"You can ask . . ."

"Okay, I'm asking."

"Well," he mumbled through the glazed sugar, wiping his hands on his jeans, "they put us in a playroom for little kids. On tiny chairs. In an empty room." He shrugged. "We had nothing to say to each other. Camille watched from another spot. Apparently, we weren't supposed to be alone this time."

"Jesus. What would you have said if you had felt comfortable enough to speak?"

"Not much. We've been through this before. I had nothing to say. I guess once school starts, I'll be able to come up with something, but today I had nothing to say."

"Well, what did she say?"

"She just asked questions. How was I, was I happy, did school start yet, was I eating . . . all the mom things she's supposed to ask."

I nodded. "Well, you can't blame her for that."

"No, but I can blame her for a shitload of other stuff."

I just nodded again. Not much to say. There was a theme here.

Chapter Twenty-One

ART CLASS CONTINUED TO BE FUN, I WAS GETTING TO KNOW MY fellow artists who had much more talent than I, but I still enjoyed the process. Suzanne was the social butterfly, bopping from easel to easel, sticking her nose into everyone's project, either praising or humming, and in general taking up the oxygen in the room.

Sally and I kept the banter up and enjoyed some private jokes and eye rolls. Marjorie and Dan were both quiet but smiled indulgently at the antics of the rest of us. They appeared to know each other, and I wondered if Dan was a patient—client—of Doc Marjorie.

He seemed to be fairly compulsive; his dress, his materials, his painting were pristine. His wipes were everywhere and in constant use. He was a musician who wrote music and played guitar, but I never heard about a job; I assumed he was a freelancer making good money, as he dressed well and was always manicured. Dapper Dan, the metrosexual.

Adam was always there but not there. Present, but quiet and supportive. Lenny sometimes came to class, sometimes not, but when he did, he kept quiet and focused on his work.

Jade Robinson from Pages next door came in once with a plateful of cookies from the catering kitchen at her place and stayed for class, encouraging us to step next door and explore the library at Pages and grab some coffee and pastries, maybe sit in on a writers' group. In turn, she took flyers of our classes.

Our little community was growing and becoming intertwined, and I loved it. The Asian store Herbs was working on refurbishing their space for an alternative health and self-care salon using acupuncture, herbs, and teas with ancient Asian methodology for common health problems. They would hold meditation classes and some what I called woo-woo art and tools: hand-made bells, drums, blankets, medallions, coins, and whatnot for feng shui practice. Choyou, Jen's former housekeeper, planned to open Herbs with her auntie from China, and had been to Pages at their opening with Chinese rice paper, writing customer names in Chinese characters as little tokens.

We only had two more houses to round out for full occupancy. That would come.

Lenny came home from his first day at school with that look of rage I had gotten to know. His hair hung in his face, his ripped jeans and baggy t-shirt at least were clean, and the new backpack dragged behind him as he went up the stairs. I heard him slam his door shut and turn on the stereo Jen had given me from her old house. Drums and guitars assaulted the air as I wondered what to do.

Do I need to report this to Camille? Bad day at Black Rock? Should I go up and ask? Should I ignore it? What the hell do I do? I called Ron just to see if a male perspective could help.

"Ron Newman."

"Hi."

"Well, hi." Amazingly, he sounded pleased to hear from me.

"So, I need some guidance."

"Yes???" I could hear his smile.

I explained about Lenny and brought him up to his first day of school. His tone changed. "My advice is to let him cool down. First days are never good, no matter who you are, but especially if you don't know anyone and feel like you're not good enough."

"Okay, thanks."

"Renee, do you know what you are doing?"

"Apparently not, but I'm doing it." *Well now, how's that for confidence in my abilities?*

"Is that all you wanted?"

"Yes. Thank you."

"You're welcome. Goodbye."

"Goodbye." *Say hello to your new girlfriend for me. Ugh.*

"I need to borrow your computer." Lenny's voice came from behind me, mumbling. "Gotta look some stuff up."

"Sure. Help yourself. Everything okay?"

"No."

"What's wrong?"

He took a deep breath and I watched as his arms straightened at his sides. His fists were balled once again, and rays of hostility came from his skin. "I didn't want to get into the system again and I didn't want to go to school and now I'm doing both. I hate this."

But you have to? Tell me what's wrong? Can I help? All these clichés came rushing through my head and I knew I didn't have any of the answers. I kept my voice quiet and still. "I understand. I get it. Give it another day. You know where to find me if there's anything I can do." So lame. "I know. Why don't you go down to Canvas? Maybe painting or drawing will help. Take the computer."

"That's okay?"

"Why wouldn't it be?" My brand new, state-of-the-art, expensive laptop. *Trust. Trust.* He unplugged the computer and took it upstairs. He was back downstairs with his backpack and out the door before I could say goodbye.

I called Adam and gave him a heads up that an angry kid was coming in.

"Bad first day, I assume?"

"He won't say, but I'm guessing it's not his best day ever. You don't mind my suggestion he go and hang out with you, do you?"

"Not at all, fair lady. I have found artwork to be very therapeutic."

"Thank you, Adam."

"Right-oh."

At seven o'clock I had calzones ready, a hit we had discovered last week from the hole-in-the-wall restaurant down the street. At eight o'clock I finally ate mine with a beer and wrapped his in foil. I resisted the urge to call and check up on him. He was with Adam, and I suspected I would have heard if anything had gone asunder. I poured a drink.

Jen and I chatted for a while, catching up. I cleaned out my bathroom cabinets and my desk drawer. I made a few phone calls and returned some emails. No Lenny. I refreshed my drink. The television had nothing to offer, so I rummaged through some magazines for "easy weeknight dinners" until I wanted to throw up.

I called Adam at ten. "No, he left here a couple of hours ago."

"Was he angry?"

"Isn't he always?"

I sighed. "Where could he be?"

Silence.

"Adam, what do I do? Do you have any children?"

"No, but I was once a teenage boy. Does that count?" He chuckled. "I say you've given him some space, maybe too much. You did give the lad a mobile (he pronounced it moe-bile), did you not?"

"Yes."

"Then call it."

"I don't want him to think I'm dogging him."

"Madam, it's ten o'clock on a school night. I think it's your job." He's right.

I called Lenny's number—it went directly to voicemail. I texted him.

> Where are you? Worried.

Surprisingly, I got a text back.

> On my way back.

He came through the door about fifteen minutes later. Time for a showdown.

"Lenny, we have to talk." The last time I heard that, Eddie had broken up with me. He plopped down and dropped the backpack, with my computer, on the floor.

"Is my computer in there?"

"Yeah."

"I hope you didn't just break it."

"So what if I did?" That look of defiance again came across his face.

"I'd not be very happy."

"What are you going to do, spank me?" What to do, what to do, what to do . . .

"I suspect they'd throw me in jail." The sarcasm was lost on him. The staring contest continued. He sat, arms crossed again, and breathed heavily.

"Lenny, I think we need to come to an understanding."

"Like what?"

"Like what time you are to be home." My hand clenched around the cold glass.

"I don't have a home." Ohgodohgodohgodohgod.

"Lenny, you are fifteen years old. I should know where you are and what time you will be . . . back. Can we at least agree that that's something I need to know?"

"I guess."

"Well, what do you think is reasonable?"

"How about if I just do what I fucking want?"

"No, Lenny, that's not acceptable." My politician speech was coming through. I am so inept at this. What the hell am I doing?

He took a long look around the room. "It doesn't matter anyway."

"Why?"

"Because I won't be here long. I'll get moved around, Mom will be better, we'll get another place, and it will start all over again."

My heart flipped over. I took a sip. "Do you have homework?"

"Yeah."

"Well, it's ten o'clock. How about if you go to bed and get it done in the morning?"

"I may not do it at all."

"Your call. But don't be surprised if you end up back in third grade."

He stood, pulled the zipper open on his backpack and threw the laptop on the chair he had been sitting on. He glared at me and stomped upstairs.

Well, that was successful.

Chapter Twenty-Two

LENNY LEFT FOR SCHOOL, QUIETLY, WITHOUT STOPPING FOR CEREAL. He just sneaked out without a word. Sigh. After working on my journal, I downloaded and began to fill out the papers to submit to the party for my candidacy. Barbara Morse had not yet announced her resignation, so I was going to have to keep this under my hat for a bit but wanted to get started.

I had nothing else to do and had not been sleeping again. Maybe getting this done would allow me to move forward. I had procrastinated long enough, but I was just so damn tired and in a fog. Coffee was missing, and I hadn't the interest to pull anything together for breakfast.

My phone trilled behind me. I reached over and managed to knock my water off the desk and almost tilted off my reclining chair.

"Yes?" I said, somewhat sharply, trying to catch my breath.

"Renee? It's Lupe."

"Yes, Lupe."

"Um . . . is everything okay?"

"Yes. Why?"

"Canvas isn't open yet. Adam is usually there before I am, and we chat every morning. This is unusual."

"Really. Well, I'm sure he'll be there shortly."

"There's a group of people waiting for a class. They are outside, waiting."

"Really. Okay, I'll be right there. Would you tell them please Adam has been detained—make something up—and should be there shortly, but I'm coming just in case."

"Sure. No prob." No prob.

I fed Gunnar, threw on some sweats, and dashed down the short trip to the art park. Three people stood outside, waiting. Some crowd. No Adam.

I unlocked the door, apologizing all the way, and asked them to be patient with me while the easels were set up. We turned the corner to find Adam had set everything up the night before. Whew.

"Great. I'm sure Adam will be here shortly. I'm not an art teacher, but go ahead and work on your projects. Use the space and have some fun!" I tried to sound enthusiastic and started back to the office. Three more people ambled in with coffee and took their places. "Great place next door! They just opened," I heard. "It's called Pages, and it's apparently for writers and readers, but they have a coffee bar set up. Good coffee!" Voices began conversations in earnest as they pulled out their tools.

Let them paint. And get coffee all over the place. I called Adam's mobile. Went straight to a full voicemail. Then I called Tricia at the law firm. It took a while to get through reception, then I was told she was in a meeting and would it be all right if I left a message on her voicemail. But of course.

I waited for a call back while looking at invoices, the checkbook, the website, and social media. Not much there, either in the bank or anywhere else. No drop-ins to look at art (wouldn't know what to tell them about the pieces, anyway . . .) no phone calls, no emails to Canvas. I drummed my fingers on the desk, listened to the chatter in the parlor, then began looking through drawers. Nothing much other than office supplies and pieces of paper.

The top of the desk was a bit cluttered, at least for organized Adam. In my house it would be normal, but I found scratch paper wadded up, a few rubber bands, and one of his leather bracelets that looked as though it had been cut clean. Wondering what to do next, I started into the parlor when my phone buzzed.

"Tricia! Where's Adam? "

"What? He's not there?"

"No . . . he had people waiting for his class this morning. So you know nothing?"

"No. I just saw him this morning at breakfast. I can't imagine where he is, but I'm sure he'll turn up."

"This isn't like him, is it? I mean, he's always been prompt, if not early."

"He always goes to work out in the morning. I'll call them. There have been no accidents reported. Is his car there?"

"No. Just mine in the back."

"Then he's off doing something . . . he probably forgot about the class." She sounded so confident. Sure he did. We rung off. With nothing else to do, and since the art students had settled in and were working on their projects, I joined them at an empty easel. I listened to them chat about their lives, talk about their children, and worry about the economy. Two of them were unemployed, one was a writer, and the others were retired. They asked me a lot about the state of the city and our new mayor, and about Adam. I had very little to say about the latter except that he had been waylaid somewhere and we would credit them a class.

The phone never rang, my phone never trilled, and Adam never showed up.

Tricia came flying through the door at Canvas at 3:00.

"Nothing yet?"

"No." I was in the office, waiting for something to happen, and on the computer checking my own emails and calendar.

Tricia slumped down into a chair and threw her bag onto the floor. "Now I'm worried."

"I am, too. Should we call the police?"

"No," she said sharply. "He left the gym at his usual time, so it's not been that long. Missing persons have to be gone for twenty-four hours before they will take it seriously." She chewed on her index fingernail. I had never noticed that habit before; it meant she really was worried.

"Tricia, is there something wrong? Does he have a medical problem or something?"

"No, he's healthy," she said through her cuticle. "Is there anything on the calendar that could explain this?"

"Nothing except for the class this morning."

"Could he be meeting a vendor?"

I shook my head. "They come here."

"Is there a note?" *Now, don't you think I would have told you if there was?* Something's wrong with Tricia. Her eyes scanned over the desk and saw the crumpled paper. She grabbed it and glanced at it quickly. "Does this address mean anything to you?" I looked at the pencil scribble and shook my head. Her eyes locked on the bracelet. Her face actually turned white, and I saw her eyes fill.

"Tricia . . ." I got out of my chair and began to go to her.

"I gotta go." She grabbed her bag and ran out of the store and down the steps. I watched as she fished her phone out of the side pocket and put it to her ear.

Something's up. But what? I stayed all day waiting for someone or something to happen. It was quiet the entire time. There were no classes scheduled for tonight, so I locked up and left a note on the door to call my cell if anyone needed anything. I felt empty, confused.

I headed over to Jen's, noting as I left that Stitches was busy with knitters on the front porch having coffee and pastries, laughing and having a wonderful time. I left and went home, not willing to socialize after all.

I sat in the living room with a drink. I heard music coming from upstairs—angry, repetitive, deep beats of anger.

Doesn't matter anyway. I won't be here long.

Jesus, this kid. What do I do? Clearly, I'm not doing him any good at all, and I don't think he likes me. When I run for office, he will be even more ignored and, dare I say it, in the way. I am not built to be June Cleaver. I cannot bake cupcakes and make boo-boos disappear with a kiss. I finished my drink and wanted to go for another, but I was too lazy to get up. So I chewed on the ice.

I am really no better than his mother.

I ran my finger over the heavy scar on my neck and remembered that night, and how alone I'd been. At his age, I had Jen and her family to fall back on, and I knew it. Lenny didn't. Jen couldn't take him, Bruce didn't want him, his own mother couldn't by law, and there was nobody else. *The truth is I don't want him.*

A while later, I found my way back to the kitchen and grabbed some ice, threw them into the glass with several plinks, and poured more scotch over them. I turned to find Lenny sitting at the table, staring at me. A textbook was in front of him and he had a pencil in his hand, held by his third finger.

"No dinner tonight?" he asked. I stared, thinking what to do. "Never mind," he said, and folded up his books and stood up. "I'm not hungry."

No better than his mother. I heard his feet stomp up the stairs. I sat at the table, feeling sorry for myself and put out that I had to deal with this.

Tricia showed up at Canvas the next morning. Adam had been missing for two days. She looked awful—like the wicked witch without the hat and striped leggings, green and sickly.

"Have you heard anything?" I asked as she clumped into the chair and began to chew her nail. I had had to force myself out of bed knowing we had customers waiting; she did not look any better than I felt. My head pounded and my eyes weren't working well. My stomach was rebelling, but I was there.

She shook her head. "No."

"What do the police say?"

"I haven't called them."

"What? Why not?" My voice rose.

She looked at the bracelet that was still on the desk. "This is a message."

"What are you talking about?"

She put her head in her hands and mumbled. "He's been taken. And there's nothing I can do."

"What are you talking about?" I repeated. I needed a drink. The fear vibe was strong and electric—I felt it coming off her in streaks, hitting me right in the gut.

She took a deep breath. "Adam is a forger. An art forger. A good one."

"What?" Now I started to shake. "What are you talking about?" I said for the third time.

She got up to close the door. "Adam is not his name." Her hand came up to wipe a tear away, and I saw she was shaking. She gathered herself by taking a deep breath and closing her eyes. She began to pace. "He's in the witness protection program because he cooperated with the FBI to nail a mob boss who was laundering money through art. It's all very complicated, and I'm not sure I understand it, but he did his job and they gave him a new identity. But the case was not closed. They must have got him."

I felt like I was in the middle of a bad movie.

She pointed to the bracelet. "I gave him that bracelet when we were together in Boston. I broke the relationship off to move home, but he came to find me. He said he would never take that bracelet off. She rolled up her sleeve to show a matching one on her slim wrist, then picked up his bracelet from the desk. "Look—it's deliberately cut. It didn't get caught on anything and nobody ripped it off him. A clear cut. That means something." Her young, wrinkle-free, dewy face was pinched and pale.

"Are you sure he didn't just leave you?" I couldn't believe I said it, but it was a possibility.

She shook her head. "No. We had sort of an anniversary. We went out. We exchanged gifts. No," she shook her head again. "There is no way he's left me. He's a good, honest man who, if he wanted out, would just say so."

"A good man who is also an art forger?"

She took a very deep breath. "Renee, yes, he was an art forger, but just for fun, not for profit. Someone saw his work and somehow a connection was made, and his skill was used in this sting operation. He never ever used it for profit. Plus, having worked at the Louvre, he knew the ins and outs of the art trade. He wanted this finished as much as the FBI did, so he helped. He got himself known and they put the word out about his abilities; they took the bait and he was in. It lasted about two years, then they pulled him out. He gave names, but it's still going on."

"And how did you meet him? I've always wondered."

She smiled. "I worked for the FBI doing legal work as an intern in Boston when I was still at Harvard. I met him there while I helped take depositions and volunteered on weekends to help with the massive paperwork they had going through their office. It earned me credits and experience, and I loved it, but the best part was meeting . . .Adam."

"So, what do we do?"

"I've called someone I know who left the FBI some time ago. His old office said they'd try to find him. I don't know if the address he wrote down has anything to do with it, but the FBI has it. I have no more contacts. I just don't know what else to do." Her hand shook as she reached for the broken bracelet.

"Maybe we should call the police."

"We can't. He's under witness protection. It will all come out and may put him in even more jeopardy."

"Okay, okay . . ."

"I have to get back to the office. Please please call me if you hear anything." I nodded.

Lenny came around the corner. "So, Adam's still missing?" Interestingly, he didn't seem sad—or surprised.

"It appears so."I wondered how much he had heard.

His head went down. "I'll set up for class tonight." Damn. Our class was tonight. What was I going to tell them?

And yet another person deserting Lenny.

Chapter Twenty-Three

THE HEARING DATE FOR LENNY'S MOM WAS THE FOLLOWING WEDNESDAY. I had asked him if he wanted to go with me. He declined. "Been there before; it's always the same." It took everything I had to get myself together to get to the courthouse after I cancelled a class at Canvas. I was worn out.

When the case was called, I entered the courtroom. Camille told me where to sit, and she took her place at the large table in front of the judge's raised platform. Lenny's attorney, a young man from the public defender's office, sat to her left.

The judge entered, a nice-looking older man with white hair and a ruddy complexion. I noticed a large class ring on his right hand and a wedding ring on his left. The court clerk read, "Rudolph case, Your Honor. The mother, the social worker, the caregiver, and the child's attorney are all present. There is no CASA assigned to the case as of yet."

So, I'm a caregiver. And Lenny has his own lawyer. Interesting. I saw Judge Sullivan's eyebrows raise as he reviewed the documents and his head came up. Our eyes locked. "Your Honor," he said with a smile.

"Your Honor," I returned.

He chuckled. "You are the caregiver in this case?"

"Yes, Your Honor."

"Thank you. We need more foster parents willing to take the older ones." He returned to the documents and took some time to review them, flipping the pages over and over again. "This is not the first time we've been at this rodeo, Ms. Rudolph." He looked at mom over his glasses.

Elena Rudolph, Lenny's mother, sat at the left side of the long table along with her own public defender. Lenny's attorney sat to her right—a young man, thin and harried. Elena wore a prison jumpsuit. Her hair was clean, but unkempt, and there were pimples and scarring on her face. She looked unhealthy and hungry. Her knee shifted nervously, just like Lenny's. Other than that, I saw no indication that she was Lenny's mother. She did not respond.

"What makes you think you're going to make it this time?" He continued to peer at her over his glasses, his lips forming the words without a smile or a hint of condescension.

"I'm serious this time. I want my kid back." Her voice was small, hushed. She did not look at the judge but at the bench in front of him.

"How far are you willing to go to get there?"

She leaned over to her attorney, who whispered in her ear. "As far as it takes."

"Ms. Rudolph, it will be no surprise to you for me to say I hope you do, but I'm not convinced, given your history with this court." He looked at the documentation again. "Where is your daughter?" *Daughter?*

Her attorney interrupted. "Her daughter is not a part of this current dependency case."

"I'll determine who should be part of this case, Mr. Linton." He turned to her again. "I'll ask again. Where is Leah?"

"I don't know, she's an adult now," Elena said.

"Do you have any contact with her?"

"No."

"And where is your son?"

"I don't know."

The judge looked at Camille. "He prefers not to attend court, Your Honor. He would rather go to school," she said.

"Good to know he's in school now. I have read the report from the social worker about how he is doing. There is no CASA, I see?"

"No, Your Honor. We are waiting for a CASA to be assigned," said Camille.

I knew enough that CASA stood for Court Appointed Special Advocate, a volunteer trained within the system to work with the foster kids from outside the system. They form a mentor relationship with the child and the caregiver, taking them to the movies, shopping or walks/hikes, whatever they have in common, and that person speaks for the child in court and ensures the best interest of the child is front and center, coordinating with the social worker, but with complete autonomy. I had known a few CASAs in my lifetime and admired the work they did.

The judge shook his head. "I see a treatment plan in place. I hope it works. Next hearing is in six months, when we will re-evaluate your progress on your case plan. I certainly hope you perform better than last time. In the meantime, the child will stay where he is and you will have visitation as is your right, to be determined between the social worker and the boy's caregiver." He closed the file. "I wish you luck. We will meet back here in six months. Next case."

That took all of five minutes. I spoke with Camille for a few minutes and we made arrangements for parameters for the mandated weekly visits.

Since I was there, I decided to head to my old office and check in on Tanya. I missed her efficiency and the easy way we worked together. I was also forcing myself to do something; I just wanted to crawl into bed and never come out.

She rose and gave me a quick hug. "Ron's at lunch, but I'm happy to see you. How is Jen doing?"

"As well as can be expected, under the circumstances," I said. "Are you free for a bite? We can go to Bobby's, my treat." Bobby's was Tanya's favorite place. She grabbed her bag and we headed downstairs to the cafe that served the best Reuben sandwiches on the coast.

As we searched out a table, I saw Judge Sullivan sitting alone at a table having a sandwich. I waved and he motioned for us to sit with him.

"I was very pleased to see you in my courtroom this morning," he said. "I'm a long-time admirer of yours."

"How nice of you to say."

"How did you become a foster parent? That's not something I would have predicted." Our sandwiches came and we settled in.

"Me neither, but it just sort of . . . happened."

"You're a foster mom?" Tanya's eyes popped open wide. "How did *that* happen?"

I laughed. "I'm not sure I'm cut out for it, but Lenny's a good kid, and it's only for the next three or four years to get him through high school. That is, unless he's reunited with his mother."

The judge put down his sandwich and cleared his throat. "Ms. Murphy, it's not a good idea for us to discuss the case in specifics."

"Please, call me Renee, and I certainly understand."

"Fine. I'm Jim." Jim Sullivan. That name sounded familiar. "Do you know Jen Conrad?"

"Yes, Arthur and I were good friends. How is she doing since he died?"

"She's sort of reinvented herself. You wouldn't recognize her." I saw no need to broadcast her medical problems.

"I heard. When we first moved here, she helped my wife meet people and get involved in projects. We often went to dinner together. We liked them very much." He frowned.

"I remember Jen telling me about your wife. She must miss Jen, now that she's no longer involved in the political and/or legal social circle."

"Claudia died last year."

"Oh, I am sorry. How did she die, may I ask?"

"Breast cancer." He turned to Tanya and changed the subject. "How is Ron acclimating himself to his new office? He must have some big plans." Jim looked at me. "But then again, he has big shoes to fill."

They chatted for a while about current city events, and I listened politely while I absorbed a breast cancer death and tried to tamp down rising panic in the realization that Jen could actually die from this.

What would I do without her?

"Do you want to know how it went in court this morning?" I asked Lenny's back as I followed him in later that night after class.

"Oh. Let me guess. She said she was going to do everything necessary to make it work this time. The judge gave her six months to prove it, and then," he used air quotes "reunification will be successful." He walked into the kitchen as he continued to talk. "I'll be forced to move back in with her, she will start using again, we will have no food, and she'll disappear for days at a time, at which point I'll go back into the system and the same thing will start over again." He was incredibly calm, his voice a monotone. "This is why I didn't want to do this."

"I got a phone call after court. They are considering letting some prisoners out due to over crowding, but will have severe restrictions as to where she can go and whatnot."

He shrugged as though he saw this coming.

"Do you want to be with her?"

"She's my mom." *That was supposed to answer the question?*

"And?"

He shrugged. "If she cared about me, she wouldn't do that shit."

"I'm not sure it's about you. I don't know much about addiction, but I understand you have no power over it." *God, I am so bad at this.*

"That's bullshit. If you have a kid, that should be your first priority."

"You're right." I stopped there. There wasn't much I could add. "Why didn't you tell me you have a sister?"

"A sister?" His eyes focused. "Oh, you mean Leah. She's ten years older than I am, with a different dad. I don't remember ever seeing her. If I've met her, I can't remember. I forget about her. She and mom don't get along and they haven't spoken in a long time."

"You know the judge ordered continued weekly visits?"

"I'm not going," he said from inside the refrigerator.

"Your mom has the right to see you."

"Do I get a choice?" he mumbled.

"I don't know, but if you don't want to, I can't imagine that you would be forced to."

He laughed. "Yeah. Riiight. Can I have this?" He held up a soda can.

"Of course. I told you, you don't have to ask. This is your home."

"For now." He shut the refrigerator door and went upstairs.

Jen was home, feeling much better, in between treatments, and almost herself. I relayed current events to her. She listened quietly as I got more and more heated about the injustice of it all. "This is the woman who put him in this situation to begin with, and she has more rights than he does."

"It's not right. Maybe you'll have to run for Morse's seat after all and make some legislative changes."

"That's not exactly how it works, but I'll have to do something. I just can't sit back and allow this to happen."

"It's unconscionable."

"Irresponsible."

"Unbelievable."

"Unfair."

"Degrading."

"Reprehensible."

We went back and forth several more times before we ran out of superlatives and started to make words up and began to crack up. It was good to hear her laugh.

Chapter Twenty-Four

"I'm going to get something to eat. Want to join me?" Sally asked as we packed up our tools and paints. The offer of friendship out of the box surprised me, and I thought about Lenny at home. Let him stew. We packed up, tossed our supplies in our cars and headed across the street.

Sally sighed as she lowered her large frame into a chair on the patio of a Mexican restaurant. The January breeze blew her wispy blonde hair into her face and she swept it away with puffy fingers. I noticed a beautiful gold band with an impressive pear-shaped diamond on her left hand.

I sat in the quiet, enjoying the birds chirp and the scent of jasmine climbing up the walls. For the first time I began to relax. I had been uptight; Tricia/Lenny, politics, a new dog, a new kid, the shop, and money issues had me in a clinch. Retirement was supposed to be easy.

Sally started in immediately. "Tell me about yourself."

I had never been the girlfriend type. Jen was my only true friend, everyone else was part of my working world. Sure, I had lunches and drinks with them, but none were intimate, and none would certainly be the source for any kind of intimacy other than for a political or city issue. I had learned early on not to trust anyone in my work world. Politics is a bitch. I filled her in on the Lenny situation, trying to amuse and entertain, but she got the gist and nodded sagely.

"You have a lot on your plate. My girlfriends were my best source of comfort when my husband cheated on me. They were the ones who told me to suck it up and pointed out the choices I had."

"You chose to stay?"

"Yes. What can I say? I sort of like the schmuck. We have three children and seven grandchildren, and, when we are together, we are happy."

"Are you always this frank with virtual strangers?"

She continued. "I'm an open book. It's who I am. No, in truth, I might even be happier now. We've established this routine where I have my own life, he has his, and we have a life together. I am sure he loves me, God knows I adore him, and what he does behind my back is entirely his business."

"Aren't you jealous?"

She cocked her head a little. "No. At first I was, of course. My ego got in the way. My drinking probably didn't help. But the truth is he needs more from me than I'm prepared to give, and if he can find fulfillment elsewhere without falling deeply and passionately in love and leaving me, I have to respect that and honor it."

Maybe she just doesn't like sex.

The waiter stood between us. I ordered a margarita and saw her hesitate. "Iced tea for me, please." She turned to me. "How's that for self-disclosure?"

"That didn't take up five minutes. Is that the abridged version?"

"No, actually. That's all there is to it. I don't know if it's even going on anymore because I never confronted him. I decided once I found out for sure years ago that I didn't want to know any more, so I don't know what's happening, to be honest. When he's home, we're good. When he's out, I have my own life."

"But what about love?"

The arched eyebrows told me my question was a surprise. "I love him. I adore him, and I believe he loves me, too. He shows it in all kinds of ways. I'm spoiled rotten. Anything I want, I get." She shrugged. "He never says no, never criticizes me, and is always loving and kind. He's always there when I need him, I know I'm his first priority. I've decided I can't ask for much more than that."

We began to sip our drinks. I inhaled mine quickly through the straw and got an immediate headache. "But isn't something missing?"

"Not really. It's molded itself into what it's supposed to be. I am secure and happy."

"Now you paint."

"Now I paint." She smiled. "Among other things. How are you enjoying being an entrepreneur?"

"The jury's out. I have no talent, and I'm sure I'm not going to be a renowned artist, but it is fun. I just don't know what to do with the rest of my life. For the first time, I have no plan." *Why am I telling her this?*

"You have no plan? Surely you thought about what you wanted to do when you retired."

"Of course I did, but those plans have gone awry," I said, and crossed my eyes for effect.

She smiled. "What have you always wanted to do?"

"Paint."

We laughed.

"What else?"

"I don't know. I thought I would be happily retired, but I am having a tough time with some decisions. Somehow I've become involved in a foster kid's life, and I'm not sure how to handle it." I talked vaguely about the issues and she listened and nodded as I went along, with sage comments and easy banter.

I began to see what she was talking about. Female support was important; the kind that mattered, not a power partnership. I hadn't felt this before, but that was probably because I always knew where I was headed. My new position created some vulnerability, and Jen had other priorities.

God, am I replacing her already?

"My mother just disappeared one day," I mused aloud. "She was a drug addict. We lived in the basement of a church and there were nights she just didn't come home. I'd go out looking for her and drag her home from some flophouse. Those guys knew me. Called me "Little Dudette." The familiar pain struck in my belly when the smells and fear came back in a rush. I rubbed the ridge behind my ear.

"Did she work?"

"She'd clean houses when she could, but she was uneducated and unemployable."

"And your dad?"

"Never knew him. Don't even know his name."

"How sad." She looked up at me. "Then how in the world did you graduate from Duke University with a master's in political science?" My radar went up. People always researched me before they came in for the kill.

"You've been doing your homework."

"No." She took a deep breath. I realized I had sounded accusatory. "Your biography has been all over the papers, a woman who has come so far."

"Oh. Sorry. To answer your question, my friend in school had me over all the time. They lived on the other side of the tracks and I practically lived there before my mom disappeared." I smirked when I remembered the natural way I had embedded myself into Jen's house. "It was weeks before they realized I was there full time and had never gone home."

"Why was that?"

"They were socialites. Patricia and Harold Palmer? Their daughter Jen has the place next door, Stitches." I pointed. "We've been friends a very long time." I chased a fly away with my hand. "Anyway, as long as Jen was occupied and kept out of trouble, they were happy. Their other daughter, Jen's sister Maggie, was older and they were grooming her to be a debutante and socialite, so she had all their attention. We were happy not to be involved."

"And they sent you to college?"

"Yes, they did, bless their little hearts, but I paid them back as soon as I could." I finished off my margie. "They didn't turn it away."

"What about your love life? Anything cooking now?"

I shook my head, "No. Thought so, but no."

"You're not dating at all?"

"I haven't had a date in twenty years."

A look of utter surprise jumped all over her face. "By choice?"

I laughed. "Not necessarily. Just busy. No time."

"Um-hm . . ." Sally reached for the sweetener and leaned back. I was sure she was after something, not that I had anything to give at this point.

I wanted to tell her the missing piece. That no one had ever truly loved me. That I had been either tolerated or abandoned my entire life, and what I wanted more than anything was to have someone adore me for me.

Lenny had been with me about three weeks during which I had been doing my ceremonial duties, going to classes, staying updated at Canvas and checking in on Jen constantly. I drove home from Canvas one afternoon after doing errands and going to the dog park with Gunnar thinking about love; it was all around me.

Jen, Sally, and Adam all found their mates and were happy. Jen had been adored by her husband Arthur for thirty-seven years. They had been unbelievably happy, poster children for happy marriages. Now she was clearly being wooed. They all came from families that stayed together and didn't desert each other. Jen and her sister Maggie were not the best of friends, but they still stood by each other.

My mother had deserted me in my adolescence. My father had never been in the picture, due to, I suspect, me. Eddie finally called it quits with me ten years ago. He deserted me after twenty years together in what worked. I loved him with all my heart, even though I knew we were never going to be together permanently. I took the leftovers and was pleased to get it.

And God only knew where I stood with Ron. Why couldn't someone love me? I shook my head at my self-pity, walked across the yard to my front door, and abruptly stopped.

The door was open about an inch. I pushed it wide open and said, "Hello?" No answer. Gunnar sat beside me, a little growl coming from him. "Shh . . . it's okay."

I called 911 and reported a break-in. I was told not to enter, but to wait for police. They were there in two minutes and, with guns drawn, determined no one was in the house.

"Clear."

"Clear."

"Clear."

"There doesn't seem to be anything missing," I said, as I checked out the electronics and the few pieces of jewelry I owned.

"You're lucky," one of them said. "Are you sure you closed the door?"

"Of course I'm sure. I'd never leave my door open. I remember putting these down," and I pointed to my canvas and painter's box, "so I could use both hands to lock the door."

"Then they wanted something they didn't find . . ." he said thoughtfully. "You sure nothing's missing?"

"Nothing of any significance that I can see."

"All's well that ends well," he said and shrugged. "Probably kids. Any liquor missing?"

"I don't keep much liquor in the house." I opened a kitchen cupboard and saw the one half-empty bottle of scotch. How did it get so low so fast?

After they left, I called Jen and reported in.

"Are you okay?" she asked.

"Yeah, how about you?"

"I'm feeling great. The first treatment is done, it's all downhill from here."

"Want to come over?"

"Why don't you come here? Bruce is coming over and we're cooking burgers on the grill. You're welcome to join us."

"No, I think I'd rather just stay here and get rid of the bad juju."

Jen laughed. "Suit yourself, but you're missing some good burgers and ice-cold beer."

That made me think of Sally and her drinking problem. We hung up and, following a whim, I called Sally and told her of my latest experience. "Want to come over and have my world-famous pizza?"

"You make pizza?"

"I make a great phone call."

She laughed. "I'm alone tonight. Sure. I'd love to."

Sally arrived within half an hour and plopped her large frame on the couch. I had ordered the pizza and a liter of soda. Both were sitting on the kitchen counter, and I busied myself slicing the pizza and pouring the drinks, the extent of my hostess duties. We chatted for a while about the break-in. Gunnar sat at attention, waiting for pizza crust. Lenny was at Canvas mopping the floors. Someone had to do it.

"Is anything missing?" she asked.

"No. That's what's so weird. The cops think it was kids looking for booze." Oops. Bad subject.

"How did you meet your husband?" I asked to change the subject.

"Oh," she leaned back against the couch. "He was my instructor in college." She giggled. "Went against all the rules. He was handsome, intelligent, and knew a thing or two about literature, my passion. When I graduated, he asked me to marry him. We had to move, of course, and started a new life here. Our kids were born here and our grandkids are close, too."

"That's so sweet. What does he do now? Does he still teach literature?"

"Literature? No. He was a political science instructor. But no, Edward is now writing."

My heart stopped for a moment. It couldn't be possible. No way. I rubbed my scar back and forth. "What? You're staring at me." Sally had a slice of pizza halfway to her mouth.

No way could I get out of this gracefully, and I had to know. I placed my glass on the table very carefully. "I once had a PolySci instructor at Duke by the name of Edward Holcomb," I said, trying to sound casual, like it was an offhand comment.

"That's him. Isn't it a small world?" Her voice was a bit different; smaller.

"Isn't it." I couldn't swallow, but took a bite and chewed very slowly and carefully, biding time.

"Did you like him?"

Like him? I loved him. I still do. I nodded. "He was tough, but thorough." I suddenly had a vision of him hovering over me, being tough and very, very thorough. My stomach started to rebel. I put my hand over my mouth. "Oh!"

"Are you all right?" I held up a finger and rushed off to the bathroom. I gave up all the pizza I had enjoyed and waited a few minutes, gaining strength and trying to calm myself down. I came out with a towel in my hands and sweat all over my face.

"My God, you look awful," she said. "Here, I'll make you some tea." She started for the kitchen. I couldn't have her in my house one more minute. I had to think.

"No, thank you, Sally. I think I just want to go rest. I'm so sorry. I was feeling a little odd earlier and should have paid attention. I must have a bug of some kind. Can I call you later?" I wanted to fall down and have a tantrum.

"Yes, of course." She shot me one more concerned look. "Are you sure?"

"Yes, all of a sudden I'm exhausted. I think a good sleep will do a world of good." I tried to smile, but my mouth shook badly.

"All right, then. I'll call to check on you later." And she was gone.

I closed the door behind her and put my forehead on the door and banged my head a few times.

"Stupid, stupid, stupid." When she told me about her husband's affair, why didn't I pick up on it? Did she ever tell me his name? Did that get by me too? Did I ever know her last name? How could I be so stupid as to befriend the one woman I never wanted to meet?

My stomach had settled down; it was a complete reaction and, I admit, I had sort of helped it along to get out of the room and have an excuse to get rid of her. Physically I felt fine. Emotionally I was a wreck.

I floated over to the kitchen and grabbed the bottle of scotch and downed a shot to steady my nerves. Then another. I needed to call Jen and run this past her. She always had good advice, and she knew all about Eddie. She didn't approve, but she knew. I stopped dead as I entered my office.

All my journals were gone.

Everything was in those journals. Everything about Eddie. In detail. Explicit. Trips, gifts, sex, money, and secrets. Everything about Ron. Hopes, dreams, meetings, innuendoes, and private thoughts about our future together, as though I were a lovestruck teenager. I even wrote my first name and his last several times. Everything was recorded there—everything about my career, my opponents, my tactics, and my younger, confident projected future to the White House. Everything.

Things that had been done by me or for me in my career, some things I am not proud of, and some that were so clandestine I didn't know how they were handled were recorded there. There are people who do that kind of thing. It's what politics is all about, I was told. That was early on, and I made it clear as I progressed through my career that I wanted nothing to do with those tactics, but still they continued behind my back and in my own best interests. It's why I locked up the journals in the first place. Why in the world did I bring them home? I realized I couldn't call Jen—she was in the middle of her sickness and I couldn't bother her with this shit.

I am alone.

My phone buzzed through the Bluetooth as I headed toward Jen's to check up on her.

"Hi." Eddie's voice came through the speakers and sent a chill through my body. I hadn't heard from him in ten years, but his voice still affected my very core.

"Hi, yourself," I said, in an attempt to appear unfazed. Gunnar growled into my ear.

"So, I had a conversation with my wife last night. It appears you are her new BFF."

"Yes?"

"I'm hoping this was just a coincidence and not something you planned nefariously."

"You know me better than that, Eddie." I pulled into a parking lot, not sure I could trust myself with nerves on the outside of my skin.

His voice came over loud and clear. "Look. I don't understand how this happened, or why. But in my own perverse way, I've lived an honest life. Sally knew about you but didn't know who you were. I never told her a thing about you just as I never told you a thing about her. You were both import-ant to me and I kept you separate. We have a good marriage."

"What's your point?"

He sighed. "I don't know. I just thought I'd connect since you've met."

"Anything else?"

"No. That's it."

"Goodbye, Eddie."

Goodbye, Renee."

Click.

"Well, well, well," I said to Gunnar. I put the car in gear and drove to Jen's house. I needed to talk to someone and didn't want to go home. My ringing and knocking produced no response.

Chapter Twenty-Five

CAMILLE CALLED ME WITH AN UPDATE. "AS EXPECTED, MOM HAS BEEN released from jail."

"Not a surprise." My nerves crawled out from under my skin and started pricking me. "Okay, now what?"

"Her attorney will be applying to get Lenny back once she gets on her feet. I am coordinating some services for her for a halfway house including drug rehab, parenting classes, and job training. Once she completes all those to our satisfaction, she and Lenny will be reunited."

That's why they call it foster parenting.

"What do I need to do?"

"Nothing. Just keep doing what you are doing. You are responsible for him until his mother is capable of taking him on again."

"What if she can't?"

"Then he stays with you until she can. Or we find another foster home for him."

"He moves *again*?"

"It's always possible. She's been going to classes while in jail, so she's been doing everything required of her so far. If she continues to do so for six months, then we will find a place for her to live and he will move in with her."

"How can that be? She's a criminal."

"She's a parent first, and she still has all parental rights."

"Have you told Lenny?"

"No. That's your job."

"What? So, what is your job, then, may I ask?" My voice sounded shrill, like a fishwife's.

"What do you mean? My job is to see that they are reunified, and I will do everything I can to ensure that happens." Her steely voice told me how seriously she took her job. "Look, I don't want to make this any more difficult than it is already. The mother has the right to get her child back if she proves she can handle it."

"So, mom has more rights than Lenny? Because this isn't right."

"It's the law."

"Fine. I'll tell him." We rang off and I stood seething with the phone in my hand when Lenny came through the front door and started up the stairs. There's no time like the present.

"Your mom's out of jail." I watched his right foot stop midway and his back go rigid. He stayed frozen for the count of four, then his foot landed on the step and he slowly went into his room and closed the door.

Adam still had not appeared. I called Tricia.

"Any word?"

"No . . . but I'm not concerned."

"What do you mean?" My radar went up. This was so different than her reaction when she saw the bracelet and ran out of the store.

"I've . . . heard from my friend and I know he's okay. I jumped to a conclusion that was wrong. I'm sure he'll be back soon, so tell people that there's something . . . we'll call it a family emergency. I have a client waiting, but please don't worry. He'll be back soon." Tricia snapped off the phone.

I sat in the office, resentful that I was left with this responsibility. This was Adam's job. We were running out of supplies and had no teacher for classes.

For that first night that Adam hadn't shown up, I'd gotten away with having them self-direct with still lives and projects they wanted to work on, but what was I going to do about the rest of the classes?

Then Fate dropped Jade Robinson, the proprietor of Pages next door, into my lap. Pages was set up for literary artists—prose writers, screenwriters, and poets. One of Jade's students had played with art journals where she combined her journaling with art: watercolors, acrylic paints, stencils, and collage. Jade had come by to show me an art journal that one of her clients had done, suggesting we share clients; they focus on the writing, and we focus on the art. It didn't sound like the traditional art I had thought of as the focus for this shop, but I was game for something to do since Adam was missing and I was lost. I showed the art journal to Marjorie, who was excited. She had specialized in art therapy with children earlier in her career and had continued to journal on her own. She offered to teach the class and we were off. We called it Artful Journaling. The class filled up quickly—not our usual painters, but writers and wannabe artists who just wanted to play. Lenny helped set up and stayed for the class.

For the first session Marjorie generously brought in all her supplies—paper, stencils, crayons, watercolors, pictures, paste, glue and several other items I couldn't identify. She also brought in a large stack of magazines: fashion, nature, art, animal, etc. Our assignment was to take a large piece of blank paper, pick up images that appealed to us, paint, scrape, wipe, whatever, and either write something on it or use something we'd already written, to make a collage using anything we wanted. It was an hour of chaos, laughter, glitter, paste, paint, and scraps of paper scattered everywhere. After an hour, Marjorie asked us to make up a story about our collage.

Everyone thought quietly about what story their collage told. There were a few really tough analyses: one of a woman who could have no children; her collage was about happy kids playing, families, and home. Her voice broke when she talked.

Mine showed glowing fireplaces, yummy casseroles, pretty houses, sailboats, picnics, and, unbelievably, a church full of people.

"I guess I just like pretty things," I said when it was my turn.

"Are you sure about that? Isn't there something more?" Marjorie asked.

"What? What does it say to you?"

"Home. Security. Cohesiveness. The whole package." Others nodded. My eyes filled, and I fought it. Lenny stared straight at his collage.

Lenny was the last to show his, and it was shocking. He had painted an area red and wrote "Love" in it. He had pictures of bicycles, soccer balls, and families. He had written something in the corner and covered it up with black paint.

"Okay, Lenny, you're last but not least. What does your piece say?"

"I dunno . . ." His nose was to the floor. Marjorie walked over to him, stood and stared for quite a long time. I heard her say quietly, " I would say it says a lot about love. That you want it but don't want it. That families are important, but you don't trust them. That you don't trust your own emotions. What was under the black paint?"

He mumbled something.

"I'm sorry, I didn't hear you."

"It said 'MOM'."

Marjorie's eyebrows knit together. "I see."

Camille called to arrange a visit for Lenny after school on Wednesday. I texted Lenny and told him of the arrangements. No response.

On the day of the visit, Lenny came back from school, very quiet and very tight.

Elena was to arrive at 3:00. Lenny sat in the living room watching television as he waited. By 4:00 she had not arrived, and I texted Camille that we were canceling since she was so late, and Lenny had something else to do for school later on (a lie). I copied Lenny on it, and when his phone beeped I watched as he read the text, turned off the T.V. and went upstairs to his room.

Did I not do the right thing? Was he pissed at me for canceling it? I just couldn't watch him anymore. I could see he was disappointed. Who wouldn't be?

Camille texted back.

> Can't get a hold of Mom, but know that we will reschedule.

Great.

I started another journal recording info for Lenny and what we were doing. I wanted to keep track of all the disappointments and all the good things that happened for however long he was with me. I began back at the beginning and took it through today.

Camille texted back that the visit was set for the next day. I did not respond. I wanted some time to think about what was best for Lenny.

Why not ask him? I texted:

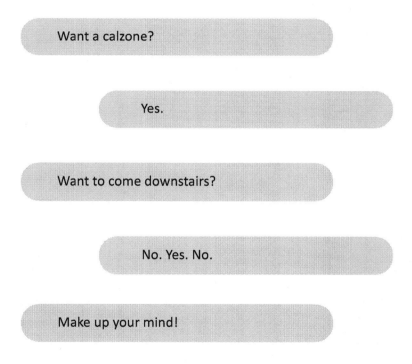

Want a calzone?

Yes.

Want to come downstairs?

No. Yes. No.

Make up your mind!

Soon I heard his footsteps come down the stairs.

"Sorry," he said.

"You don't have to apologize to me. Let's go." We jumped in the car and went down to the calzone place, which was teeming with kids his age. Lenny and I ordered at the counter, paid, and found a table in the corner.

"God, you guys are loud," I said as I looked around the place. Everyone was on their phones and talking to each other at the same time. The guys were punching each other on the arm, switching hats, and throwing straws around.

"I guess," he said. Over his shoulder I saw a group of four girls together, leaning in toward each other, whispering and looking at Lenny.

"Don't look now but I think you have a fan club."

"What???" Lenny said with his mouth full.

"There are four girls behind you, and I think they are whispering about you."

"No way."

"Way. I was once a teenage girl, and I'll buy their dinner if I'm wrong."

"How you gonna prove it?"

I shrugged. "I'll bet you five bucks that fairly soon one of them talks to you first."

"You're on. Nobody talks to me."

"That's because you're new; they're still trying to figure you out. Where you belong, what side of the fence you'll jump on when things get rough, whether you're a good guy or not."

"Am I?"

"Are you what?"

"A good guy."

"Uh, *yeah* . . ." It occurred to me that no one had ever told him who he was, what he represented in other people's lives. He didn't see himself as anything but a burden on his mother and society. How familiar. My heart melted a little with this realization. It was up to me to shore him up. Me and maybe a teenage girl.

I told him about Camille's text. He shrugged. "If she shows up, I'm not going. I just won't be here tomorrow." He took a huge bite.

"Your choice."

I texted Camille that unfortunately he would not be able to make the visit; he had other plans. I copied Lenny and decided I would copy him on every piece of communication I had with her, no matter what. He deserved to know what was going on in his life.

I felt like I was making progress.

Chapter Twenty-Six

ADAM SHOWED UP ONE MORNING A FEW WEEKS LATER AS THOUGH nothing had happened; he had been gone four weeks; he looked thinner and grayer, but was presenting himself in his usual casual perfection. I walked into the shop and smelled coffee and turpentine. He sat at his easel working on a portrait and looked up at me and smiled.

"Welcome back," I said, not a little sarcastically.

"Apologies, dear lady. I had not meant to put you in this position, but it couldn't be helped."

I stared.

"My wife tells me you know the story, and I am grateful you are aware, but I cannot discuss it. I had an opportunity to finally accomplish a goal I had set out to do three years ago, and I took it. All is well now, and that chapter is closed."

"You have nothing else to tell me?"

"I dearly wish I could." Those blue eyes stuck to mine; I was the first to turn away.

"Fine. Let's just get on with it." I turned and walked out of the shop. Adam was in control; there was no need for me to be there.

Now what? I headed over to Pages. Jade Robinson had taken over the shop from a previous owner who had only opened the coffee shop to support the park, but had run into difficulties, and Jade and Robert Graham, the social journalist in town, had turned it into a writer's paradise, complete with a coffee bar, pastry shop, library, a spot for readings, workshops, and social events for the literati. They were still working things out, but it looked promising. The Writers' Guild was considering moving to the art park, which would be a great boon.

"I'm so sorry to hear about Jen," Jade said. "I know she's your friend." She said quietly. I gave her credit for coming out with that much.

"Thank you, Jade. She's doing as well as can be expected." What else am I going to say? "How is Pages coming along? I mean, other than working with us with the art journal program?"

She smiled. "Robert and I are working on some projects. Iris left a huge box of memories, and we are going through them with the idea of maybe putting together a biography of her."

"Really . . ." Iris, sentimental enough to leave memorabilia behind? That's a shocker. "You know, that makes sense. She had so much wisdom. If you can find some stories or background to go along with the pictures or whatever it is you have, it might help the next generation understand how women progressed. Maybe make it an investigative piece . . ."

Jade smiled and showed some dimples I had not noticed before. "I've been to the Library of Congress in Washington and picked up some things; I've also done some research online and have contacted a few people who knew her or knew of her. There's some missing spots, but it just makes me want to dig deeper."

"Iris had a lot to say, but I'm afraid she ran out of time to say it." My heart dropped a bit as I realized how busy I had been and had not mourned her much since her death, but I recognized how much I missed her and her guidance.

Jade nodded and lowered her head. "I miss her," she said quietly. "She was the only one who gave me a chance."

I didn't know what to say. "You're doing fine. The shop looks great, I know you are doing some writing labs and classes, and your project sounds great." We weren't close, but I wanted to support the business side of her life. "Drop in at Canvas any time and play," I said. "You're always welcome. We have to support each other."

She nodded. "I will. And thanks."

Lenny was quiet the rest of the week. He did go to art class with me, and his work was rough and hard. Black lines everywhere, no shading, and he almost ripped the paper, he was pushing so hard with his charcoal.

"Perhaps you'd like to try this, lad," Adam said, and handed Lenny a big, wide brush and a palette of oil paints. Lenny immediately began to brush the paint over and over, back and forth, until the entire page was obliterated by different colored paints. I watched as he then tore off the sheet, crumpled it up, and threw it on the ground.

Adam deliberately sauntered over to the paper, picked it up, and uncrumpled it. As he did so, he smiled. "Anger can sometimes be a very good thing for the arts," he said, turning the page around to show the class. The page looked like a beautiful piece of abstract stained glass. Like in the magazine Highlights we had as kids, I found hidden treasures. Lenny stared at the paper.

"All art is good art," Adam said. "Even that which you think is not. Energy and passion go into your art. It's evident." He shook the page. "Right here."

He handed the paper back to Lenny, who carefully held it by the edge and put it on a stool to dry completely. I looked over at Marjorie, who winked at me. This was good. Art therapy was something Marjorie did in her practice; I knew this was the right track.

Chapter Twenty-Seven

GUNNAR MET ME AT THE DOOR, ALL EXCITED, AND WOULDN'T CALM DOWN. I had had a doggie door put in so he could let himself in and out to the back yard, and when I was gone, I knew I didn't have to rush back. He ushered me to the sliding glass door in the back.

It was open about three inches, with a piece of blue fabric hanging off a jagged edge. Gunnar sat, wagging his tail proudly. I bent down to untangle it from the jamb and examined it. "Well, did you stop a burglar from coming in again? Good boy!" He stood and turned his body into a Jack-in-the- box. I laughed and gave him a doggie biscuit, then sat with the piece of fabric. About two inches by four; blue with some watercolor-y print. My memory was juggled a bit. Then I remembered.

When Eddie had moved to San Diego all those years ago, I had memorized his address and shamelessly driven by several times. I stopped when it lost its excitement, but I still remembered the route and got there in record time. I raced up the brick pathway to the east-coast-flavored house and rang the doorbell, then pounded on the door. Sally opened it and her face fell. She stepped aside and motioned for me to come in.

"What were you doing at my house?" I asked. "What could you possibly want with me?" She wore a top of the same fabric I had in my pocket. I saw where it had ripped on her right hip.

She wobbled a little and tried to get her balance by grabbing the door. She missed and started to slide. I caught her arm and helped her right herself and smelled alcohol.

"Did'n mean to . . . went to your place to return those . . . never read 'em . . . your stupid dog . . ." her left arm came up behind her and she pointed to a box on the dining room table. I let go of her and she swayed,

150

clearly drunk. She wobbled over to the sideboard and grabbed a bottle and started to pour. "Wan' one?" She pointed a glass at me. "Friend?" She smirked, then said, "You're not my friend," she shouted, her arms raising above her, pointlessly. "You're my emeny. 'S all for me." She opened her mouth and let a couple of fingers full of amber liquid slide down her throat. "Nope. You can't have any. Oh. Bottle's empty. Gotta go." She grabbed a set of keys and started out the door.

"Oh, no. You're not driving." I grabbed her hand and she wrested the keys from me, holding them high in the air. "You're too small to get them. Too small, too small, too small." She tried to open the door, but I barricaded it with my body. "Let me out. Get OUT!" Her face was nothing but rage, saliva dripping from her lips. "GET OUT!"

My cell was in my pocket. I looked through the "recents" and found Eddie's number and called. "You better get home. Sally's in self-destruct mode."

"What? Who is this?"

"Who the hell do you think this is? Get home NOW!" I clicked off.

"D'jou jus' call my husband? MY HUSBAND?" Her right hand with the keys in them came at my face. I ducked and heard a loud crunch right next to my ear. I heard every splinter that shattered with the force of one drunken woman's wrath. I grabbed her around the waist and marched her into the kitchen. She was not happy. "Get your hands offa me!" I put her in the padded breakfast nook and turned to find a bowl, then filled it with ice and water. I stuck her hand in it and she yelped. "Ow. Now look." Her voice lowered and she became a bit recalcitrant. "I don' like you anymore."

"I'm sure you don't, but I'm not leaving you." I turned from her to pull out a chair and heard the bowl tip over and spill onto her as she passed out on the bench.

"Well shit." I took her pulse and found it slow, but there, mopped up the water, put the bowl in the sink, and walked out of the kitchen to inspect Eddie's house.

Pictures of children, grandchildren, graduations, weddings, new babies, and all of the major life events surrounded me. All the events I'd heard about, congratulated him about, and mourned over, right in front of me. This was someone else's life.

A portrait of the two of them, in the same posture as in the wedding picture next to it, young people before the children, the drama, the drinking. Before I knew him. Wide lapels, a seventies' moustache, her with hair in a shag, his hair long and curly, tinted aviator glasses. The color was almost red, a color I never knew of him.

I wandered into the dining room to find beautiful china, crystal and silverware—probably wedding patterns—perfectly displayed. The box Sally had pointed to sat on the edge of the table. I opened it and gasped.

My journals. All twenty-two of them.

Eddie came crashing through the door, older, grayer, and panicked. "Sally? Sally?" He looked around wildly, and I surprised myself by staying calm.

"She's passed out in the breakfast nook."

"You! What are you doing here?"

"Long story. Take care of your wife." As he hurried into the kitchen, I took the box and left them to their own devices. If he wanted an explanation, he could call me. I doubted Sally would remember any of it.

After finishing a Rotary luncheon in which I pitched the art park, my phone rang—a familiar number, although I had not input a name to it.

"Hi." Eddie's voice came roaring through my brain.

"Yes?"

"I want to thank you for the other day."

"How is she?"

"Home from the hospital."

"She had to go to the hospital?" I was surprised. I thought drunks just slept it off.

"She was toxic. You saved her life. They cleaned her up and sent her home. She's committed to a program again. She was doing so well."

"I'm afraid I'm the cause of this last episode."

"Bullshit. She's the cause, not you. I've learned enough to know that an alcoholic will take any reason, any excuse, to check out."

"Well, I think she had good reason to, don't you?" I explained about the journals.

"Holy shit. You mean you wrote all that stuff down? How could you?"

"Relax. I kept it all locked up until I retired, then apparently she figured out who I was before I did, snuck into my house and stole them. I had a burglary a few weeks ago. I suspect she played both of us."

"That's what she meant when she said she was just trying to return them. I had no idea what 'they' were," he mumbled.

"What I want to know is how she even knew they existed."

"She probably didn't. She probably got drunk and decided to go to your place and see what she could dig up—she got the motherlode, from what you tell me."

"Well, thanks for calling. Have a nice life." There was no reason for me to talk to him, and I didn't want to stir anything up.

"Wait."

"What."

"She has no friends. All I know is she was so happy when she met you. She felt like she had made a good friend, one she could trust."

That's a laugh. "What are you saying? Jesus Christ, you want me to be her BFF?"

He was very quiet. Then, "Yes. That's exactly what I'm asking. I know it's not right, and I'm asking a lot, but she really could use someone right now."

"Not you?" That was mean.

"No, not me, as it happens. Her therapist thinks she should have more of a foundation. She didn't leave the house for a long time. That painting class was her first dip into the social pool."

"And she comes up with me."

"And she comes up with you, thank God." I breathed into the phone.

"Just help her, please?" The whine in his voice almost did me in. He really loves her. And I can help.

Well shit.

Chapter Twenty-Eight

"DO YOU EVER WONDER ABOUT YOUR MOM?" LENNY ASKED ME AS HE inhaled a peanut butter sandwich after school. Electrical shocks wove their way down to my fingertips. *He's talking to me.* "Sometimes. Why do you ask?" I was so tired, but I forced myself to continue.

"Because you and I are in the same situation—our moms are unreliable and untrustworthy." I thought about my mother and what I knew about her so far. She was sober and had her own family.

"Sometimes people turn their lives around."

"Don't believe it for one second," he said in a monotone, and threw the rest of his sandwich on the table. "Fuck it. I'm going to Canvas. Adam has another class tonight and needs help setting things up."

I didn't respond. He gathered his things and left. I poured a drink after wondering if I should address the swearing.

The Lenny journal was in a drawer. I pulled it out and updated it with the latest info. As I put it away in the locked drawer, I looked over at the box of twenty-two journals I had yet to replace in their bookshelves. *What the hell good are they, and why am I keeping them? Move on.* I pushed the box into the closet and behind some old coats.

The doorbell rang. Ron??? No. Standing on the stoop was the woman I had seen in court, Elena. Lenny's mom.

"Yes?" I said as I opened the door further, my arm bracing against it so she got the very clear message she wasn't entering my home.

"I'm here to see Lenny."

"Well, you are here on the wrong day, and he's not here."

"He's my son."

"And he's my responsibility. Look, he's not here. Did Camille not tell you he had other plans?"

"What other plans?"

"I'm not sure it's important for you to know that. Suffice it to say he's not here."

"Then I'll wait for him." She tried to bulldoze her way into my house.

"No. I can't let you in." My voice rose. She dodged under my arm and took two steps. Then I heard Gunnar growl. He showed his teeth and began to very slowly march toward her.

"Gunnar, SIT," I said. He sat, but watched her very carefully, growling lower, letting us know he was not happy, and ready to pounce at the slight provocation. Dogs know.

Elena had flattened herself against the wall. "Call him off."

"Maybe you'd just better go. He's a new dog and I'm not sure I know how to control him yet. We'll make other arrangements."

"I'll wait for him outside."

"Your choice." I seemed to be saying that a lot lately. I texted Lenny with the latest update.

No answer. I didn't dare jump in the car and have her follow me. Brilliant.

"Do you have room for Lenny tonight?" I asked when Bruce answered the phone. "I know things are a bit hairy for you and Jen right now, but . . ."

"I think Jen can use a night alone, as a matter of fact. Yes, I'll take him." I filled him in on the sitch. God love him, he jumped into action. "I'll come to your place now and pick up whatever he needs for school and a change of clothes, then go get him and take him to my place. I'll get him to school in the morning. But . . . Renee? I'm happy to help, but let's not make a habit of this."

"Of course not. Thanks." Bruce was there inside of fifteen minutes and I handed over the backpack inside of a cardboard box for subterfuge. I saw a broken-down Toyota across the street. "That her?" he asked.

"I'm thinking so . . . thanks again for doing this."

"You're welcome. I didn't mean to be so abrupt when I said not to make a habit of this. I think he needs to have some stability, not go from house to house."

"You're right. Just right now I don't know what to do and I have to think. I suspect Lenny does, too. If he doesn't want to go, or if you have any trouble with him . . ."

"I won't." He turned and walked back to his car, slid in and cruised off at a slow pace. She didn't follow.

He's right. I have to take control, have boundaries like the parenting classes said. I can't go selling him off to anyone who offers to take him. I'm in charge. I need to do this. And do it well.

I texted Lenny and told him what was happening, giving him the choice of coming back or going with Bruce. Bruce would honor whatever he wanted to do, but I wanted Lenny to know what he was up against if he came back here. Then I texted Camille and told her Elena was stalking my house.

Camille:

> I'll be right there. Do you want me to call the police?

> No. I just wanted you to know.

> I need to tell her how inappropriate this is.

> Thanks.

> This is why I didn't want her to have your address. You should be protected.

I had said no to a "confidential" placement, thinking we could all be adults and get along. Apparently, I was wrong. I know that now. My phone buzzed with another message.

Lenny:

> Going with Bruce

> You have a choice, you know.

No answer. I didn't copy him on the message to Camille, already breaking my vow to him. Half an hour later, I watched as Camille drove up and approached Elena. There were words. Elena drove off in a huff and Camille got back in her car and drove down the street.

Camille:

> You might want to get a restraining order. She's very angry.

Why was I so stupid as to not take the confidential placement? I didn't think it would be a big deal. Another bad choice. I'm getting good at this bad choice thing. Wait. Wasn't I the most powerful woman in the city just a short time ago? What happened to that woman? I watched my hands shake as I put down the phone.

When South Bay flooded last year and thousands of people were hurt and displaced, I handled it. When the fire destroyed an apartment building and killed five people, I handled it. When someone threatened my life and sent awful messages to me, I handled it. When conflicts arose and things got heated, I handled it and slept well.

But this? This was getting to me.

When Lenny came back after school the next day, Gunnar growled, barked, then jumped and down on his hind legs in ecstasy. I came around the corner and had to do a double take.

Lenny's hair was cut short. It made him look very handsome. I could actually see his face and his gray eyes.

"Hey! Look at you!" I said.

"Yeah. Bruce made me do it." He put his head down and slowly clomped upstairs. Time to take control. Set boundaries. Show him who's boss. The stereo came on loud. Very loud. I texted him to please come downstairs.

Thankfully, the stereo went off and he came down.

"What."

"Are you mad at me?" So much for taking control. I was now the victim.

"Yeah."

"Why? What did I do?"

"You don't really want me here."

"God, I am just so bad at this." I said it out loud. "Lenny . . .I don't know how to do this. I do want you here. You keep shutting me out."

"You shut me out last night."

"That was to protect you. I told you why."

"You don't think I can take care of myself?"

"So, I should have let you walk into it?"

"Yes." His face was red and his upper lip began to glisten. "It's better than being shoved around from one house to another."

"But . . . you're fifteen."

"So? Does that give you the right to tell me what to do?" Tempting as it was, I withheld my original thought—telling him I had a piece of paper that said just that. I didn't know what to say. He was probably far older than fifteen, and didn't I know it. I thought back to my own maturity, far faster than my friends'. Life was hard. I wanted a team, a family, not necessarily a parent. Time for a new tactic.

"Let's try something. Let's each take ten minutes and write down what we want to talk about and see if we can come to an understanding. If we can't, then you are free to do whatever you want. Live on the streets, wait for your mom, whatever. I won't stop you. If we do work things out, we are a team. I am not a parent, but I am your guardian, so we need to have some guidelines to live our lives."

The next four hours were brutal. He argued with me on everything: curfew times, homework assignments, chores, and allowance. Who was going to pick out his clothes and how loud the stereo could be. Friends, school, clubs, sports . . . we talked about it all. He hung in there even after I wanted to throw in the towel. The only thing that kept me at that table was his energy. He fought me on every detail, but we finally came to an agreement. I had him sign the page with scribbles and changes on it, and I signed it, too.

"So . . . about your haircut. Did Bruce really make you do it?"

He hung his head. "He took me to the haircut store and said I was getting my hair cut."

"He didn't ask?"

"No."

"But you could have objected."

"Yeah."

"Why didn't you?"

"He was just so . . . strong about it. I felt like I didn't have a choice." Like a parent.

"Should I talk to him?" I asked.

"Nah." He shrugged and looked at me. "Are you going to find your mom?"

Hard to admit, but it is the truth. "She doesn't want me. She has a new life."

"Hunh. Going to bed."

And that was that.

Chapter Twenty-Nine

WHY AM I DOING THIS? I CERTAINLY DON'T NEED A PISSED-OFF KID IN MY life. He's not mine. He's somebody else's kid. How did I get here?

Retirement sucks. I did a mental checklist of everything that was going sideways, and counted them off on my fingers. Once again, I just wanted to crawl away.

I dreamed of sailing away into the sunset with Ron. Instead, my mother will not even acknowledge my existence, my best friend may be dying, I have an investment in an art store that may or may not have been wise, and I have a steady case of anxiety—new for me. On top of that, my ex-lover has asked me to be his wife's BFF. And I could handle all that. Not willingly, but I knew I could. Where will I get the energy? I just wanted to fall.

But Lenny's situation had me all churned up. I am not sleeping, my stomach is in constant knots, and sometimes my hands shake. I knew I could hand him back over to the system. Call Camille and throw in the towel. Make my life easier. Get this monkey off my back. *I'm tempted.*

I called Ron, and was put through immediately.

"Hello, Renee."

"Hello, Ron." *How's Suzanne?* "Ron, I need some help."

His tone changed immediately. "What can I do?"

That's why everyone loves you.

"It's the kid. I can't do this."

Ron waited three beats. "What makes you say that?"

"He hates me."

"I suspect he hates his life." A few more beats. "Do you want to meet for a drink?"

My heart flipped over. "Sure. Why not?" We made arrangements and clicked off. I went into my bedroom and looked over my wardrobe and dressed girlie, and even put on some makeup. I felt like an idiot.

The former mayor of San Diego meeting the current mayor for drinks would be noteworthy. I wanted to make an impression, but I didn't want to send the message that I'm available, looking, or that we were a couple. Just old friends meeting to discuss something. I put on the one suit I had with a skirt, but added a silk blouse. Even pantyhose. Ugh.

Won't he be surprised.

We met at a small place on the coast in North County, and indeed we did get some looks, but nobody came over to chat. We ordered drinks and began to chat about city business. I caught him up on some old business and he caught me up on some new. I was happy to know I could fill in some blanks for him. We were very cordial and correct.

"So, what are you thinking about the kid? What's his name?"

"Lenny. He's very angry. He's far behind in school, has no friends, has had God know how many placements, and doesn't know where to go. He doesn't trust me—or anybody." I took a sip, then got going. "He's smart, Ron. He's cute, he's curious, has a great, if quirky, sense of humor, he's every-thing a fourteen-year-old girl would want, if he would just clean himself up a little. He's sensitive, like a poet. He's got something. That sense of power, of reasonableness, of . . .I don't know, a solid citizen." My heart raced and I found myself using my hands as exclamation points.

Ron kept staring at me as he took a sip, then said, "I have never seen you so passionate."

"What?"

"Usually you are factual, precise." He threw his hands in the air. "Take it or leave it. But now you are showing some emotion." He cocked his head and pointed a finger at me. "You care about him."

"I do not." Knee-jerk reaction. His hand was warm and left a cold place when he retracted it.

He laughed. "Oh, yes you do. You're not about to give him up for yet another placement." He cocked his head. "You think you need help. You

161

don't. You're fine the way you are. Just talk to him. If he doesn't want to talk, let it go, but keep at it so he knows you're there and not shutting down."

My brain froze. I'm good enough? I didn't know what to say.

"Renee, you don't have to be anyone but you, no matter how you dress. You look fantastic, by the way."

The bottles over the bar had held my attention while he talked, and I jerked my head around to face him. "Now that's sort of contradictory."

He smiled. "Yes, it is. I'm going to stop while I'm ahead." He stood, took a twenty out and slapped it onto the bar.

"Who says you're ahead?" I asked. He smiled and ambled out, hands in his pockets. Probably has a date. Deflated, I sat in the car and wondered what to do next. *Why is nothing working?* Ron so clearly was not interested. I had to let that thought go. I was crazy to think that he ever was.

But wait. He did hold my hand at Jen's that night we went for dinner, all that time ago. What did that mean? I had taken it as a signal. Maybe Jen can help me make some sense of this. I drove over there, but Bruce said she wasn't up to company.

I stopped at the grocery store and got more milk and cereal, then sat back and took a few deep breaths, then bolted upright. *Damn. There's a class tonight, and I'm already late.* "Shit!" I turned the key. Nothing happened. Turned again. Nada.

Okay, now what? The auto service was there inside of ten minutes, jumped the battery, and had me on my way quickly. I ran by the house, left the engine running, grabbed my painter's kit, fed Gunnar, then jumped into the car and sped off to the art park.

Lenny was not there. Surprise, surprise. *What do I do if he's doing drugs, drinking, or robbing stores?* I shook my head. Lenny's got a good head on his shoulders. I want to keep it that way. But is that my responsibility? Uh, *yeah*.

And Gunnar? He's not getting the kind of attention he needs. And Lenny is afraid of him. So is Adam. Do I have to get rid of both of them? One of them? I screamed into the interior of the car.

Didn't make me feel any better.

I flew into Canvas, made my excuses, and took my place at an empty easel. After I set up, I looked around to find Suzanne, Marjorie, and—oh God—Sally at their easels. Too much. Way too much.

Shouldn't have come. Adam walked around the easels giving suggestions and encouragement, while I began to work on my project. My hands were shaking. I took several deep breaths and tried to calm down. This is so not like me. What is the problem? Is it that Sally's here? No, I can handle that. It's Lenny. I don't know where he is, and I'm responsible for him.

"Have you seen Lenny?" I asked Adam as he came to me.

"Yes, dear lady, he was here earlier and helped me set up. Then he was gone."

"He wasn't at . . . the house."

His eyebrows rose and he turned to Marjorie, engaging her in a conversation about mixing paints.

What am I doing, painting like there's nothing wrong? There's a kid missing. I packed my things up again and left. Adam nodded to me as I turned to go out the door. Sally kept working.

My car wouldn't start again. I slammed my fist into the steering wheel and for the first time in my life I wanted to break down. So, so much. I cursed up a storm as I stomped back up the stairs to Canvas. "My car won't start. Does anyone have jumper cables?" I looked around the class. Sally wouldn't look up. "No, I'm sorry," Marjorie said. "I should, but no."

Suzanne, of course, didn't have any, nor did Adam, nor Dapper Dan.

"Oh, for God's sake, I have some." Sally threw down her brush and brushed past me out into the parking lot. She moved her car to the empty space next to mine and we hooked it up and got me up and running again.

"Thank you."

"You're welcome."

"Sally . . ."

She held her hand up, said, "No," and walked away.

Chapter Thirty

WHEN JEN ANSWERED, I TALKED INCESSANTLY AND FILLED HER IN ON everything that had happened, from my meeting with Ron to Lenny's situation. She was very quiet and listened as usual. When I wound down, she took a deep breath.

"Do you know this is the first time you've ever told me your problems?"

"What?"

"I have never heard you talk this way before. You've been talking for fifteen minutes non-stop. Not a sarcastic line, no innuendo, and no humor. You ran through some of your accomplishments like they were nothing. Not even when Eddie broke up with you did you talk like this. It was just a fact. Everything has been just facts to you."

"And?"

"And now you're on the other side of the fence."

"What do you mean?"

"Renee, this is personal."

My heart dropped. Personal. "Apparently I'm clueless in that area."

"That's because it's so new to you."

"What do I do?"

"About what?" She took a deep breath. "Sweetie, I can't help you with this one. You'll have to work this out through your own methods. I have enough on my plate." The new Jen.

"I'm so sorry. How are you doing?"

"As well as can be expected. Chemo tomorrow. Not looking forward to it."

"What can I do?"

"Can you pick something up from Stitches for me and bring it here? Lupe will have it ready."

"Sure. What else?"

"Pray."

I heard Lenny come in the door, Gunnar's tail bouncing off the base-board, and go upstairs. I said nothing.

Coward.

A few hours later, we were contemplating dinner when my phone buzzed.

> Are you coming over? Jen.

Why would I . . . oh shit. I forgot I was supposed to get something from Stitches. Damn.

"Want to come with me to the art park?" I asked Lenny.

"Weren't you just there?"

"Yeah, but I forgot something. Come on, we can grab something on the way."

He shrugged and walked out the door. Gunnar was despondent, so I put him in the back seat.

"Does he have to?"

"Why not? You guys are buds, right?" I punched him in the arm.

"Ow."

"Sorry."

"No, I hate dogs."

"No, you don't. Just look at that face." Gunnar was hanging his head down and breathing into Lenny's face, tongue out, and very sad eyes drooping.

"Let's just go."

"All righty then." Silence all the way to Stitches. When we entered, Lupe gave me a hug and looked at Lenny. I introduced them, and Lenny was just as quiet as he could be.

"Who's this?" she asked, looking down at Gunnar, who slobbered all over her floor and cocked his head at her.

"This is Gunnar. He's a great watchdog."

She knelt down and he licked her face. "Some mean guy you are! I could have used you last night."

"What happened last night? Were you robbed?"

"No, nothing like that. Hal came by and threatened me."

"Your ex-husband? I thought he was in jail."

She shook her head. "Out."

"Don't you have a restraining order?"

"Yes, but he breaks it all the time. By the time the cops come, he's gone." She shrugged. "But I'm okay. It helps to be dating a cop. Here's what Jen wanted. Tell her I said hi."

"I will." I took the package and we got back in the car.

"What's a restraining order?"

"It's a piece of paper that says someone's not allowed to come within five hundred feet of you or something if you think you're in danger. A judge awards it if you have proof of imminent danger, usually only if you've already suffered at that person's hands in the past."

An image of Lupe's black-and-blue face floated in front of me. It was horrific. She put up with it until she found out she was pregnant. Then she left him. It was a tough time, but now she has little Catie and a new life.

Lenny folded his arms across his chest and turned into himself.

I had been at the shop and doing public events and a few board meetings. I was fairly exhausted when Gunnar met me at the door, grinning from ear to ear. His tail made his entire body shake and I had to laugh at someone greeting me with such glee. Lenny, on the other hand, was in his room and didn't even know I had come home.

"Want a friend, get a dog" was actually proving itself true. He never failed to be happy to greet me.

My brain was getting foggy with so much to worry about. I took out my journal and listed everything in my brain. It's my method for compartmentalizing and dealing with various areas, and it's always worked well. I labeled it my Items of Concern.

Tutor for L?
Jen—what can I do?
Bruce—how can I support?
Ron—what's happening?
Canvas—was this a mistake?
Senate—need to get moving
Cooking—casseroles and home-cooked meals?
Groceries—how to keep milk in the house
Clothes for L—how do I shop for a 15-year-old, and should I?
Personal—makeover?
Hobby—do I need one?
Tricia—what's going on with her?
Sally—friend or foe?
Am I retired or not?

"Jesus." I threw down my pen and went into the kitchen to pour a drink. I was out of scotch. Damn.

Later I texted Lenny, even though he was fifty feet away.

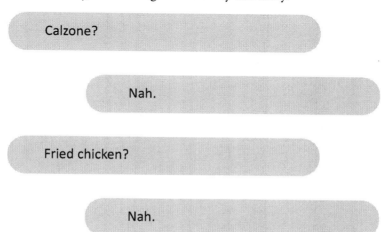

Calzone?

Nah.

Fried chicken?

Nah.

> Waddya want?

> Nah. (Smiley face)

> Anything you want.

> Seriously?

> Nah. (Smiley face back).

Stomp, stomp, stomp. God, he was big.

"Sushi."

"Sushi??? Are you kidding me?"

"No. Adam took me once. I really liked it."

"Okay, then. Raw fish it is." I could always get teriyaki or something. I wanted to puke. We went to the same sushi place Adam had taken Lenny to, and he ordered a California roll. I ordered miso soup and chicken. I also ordered a beer. Lenny had green tea.

"So, Adam brought you here, huh?" I said as I watched him inexpertly manipulate the chopsticks. He dropped more than he got in his mouth, but he kept trying.

"Yup." Shovel, shovel. "Take one. It's really good."

So, I did, and had never had anything so wonderful in my life. The crab, the avocado, the spicy sauce and cucumber wrapped in rice was definitely a winner.

"You like?" the sushi chef asked as he watched me.

"Me like!" I said, inappropriately, and laughed.

"You want try something else?"

I hesitated. "I'll try something else!" Lenny said.

The chef nodded and smiled, and shortly handed over a pressed seaweed cone something with rice inside and some creamy something. "Hand-rolled spicy tuna," he said as he nodded to me. I took a bite and, once again, was ecstatic. Lenny took it from me and took a huge bite, nodding the whole time. Chef Araki was pleased with our progress and brought us some other things to try—a small sushi rice piece with salmon eggs—something I used to cringe about—but I put on my big girl panties and tried it. Salty, melting, and delicious. Lenny was grossed out by the texture, but I loved it.

We rolled home after a long, expensive dinner. We had finally found something to have in common. Who knew it would be raw fish?

I still hadn't filled out the campaign registration forms. I sat and stared at them for at least an hour, shuffling the pages and procrastinating putting pen to paper.

If I did this, it would have all sorts of repercussions. I would have to focus only on the campaign. I would have to surround myself with other politicians, volunteers, and aides. My blood sang when I thought about the excitement of running for office and living in Washington, or, at the very least, going back and forth. It was no longer about just me. Running for office meant leaving everything else behind—my house, my business, my dog, and my kid.

My kid? My *foster* kid.

And Jen. I would not be able to be by her side. I'd probably not be able to help her at all with going to therapy and hospital visits. That's why she had Bruce. I had not been helpful. She didn't need me, but still.

What would I do without her? If she died, and it was looking more and more possible that that would be the outcome, what would I do? I'd have to have something to sink my teeth into and being a senator would fill that bill nicely. It would be all-consuming.

Life without Jen was unthinkable. Painful. Just unbelievable. And yet, a possibility. No.

The kitchen beckoned. I should say the new scotch bottle beckoned. I poured myself a big one over ice and cradled it against my chest as I thought about the many reactions I would have to this decision. I took a quick glug and schlepped my way back into the office. I pulled out my Items of Concern and realized that out of the eleven issues I had scribbled down off the top of my head, only one of them was about my career. The rest were personal. *But I want to have an impact on the world. I want to make changes, big changes, and have a voice in government. I want that.*

Ordinarily, I would call Jen and hash this over.

Chapter Thirty-One

"HOW ARE YOU FEELING?" I ASKED JEN WHEN I STOPPED BY. SHE HAD answered the door in one of her newer caftans that used to cover her weight gain. Now she looked like a scarecrow. My tongue dried up; I was afraid I was seeing my best friend literally disappear in front of me.

"And how are YOU feeling?" she asked as she opened the door wider. "I'm sick of talking about myself."

"Oh, I'm okay . . ."

"No, you're not."

"No. I'm not." I plopped onto the couch.

Jen sat in her overstuffed chair, leaned over to the table at her side and took out a joint. "Chemo yesterday. This helps." She lit the joint with an engraved silver lighter. "A leftover from my smoking days . . . what's up with you? You're not worried about me, are you?" She stared at me through the smoke.

"Yes. Of course, I am. I don't know what I would do . . ."

"No. We're not going to talk about that just yet."

"Just yet?"

She shrugged. "We don't know at this point. I'm hanging on to positive thoughts, but I have to be prepared for the worst. I'm in the biggest fight of my life."

I nodded and tears streamed down my face.

"Oh, Renee . . ." She sat up, back ramrod straight.

"No. It's not just you, it's everything."

"Everything? Lenny? The shop? Spill." She took another toke.

"I'm alone, Jen. For the first time, I'm not connected to anything. No job, no friends except for you, and Sally, well maybe . . ."

"Sally?"

"Oh, God. I didn't tell you. Yeah, Eddie's wife."

Her eyes went wide. "His *wife*? Good God. How did you manage that?" She started to giggle.

"Just lucky, I guess. Now Eddie wants me to be her BFF."

"You've spoken to him? Oh, this just gets better and better."

"Uh, yeah." And I proceeded to tell her the whole story.

"How did you manage to get into this situation?" She laughed.

"It's not funny."

"Yes. It is." She giggled again.

"Then there's the shop. Adam is somewhat off-limits. He seems to keep to himself and is not interested in a friendship, just a partnership. There's no connection there."

"I see. There may be a reason for that."

"What do you mean?"

"Just trust me when I tell you that there's a reason Adam is holding himself at a distance." She took another hit. "It's a good reason. He's one of the good guys. That's all I can say."

"Ah. So you know." She nodded and held up her hand in a stop signal.

"Then there's Lenny. God, Jen, I have no idea what to do with the kid. He's sulking around, hates school, won't talk to me, and eats like a horse. His acne is awful and he doesn't like to shower. He's angry and pissed off and I think he wants to murder somebody."

"He's fifteen. That's his job, I think."

"No. It's really uncomfortable."

She cocked her head at me. "What's really going on?" She waited while I gathered my thoughts.

Something caved. "For the first time in my life, I'm feeling worthless." I had to move. I stood and began to pace. I was nauseous, itchy. "I had a good job, lots of people who supported me and allowed me to do what I needed to do. I was respected, I now realize, not for who I am, but for what I was."

"Go on."

"Ron wants nothing to do with me, you are sick, my own mother denies my existence . . ."

"What?"

"I called her and she hung up on me."

"Oh, Renee . . ."

I started to cry again. My throat hurt from trying to force words out when they just weren't willing to come. "And then you . . ."

"Don't you dare put this on me." She fired back. "I will not allow you to wallow in pity for me or for yourself. If it's my time, it's my time. Accept it. I hope it's not, but if it is . . .I'd like for us all to work together so it's not a painful process, like it was for Arthur. I learned a lot from that, and I won't go the same way."

"Jesus, Jen." I reached over, grabbed a tissue and blew my nose.

"I'm serious. What else?"

"The biggest thing is Lenny." I dropped my head. "I just don't know if I'm doing anything right."

"Are you there? Are you feeding him? Are you listening to him? Have you provided anything he could possibly need? Not want, but need?"

"Yes, yes, yes, and yes, I think."

"Then you are doing what you can." It was a whisper. Her eyes closed, then she said, quietly, "I think you would benefit from some counseling. Pour all this out and get some feedback on what's working and what's not. Do you know of anyone?"

"Yes, there's one in our art class. I know her by reputation. Marjorie something."

Jen sort of laughed. "Oh, her. Yes, she is great. Very direct, won't let you bullshit her at all. Gets right to the point, gives you your options, and lets you get on with your life on your own terms. She's really good."

"Maybe I will."

"She's so good that Maggie fired her."

"Then I definitely will."

"What else? There's something else that you're not telling me."

"I don't know how to put it onto words."

"Try."

"I'm fifty-nine years old, not terribly attractive, a little overweight, with very little in the way of social skills other than political lessons learned the hard way. I have an impressive list of contacts and accomplishments, but nobody to share it with. I miss Iris." I stopped, and finished with, "Why won't anyone love me?"

She thought for a moment. "Oh, you definitely need to go see a shrink."

My cell phone trilled on the desk next to me. I put my green pen down and stared at the name—City Hall. Tanya.

"Hello, Tanya, what can I do for you?"

"It's Ron," followed by a chortle. "Sorry to interrupt you."

So, he called from the City phone. It will be logged in.

"Hello."

He got right into it. "I received a phone call this morning asking about our relationship."

"Our what?" Couldn't help it.

Another chortle. "Our relationship. Ed Knowles wanted to know if I had received any special favors from you."

"Ed Knowles? That slimeball?"

"The very one . . ." I could just see that smile. I shook myself. And took a gulp of Jamaican Java that I had poured a little coffee-flavored liquor into.

"So, what was he implying?"

"More importantly, why would he be interested? Are you running for something?" Busted.

"Possibly." Silence.

"Really."

"Really." Silence.

"So, how's Jen?"

"She's holding up, last I heard." I wasn't going to get into specifics.

"Last you heard? Aren't you in touch every day?"

"Not lately. I've been a bit busy with Lenny and the shop."

"And you're going to run for office with all of that going on?"

I bristled. "Why wouldn't I? Because I'm a woman?"

Hesitation, then a very calm monotone. "No. Because that's a lot on your plate without someone, like a spouse or a significant other, to take half the burden."

"You did it alone."

"Yes, but I wasn't raising a child or starting a new venture."

I sighed. "Ron, what I do is my business."

"I hear that." He hesitated. "Loud and clear."

"So, about the phone call you received. We have nothing to hide. Tell him the truth and I'll be vetted by the party. It's just part of the process."

"Already done. I told him of our torrid affair and he thanked me profusely."

"Whaat?" I spit out my coffee.

"I'm kidding, Renee. Lighten up."

"This is my life we're talking about."

"I know, and I'm sorry. Can I ask you a question?"

"Sure."

"We've had this discussion before, and I want to revisit the homeless situation. I get that we have different attitudes towards the homeless, but can I ask why? Is there a concrete reason?"

A concrete reason. Yeah.

I gave him my history, Mom in flophouses and me going to get her at seven years old. "I knew she was there and couldn't get out because she owed this guy forty bucks. I stole the money from Mrs. Putnam's purse and had it in my pocket. I was going to put it back if I could sneak her out, but it didn't work that way."

"What happened?"

"Let's just say I almost lost my ear and have a deep scar on my neck that reminds me every day."

"Did he get his money?"

"It's a forty-dollar scar, so, you know . . ."

"Jesus. No wonder you have no sympathy. You've only ever known the bad side."

"There's a good side?"

"Yeah, look at your kid."

Silence.

"Okay, then. Catch you later." *Catch you later?*

Click. I threw the phone down and went to get more coffee and a dash more enhancement.

Chapter Thirty-Two

ALL DAY LONG, THE PHRASE "BUT SHE'S MY MOM" KEPT COMING BACK at me.

Lenny wants his mom. Doesn't everybody? I did. Even though I'd had a nice life with the Palmers, I was still missing that piece of the puzzle that connected me with someone by blood. The difference is, she made it very clear she didn't want me in her life.

Reunification was the goal. If Elena could get sober and productive, she would be able to see Lenny through high school. But if she couldn't, I'd be there. So, I knew I shouldn't invest too much emotionally because he could leave me.

Too late.

Breaking my vow with Lenny about telling him everything, I called Bruce to find out exactly what happened.

"How's Jen?"

He chuckled. "Smoking weed and loving it. So far, it's staved off the nausea." I heard Jen's voice in the background. "Tell her to come over!"

He laughed. "Do you want to talk to her?"

"Actually, I called for you. How did things go with Lenny?"

"You mean the haircut?"

"Yes. How did that come about?"

"I suggested he might want to get cleaned up. He said, 'I guess so,' and we were off. He seemed okay with it. Why?"

"He said you made him do it."

"That's bullshit. Sorry. If I thought for one second he didn't want to, I would have pulled the plug, but I was strongly suggesting this. Did I overstep?"

"No . . .I'm just trying to get a handle on this kid."

"Look, I was once a fifteen-year-old boy. What he wants is someone to tell him what to do, not give too many options." *So, had I just blown it by trying to be a partner? If he didn't like something, I could at least say he agreed to it. Coward.* All these thoughts came scrambling through my brain as I listened to Bruce talk to Jen.

"Okay, thanks." I rang off, knowing Jen would be dozing soon. Besides, I didn't want to have the smell of grass all over me again when Lenny came home.

Gunnar and I went for a long walk. When we got back, the mail was in: the usual bills, credit card offers, and a check from HHS. An envelope dropped to the ground. From Iowa. My heart in my throat, we walked back to the house. Mom.

In a daze, I took the leash off of Gunnar, gave him some water, and took the mail into my office. What could she possibly have to say?

The handwriting was not familiar. But then again, I had never seen her sober handwriting. It was elementary, like a fourth-grader's. I stared at the envelope and turned it over and over again. I smelled it. Nothing familiar about this. I opened it and spread the single lined page flat on the desk.

Dear Renee,

I am sorry to cut you off when you called. I've been thinking about this a lot, and I thought I should write to you.

First off, I want you to know that I've been following your career and I am very proud of you. The Palmers did you good. I gave you up because I knew they could do a better job than me, and I was right.

I have been sober for twenty-five years. I have a good life with three stepchildren and two grandchildren I love. My husband is good to me and is a good man. He knows

I had a baby years ago, but doesn't know any more than that, and I aim to keep it that way. I am happy.

Life goes on, and we make of it what we can.

Lorna

And that was it. No 'Love, Mom.' No affection at all. Just a howdy-do and don't contact me. I read it about ten times, looking for something intimate. Gunnar came over and put his chin on my thigh. I read it again while I went from white hot to chills.

But she's my mom. My eyes pricked and burned. Gunnar's tail flapped at something at the doorway. Lenny stood at the entrance to my office and watched me.

"I'm back," he said lamely.

"Oh, okay." My hands handed over the page. We were in the same boat. He might as well know what's happening. I handed it over to him. He sat on the chair opposite me and flattened out the page and began to read. It didn't take long.

"That sucks." He stood and went into the kitchen. I heard the refrigerator open, close, then the pop of a soda can.

"What are you going to do?" he said as he plopped back down.

"What she asks. I can't disrupt her life." I shrugged. "I've lived without her this long." I explained how she left; that Jen's parents had manipulated her exit.

"So, she jumped bail?" He was far more educated than I about court proceedings.

"I guess so . . . maybe they did something on this end. I don't know."

"Yeah. Sucks." He took a big gulp. "Tried out for the wrestling team today."

"What?"

He laughed. He had some cute dimples I hadn't seen before. "They had tryouts today."

God, he's going to kill somebody with that rage. Then I remembered that's why God invented coaches.

"When do you find out?"

"Couple weeks."

The doorbell rang. We locked eyes. "Whatever it is, we'll handle it," I said quietly.

Gunnar made a racket at the front door and I had to pull him away. Elena stood on the stoop.Lenny said, "Hi, Mom." Just as calmly as he could. "Come on in. He's just a big baby," he said as he gestured toward Gunnar.

"No, thanks. I thought you might want to go get something to eat."

"Sure." He turned to me and said, "Back by," he checked his phone, "seven."

"Great!" I said with more enthusiasm than I felt. "I'll be at class." He nodded. I closed the door behind them.

Chapter Thirty-Three

My home phone rang. Uh-oh. "Ms. Murphy? Dick Ambrose here." "Yes, Dick?"

"We have been hashing this over for a bit, this situation of yours . . ." It took me a minute to think about which situation—ah, yes, the apparent preference I showed to Ron Walker.

"Yes?"

" . . .And we've decided to look into it a bit further. Some things are just not adding up." I waited.

"I am sure there is nothing to it, just some rumors somebody started, but things are coming out now that I won't bother you with unless we need a full explanation from you."

"Does it all have to do with Ron Walker?"

" . . . and others . . ."

"What?" I took a deep breath and dove into the deep end. "You know what, Dick? I think I'll back out. I have not filed any forms yet, and I do have a lot on my plate. I think maybe I will just back off for now. Barbara Morse has not announced her resignation yet, so there is time."

"If you think that is best."

"I do."

"As you wish." Click. So much for the backing of the party. And so much for a hard decision to make. It just got made.

I had hit my limit. I made a call to Marjorie's office and made an appointment.

"I think I'm going crazy," I said.

Marjorie-from-the-painting-class threw her head back and roared. Tiny, with a string of pearls and a wool skirt and matching sweater, she looked like a throwback to the fifties, ready to head off to a PTA meeting, a costume. Her response irked me.

She wasn't taking me seriously. Nobody did, and that was the crux of my problem. As a therapist, she should have at least shown some concern, and it pissed me off.

"If you knew how many times I've heard that . . ." she sputtered out. "Hang on." She took an enormous water bottle from the end table and drew quite a lot of water through the straw. She adjusted herself and pulled her leather notebook onto her lap and clicked her pen.

"Okay, now. Is this better?" She sat upright, poised to take notes, then roared again. "So much for reaching expectations," she said. "You'll find I like a bit of sarcasm and humor in my sessions. It tends to loosen people up and I can get to the root of the matter much more quickly. Saves me time, you money, and the next person on my waiting list gets in faster."

It was true she had a major waiting list. I was only able to see her tonight because I begged. I knew Ron used her for extra help with an officer who needed additional support after an incident, so I knew she could be trusted.

Being mayor certainly had its perks, but I discovered I was paying double her fee for seeing her after hours. I snuck in the back door, which was fine with me.

"I just don't know which way to turn."

"Why? Because you are no longer in a power position?" Ouch.

"Not so much that, although I have discovered who my friends are. No, it seems that everyone in my life has deserted me."

"They aren't really in your life, then, are they?"

"What?"

"Think about it. It's a blanket statement, but if they aren't paying attention to you when you need them, then are they really 'in your life'?" she used air quotes, which irritated me no end.

I didn't quite know what to say.

"All right. Name them."

"Name who?"

"The people who have deserted you."

"Oh, let's see, my best friend, who has found a new, shall we say, companion, and who may be dying; the man I thought I had a future with; my assistant has a new mentor, my supporters in the party, and, oh yeah, my mother. My foster kid is ignoring me, a friend I thought was a friend actually set me up, and my store manager is distant."

"Any more?"

"Isn't that enough?"

She tapped her pen against the legal pad in her lap.

"What have you done in the past for a trusting relationship?"

"What do you mean?"

"How do you know you can trust someone?"

"I don't."

"You don't. Is that because of your profession?"

"It's because of my life."

"Maybe we'd better start at the beginning." She looked at her watch and placed her prop of a notebook on the end table. "I have three hours. I have a feeling this is going to take every minute of it."

I told her everything. Everything about my mother, Eddie, Sally, Jen, the Palmers, my career, and my dreams and projections about Ron, the store, and my political career.

"Do you really want to get back into politics?"

I thought for a moment. "You know what? I'm not sure. It's just all I know. I've put it off for the next election, but I may jump back in once things are . . . resolved."

"Hmmm . . . so it's not a passion to have an impact? Like the environment, children's rights, I don't know . . . higher wages for the working class?"

I laughed. "It would be nice if that's the way it worked."

"You sound cynical."

"It's a cynical business," I shot back. "I hate it."

She cocked her head and kept her focus on me.

"Wow. I can't believe I said that."

"Oh, I'm goooooood," she said with a smile. "You realize that as a single person you cannot run for office and give a child the attention he will need."

It was my turn to be silent.

"So, Lenny," she said, as thought finally . . . finally getting to the real stuff.

I sat up. "Yes, Lenny. I really don't want to raise a kid, but for some reason I'm stuck with a very angry adolescent and I have no idea what to do with him."

"Do you see the correlation with your own life?"

"Yes, of course I do." Was she an idiot?

She took a deep breath. "Do you believe in God or the Universe, some major power controlling what happens to us?"

"God no."

"Okay, then . . ." she took another deep breath. " . . . then what do you think about the idea that Lenny's been put in your life for a reason?"

"What?"

"Stay with me here. If there is no one else to take Lenny, and you are the last person standing, maybe, just maybe, there's a reason for it."

"Like what?"

She shrugged and leaned back. "Maybe that's for you to figure out. Something's missing from your life. Maybe this is it?"

I didn't quite know what to say. Too woo-woo for me.

Somehow, she got me to succinctly and correctly tell her every pertinent detail of my life, and in the telling I got a handle on it. While most of my relationships were political, meaning those that offered tit for tat, the real ones, the ones that meant the most to me, were not about me, and I had a hard time sliding into that mode. She told me to think of it like a game of chess. Sometimes your piece has to slide over to make room for another piece. Jen having a new relationship did in fact scoot me over to the side, and rightly so. Love does that.

My mother having a new family scooted me over to the side; a part of her life she'd rather forget. Right or wrong, it was the way it was. Some relationships are finite, even family ones. Sally chose her husband over me; Eddie had already chosen Sally over me. I not only got shoved aside, it was check and mate. And, again, rightly so. A marriage is about that.

Marjorie helped me see that I was stuck, and spinning like one foot was nailed to the floor, unable to stop. I needed to choose another game, one with new players. She advised me to go back to the people who really mattered to me and try to mend things, not to let them go, which would have been my normal mode. Go back. Talk. Open up. Then try something new. Take a chance.

I wrote a check for her time, thinking once again that someone to whom I had spilled my guts was only in it for the money.

Chapter Thirty-Four

CANVAS WAS SWARMING WITH PEOPLE. APPARENTLY, ADAM HAD BEEN doing some marketing. All the easels were taken, and people stood around waiting.

"Do you have the lad with you?" Adam asked me.

"Not today."

"Could have used the help setting up, but not to worry, all shall be well." He smiled. "We'll use the dining area and spread out." He waved in the direction of the dining room and I saw the easels were set up and ready to go. I took one and several other people joined me. Then Sally came in. The only easel left was next to me on the end. She hesitated, then walked over and set up.

"Hello."

"Hello."

My heart was in my throat. Conflict has never been a problem for me. I fix it before it becomes a problem, and if it's not fixable, it's done. Gone. But this time I was torn. I liked her, and God knows I needed some new friends. Plus, Eddie asked me to help. Jesus.

Marjorie waved to me across the hall. It occurred to me I hadn't told her that Sally was the woman married to the man I had a twenty-year affair with. Suzanne watched, leaned over, saw me, and came clonking over, her bracelet banging against everything she touched, and sidled up. "Renee! How are you?"

"I'm just great, Suzanne, how about you?" *God. What does she want?*

"Couldn't be better. Happier than a randy man in a whorehouse."

"Well . . . good for you."

"Yes, I am happy and satisfied, if you know what I mean."

"No, I don't. Could you please explain it to me?" Sally interjected with a firm tone.

"Well, I just . . .I just mean I'm happy." Suzanne's brilliant smile almost knocked me out. She looked over at me and said, "Ronnie says hi!" and scampered off. We both watched her as she crossed the hallway into the living area to her easel.

"Bitch." Apparently, I said it out loud.

Sally continued to set up her station. "Is she interfering with your life? Your territory? Isn't that a goddamn shame," she mumbled.

"I'll ignore that."

"Do what you please."

"Why are you here if you hate me so much?"

"Because I have to have something to look forward to, and this is it. One of us has to go, and it's not going to be me."

"I'm not going anywhere. I own this place."

We were talking quietly, but others began to give notice they were sensing the tension between us.

Adam came in with instructions and we set to work.

At the end of class, Adam followed me out the door and asked again about Lenny. I gave him the latest and he clicked his tongue. "Never having had a child, I cannot advise you on this. But I say trust your instincts and do the best you can. You're in a difficult spot."

Sally almost bumped into him as he turned back. We walked together to our cars.

"You know," she said, "I don't fight with people and I certainly don't get into other people's business without their permission, but I will stand up for an animal or a child and break all the rules."

"You have something to say?" I held my painter's kit by the handle, and I felt my fingers clutch hard at the plastic. They began to tingle.

She went on. "I entered your house. I took your journals. I did not read them." She looked over my shoulder. "So I'm trying to be good now." She took a deep breath. "I've raised four kids. What I do know is they want someone to show them they care, and you do that by setting limits and being firm. Don't let him run all over the place. Keep a firm hand on what he does and where he goes. You're going to have to dictate his life for a bit."

"Thank you, Sally. I'll take it under advisement." I began to walk toward my car, then turned to find she hadn't moved. "Did you set me up?"

"I beg your pardon?"

"When you were confessing your marriage secrets to me, were you waiting to see what I'd do? Did you think I'd confess? Beg your forgiveness?"

"I don't know." Her eyes looked over my shoulder.

"Right." I pushed the unlock button, threw the kit in, and slid into my car.

You're not the only one to be pissed, Sally.

I came home to find music blaring from upstairs. The kid was back.

Chapter Thirty-Five

"Dear lady, I believe it's time for a grand opening." Adam peered through his ice-blue eyes. "We are organized and ready."

So, I had my marching orders. We were closing up after a class. Adam had been putting things away and Lenny was sweeping the floor. Gunnar curled up in a corner snoozing, exhausted by all the attention he had gotten—and from being ignored by Lenny.

"Oh? What do you propose?"

"An event that showcases the artwork of professional artists around town as well as the students in the class. We have a class going on at the same time and people can come in and try their hand at a canvas—we can set up smaller canvases for free or they can pay to have access to a larger canvas—we will provide the paints and instruction on an informal basis, and they take their product home, or bring it back to continue it in another class."

"Which is what we're after . . . more students."

"Exactly."

"Will there be food?" Lenny asked, leaning on the top of the broom.

"Of course, dear lad. I'll put you in charge of the food."

Lenny blanched. So did I. It would be peanut butter and chocolate and jellybeans or something. "Pages has a coffee bar and there is a group of women who make pastries and stuff for special occasions—we can get them to do it."

"Brilliant as usual, young man," Adam said, and swung back to his canvases. Lenny went back to work.

"I have made the acquaintance of several local artists; I'll put some feelers out about contributing and being a part of this exhibit. I am sure if we allow them to sell their artwork, they would be more than happy to contribute.

Artists really are starving, you know." He grinned a bit. "We can have personalized invitations for special people; I am sure you have connections to make this a social event?" He looked over at me with he continued his brushstrokes.

"I'll see what I can do . . .Robert Graham is the social writer . . .I'll try to find him."

"He works upstairs at Pages now," Lenny mumbled. "Cool guy."

Hunh. Lenny was making friends. Of people I knew. At least he was participating. So it was set. I had nothing to do but pay the bills. And I was getting nervous about money.

Over the next few days, what I called The Beast grabbed hold and wouldn't let go. I did what was on my calendar, performing like a circus animal, and received no pleasure in any of it. Once my duty was done, I found myself alone and heading home with a headache. But Jen's words kept nagging at me: Get a life.

Kind of hard when you're severely depressed.

I had a life. It wasn't a very good one, but it was a life. My best friend may be dying, my business partner had huge secrets, I was beginning to think I had made a huge mistake in opening up the shop; there had been no uptick in business, I had no sex life, and my career was seriously in jeopardy. Plus, my mother had definitively slammed the door in my face. But none of that really mattered.

I was responsible for an unhappy adolescent with whom I had no real connection, and it was beginning to interfere with my sleep and my daily existence. Marjorie had talked to me about anti-depressants, but I had knocked it out of hand.

Several fingers of tequila went into a glass and I took it and my attitude into my office. I took a long look around at a space where I was supposed to feel productive and supported. How depressing.

Decorating efforts had stalled. One wall was half-finished, drop cloths were piled into the corner, and furniture was in the center of the room. Great. I sat in the gray office chair and opened up the computer, surfing for a bit, looking for emails (none), and picking up the news. More gray overhead.

The Beast was having a huge impact, and I was losing it. Marjorie said to take some risks, try new things. Basically, get a life.

No time like the present. I had never used any social media, but Lupe, bless her heart, had set up some accounts at various sites for Canvas and I went hunting for them, surprised to see so many ads among the posts.

Duh—that's how it's free, stupid.

One of them was for a dating service for "olders," free for the first three months as a try-out. Then I found the Baby Boomer site Jen had discovered. I sipped some tequila and felt it tingle down my throat and burn its warm way down, then my finger clicked on the mouse. I uploaded a picture of Gunnar for my profile, and I used the name Anne Addams as a pseudonym. I wanted to see what was out there. Keep my distance.

Maybe that's your problem.

Now to the profile:

What do I like to do? What music do I prefer? What do I look for in a man? What are my hobbies? What's my idea of a perfect date? Where do I come from? What's most important to me?

Hoo boy.

I didn't know the answer to any of the questions. I failed the test. I schlepped back into the kitchen and poured more tequila, leaning against the counter with the glass cradled across my chest, determined to do this. For Jen.

Favorite music? I don't really listen to music . . .

Hobbies? Meh.

Where do I come from? Hell.

Not exactly titillating stuff. I finished the tequila and sloshed more. Time to get creative and invent an interesting person. I am, after all, what you would call a blank canvas. Ha. Ha.

I poised my fingers on the keyboard and let them fly.

Music: love it all.

Hobbies: painting, writing, hiking (no, strike that), attending civic events, plays, dinner parties, and long walks on the beach (strike that).

Favorite Date: Skipping dinner and going right to bed (strike that). A nice dinner, a long walk, maybe some window shopping (strike that).

What I look for in a man: Well-hung (strike that). A sense of humor and well-read. Maybe red hair (strike that). Nice body (strike that). Fit, takes care of himself, not a metrosexual (strike that). No kids (strike that). Believes in equality. Kind to his mother and waitstaff.

I finished after changing it up a bit and then pushed submit.

Bruce answered the door, and I could see he was rattled. His normally combed curly hair was messy, and he had a stain on his work shirt. Not good.

"Hi, there," I said brightly. "Just thought I'd drop in for a sec to see how she's doing." He stepped aside without a word. Jen was not in the living room. I turned and looked at Bruce, who pointed up the stairs. So not good.

I took my time, knowing instinctively that any panic or rushing wouldn't help. Besides, I had to gather myself. God knew what I would find. Every step was agony. It felt like this was the fork in the road.

Jen sat, propped up, in the dark bedroom. She'd had it furnished all in white a few years back, thinking the decorator knew what she was doing—very chic, very sophisticated. Arthur had laughed. "You could lose a ghost in here," was what Jen had relayed to me with a grin. She'd added a few colorful pillows and touches here and there, but at the end of the day it was still all white. And I couldn't really see her. She was pale, breathing through her mouth, staring straight ahead. No light, no knitting, no books, no television, no music. This could have been someone else.

"Hey, Gigi, how are ya?" I asked once I had gathered my wits.

She slowly turned her head to me. "Water," she said.

I picked up the glass on her white bedside table and lifted the straw to her lips. She took a semi-sip and collapsed against the pillows. I could smell the cancer, if that's at all possible. I watched something clear drip slowly down into a plastic bag from the pole on her bedside. Gingerly setting myself on the edge of the bed, I asked, "What's going on inside there?"

"A war," she warbled out.

"Are you eating anything?"

She shook her head. "Not hungry." Her eyes closed and I heard her slightly snore. Oh God. Ohgodohgodohgodohgod. I headed down to the kitchen, where I found Bruce putting cartons in the freezer.

"Somebody's been busy," I said as I recognized soups and stews.

"Yeah, well, she's not eating, but when she gets better, she's going to want something but won't have the energy to cook, so I had to do something. My son is here, and he's been really helpful."

"At least you can do that," I said as I realized there was absolutely nothing I could do. "What happened? The other day she seemed fine."

"A bad reaction to the chemo. Her bone marrow has been decimated. She's on all sorts of meds. I don't know what half of them are, but we have a schedule to keep to."

I hated to ask the question that needed to be asked. "What's the prognosis?"

He shook his head and I saw a tear drop to the floor. "I don't know, but it doesn't look good."

I was helpless to do anything for either of them.

Over the next few weeks, Bruce continued to keep me updated; some days were good, some bad, but slowly the good outnumbered the bad. We just waited for the war inside her frail body to be over. To win.

Weeks after my visit, I had just poured a drink to get ready for a deep, dark pity party when my phone trilled. I knew Jen was feeling better and had waited to hear from her. Finally, Jen's voice came over, loud and strong. "Sorry to not be able to talk lately. I'm winning the battle and determined to keep up my end of the deal. What's going on with you?"

"Are you sure you want to hear this?"

"Of course, I'm tired of thinking about myself. Dump."

So I did. Everything about Lenny and his mother and the social worker and the system. How frustrated I was that he was not doing well and neither of us was happy. I wanted out.

"You don't mean that."

I sighed. "I don't know . . . this is not at all where I thought I'd be at this point."

Silence.

"Oh, God, Jen. Neither did you. Here I am thinking about myself again." I went into the kitchen and poured another scotch, adding ice. Clink, clink.

"Tell me about Lenny. How's he really doing?"

"Not well. He's just so angry. He's not listening, does what he wants, and just goes through the motions. He disappears from time to time and I have no idea where he is. He comes back late at night and just walks by me without saying a word."

"That can't be fun."

"I should be sailing around the world, or traveling to exotic places, or having an affair, or writing the Great American Novel or something. Instead I'm stuck with Edward Scissorhands. I took a drink, the ice clinked against the glass.

"If you want to make God laugh, tell Her your plans," she said. "Are you drinking?"

"Yes . . ."

"A little early, isn't it?"

I looked at the clock. 3:00. "Maybe, but it helps."

"Helps what, take the edge off? Help you cope? Does it really make it better?"

"Yes."

"You know better. Don't fuck this up. He doesn't deserve it."

My eyes filled. "I know."

I had a telephone appointment with Marjorie to fill her in on progress with Lenny.

"Time to turn it around," she said.

"How?"

"Well, for God's sake, talk to him. Tell him what the rules are. Give him some consequences for his actions."

I knew that Marjorie was tops in her field, but my guts told me that was the wrong approach. Maybe I didn't know what I was doing, but I knew this kid and knew if I put some clamps on him he would just shut down. No, I needed another way, and it wasn't the normal parental approach. He had no reason to respect me. I hadn't given him one.

Chapter Thirty-Six

"SO, YOUR MOM HAS FINISHED THE FIRST PART OF HER REHAB TREATMENT. Apparently, she did very well and is on limited lock-up. She's in a halfway house."

"That's nice."

"Lenny, give her a chance. She's working hard."

He shrugged. "She always works hard."

"And?"

"It doesn't stay good."

Silence.

"Maybe you should tell her how proud you are."

He stared at me. "Yeah, that's gonna work." He pounded his way upstairs.

I poured a drink and sat down to watch the idiot box but watched a sit-com I didn't understand. Lenny's pain just cut through. He had no one—no one but me.

The home phone rang and I jumped. Maybe it was Jen.

"Ms. Murphy?"

"Yes."

"It's Camille. I wanted you to know that Elena was arrested downtown tonight for attempting to buy narcotics from an undercover agent. She's back in jail, and this time I'm afraid it's not going to be so easy. You know what the judge said last time, and he's very good about following through."

"I understand."

"I wish I had better news."

"Me too. At least he's not going with his mother. Drug addicts and criminals belong in jail and away from the rest of us. Lenny cannot be subjected to that." I knew my voice shook and recognized I was about to go over the edge.

Silence.

"On the good news side, Voices for Children has finally identified a CASA for Lenny."

"Now, that sounds like progress, but what does it mean for Lenny?"

"That means there is someone who will be checking in with him twice a month or so, maybe have an outing or two, and make sure he's represented well in court."

"Tell me about this person." We chatted for a while, then hung up. I poured another drink. Now I'm committed. The possibility I was holding onto of having my house to myself again and Lenny being back with his mother, which is what he really wanted, disappeared. I was going to have to see this kid through high school. Unless someone were to adopt him.

Not bloody likely. And I am going to have to tell him.

After school, we went to get calzones again and talked about the CASA, trying to put it in a good light. He could take it or leave it. He didn't seem impressed. "You don't have to, you know, but give it a chance," I said. He shrugged. We finished up and went home. I was actually nervous, not knowing how he'd react and sat at the kitchen counter with ice cream.

"I have something else to tell you, and I really don't want to."

"What."

"Well, it's not good." He stared at me over his ice cream, spoon hanging, rage all over his face. "Your mom relapsed. She's back in jail."

"Is that all?"

"Yup."

He dropped his spoon in his bowl with a clang, hopped off the stool.

"Do you want to talk about it?" I said to his back.

"No." His steps back up the stairs were pounding, and soon the music was, too.

I poured a drink. Ice cream a scotch. Yum.

CASA Juan called to make arrangements to meet with Lenny. I gave him the lowdown, which he already knew, and he asked a few questions I couldn't answer, like what Lenny liked to do, hobbies, etc. I couldn't answer them. I had no idea. *Why don't I know this?* "What if he doesn't want to meet with you?"

"That's his choice, but I'd like to try." He sounded young, a bit insecure.

"I have to warn you that he's resistant to being 'in the system' and probably won't want to. He's a bit of a loner."

"So am I; maybe we can find something in common. Does he like to eat?"

"Does he like to EAT?" I laughed.

"Okay, we'll start there. I'll make it clear to him that he's not obligated, but maybe we could just hang out." He was quiet for a bit. "I hope he likes me." *Buddy, I feel the same way.* I gave him Lenny's cell number so they could communicate in private. I had to trust them to make it work.

Juan showed up on Tuesday after school, dressed in jeans and a black tee-shirt, with a black baseball cap turned backwards. He appeared to be mid-thirties and drove a muscle car. An older Lenny. I wondered what Lenny would think of him but decided to let it be.

I went to Jen's to check up on her and get her caught up on Lenny, as she requested. She looked tired but her energy level was higher than I'd seen before. She smoked a joint as I sipped my one scotch and we chatted for a bit while the puppies stuck close to her, one on each side. I was aware she watched my drinking, so I took it slow.

Things had changed between us. Her illness was front and center, but she didn't want it to be. She kept asking me about my life, about Adam, about the shop, my plans, and then we got down to Lenny. I told her about the CASA, and she laughed with me about what a match it was, and that Lenny might hate him.

After a while, I noticed she was wearing thin, so I stood to leave. She didn't object. "You know I love you, right?" I said as I left.

"Yes, I know." She smiled brilliantly. "I know." I had been there half an hour.

Canvas was open for classes, but before I went in, I dropped into Pages to get some coffee and see how they were doing. A young girl was behind the coffee bar; she had a black eye but a great disposition and managed the hissing espresso machine beautifully. I noticed several people in the lounge pouring over books, some with laptops, and a fire in the fireplace. A cozy scene.

"Is Jade here?" I asked the young girl.

"Upstairs, I think," she said. I trooped up the stairs and found Jade in her office surrounded by boxes of files and pictures. She had posted articles, pictures, and mementoes on a cork board and it looked like a huge investigative process taking place. A framed picture of Iris sat in the middle. My heart took a tug.

"Hi, Ms. Murphy!" Jade said as I knocked on the door frame. "What can I do for you?"

"I just thought I'd check in and see how you were doing. Who is tending bar downstairs?"

"Tending bar? Oh, you mean the coffee bar. That's, um, Rosita." She stopped abruptly. There was more to the story.

"Oh?"

She nodded. "I guess you should be aware, but please don't tell anyone. Confidentiality is huge on this, okay?"

"O . . . kay . . ."

She lowered her voice. "I have turned Iris's house into a safe house for domestic violence victims while they are waiting for their court dates. You know Lacey, Tricia's law partner? She's doing all the legal work for them. In the meantime, they are safe behind that big iron gate."

"That's amazing. Iris would be so proud of you. How did this happen?"

"I honestly don't know, but it just fell into my lap. I didn't understand how someone could let themselves get beat up at first, and I blamed them, but now I get it."

"I have the same problem with people who abuse drugs. I just don't get it. How can they let it happen, especially when they have kids?"

She sighed. "I don't have all the answers, but I do know that sometimes the situation is so powerful you just can't get out. You just can't. It takes over." That was the longest sentence I had ever heard come out of her mouth.

"So, what's all this?" I asked, pointing to all the tickets, invitations, cards, and pictures on the wall.

She blushed a little. "I'm putting Iris's life together."

"What do you mean?"

"The speeches at the funeral showed me an Iris I had no idea existed. I found a huge box in her closet where she had kept everything; there are pictures, articles, and journals, and I decided to recreate her life. Robert is helping me put it into a book format. I may just do a biography of her." She stopped. "Or Robert will, if I can't. He's as enthusiastic as I am about her. He adored her."

"Me too, but don't sell yourself short. I'm sure you are capable of writing this bio; you lived with her. Keep going. I'd love to read it."

"Thanks for the support. I really appreciate it." She smiled and her eyes lit up. Iris had given her a life.

If I can do the same for Lenny, I'd consider myself a success.

I headed over to Canvas. A watercolor class was in session with several painters in the studio working on their own projects. Adam waved at me as he worked at his easel, then put his brush down and sauntered between the two rooms, affirming, guiding, and supporting. Everyone looked so pleased. I wandered back to the office, where I sat with some bills and notifications and went through the mail.

I was about to leave when I heard Lenny and Juan come in to browse the studio. Adam met them and was introduced to Juan, and they had a nice chat. It sounded as though things were going well, but I did not get up from my desk, thinking it might interfere with their time, so I stayed put and out of sight.

Lenny stated that he "worked" there, and it was then I knew that Canvas was more than work to Lenny. It was a place he could feel comfortable and express himself, and it was important to him or he would not have brought Juan there. I smiled as I waited them out, waved to Adam, and went home.

I was on my second drink when Lenny popped in, Gunnar tail-wagging and leaping. "How did it go with Juan?" I asked.

"Okay," he said.

Hmmm . . . "What did you do?"

"We went bowling."

"Bowling???" That was the last thing I expected Lenny to enjoy.

"Yeah, it's kind of cool." He went upstairs, Gunnar at his feet, and closed his door.

Well, okay then.

Chapter Thirty-Seven

I SAT OUTSIDE THE COURTROOM WAITING MY TURN TO HEAR LENNY'S CASE. Again.

CASA Juan was already there, waiting on a bench. We chatted a bit about Lenny and how the visit went. He said he thought it went well and that he would contact Lenny soon to set up another visit. I honored their privacy and didn't ask too many questions, although I really wanted to grill him.

The court reporter came out of the courtroom with reams of paperwork. I had checked in with him earlier and he knew my case; he handed me Camille's as well as Juan's reports and the recommendations by the City attorney. He opened the door and motioned to me and Juan to enter. Camille sat up front at the long desk. Juan found his chair beside her, and I sat in the back in one of the wooden chairs.

Judge Sullivan was on the bench. The case was called, and Elena was already at the table. She stood at the desk next to her attorney, in handcuffs, head down. Long stringy hair covered her face, and she wore a look of total defeat, like a small child who waited for her punishment.

"Ms. Rudolph, good afternoon," the judge said, looking directly at her.

She didn't respond.

"I said good afternoon, Ms. Rudolph."

Her attorney elbowed her, and she mumbled "Good afternoon."

"Thank you." He leafed through the report in front of him, sighed, and closed the file. "Ms. Rudolph, how sad for you. I know that you have tried to get clean. I know that you attended classes and participated well. The reports of you in prison are exemplary. You have what it takes, and I will continue to support your efforts for rehabilitation, because I believe every human being deserves the chance to be better."

She turned her head up and looked at him directly.

"However." He took a long breath and seemed to reconsider his opinion, then shook his head. "I also believe that children need the support and the backing of a strong parent who can set examples and let them know they are loved and respected, and you have failed in that regard in a very big way. Ten years ago you failed your daughter, and you lost your parental rights because you were not able to give her the support every child needs."

He placed both hands on the desk and leaned forward. "Your son is now in the same position and try as we might to get you the help and support you need to be a better parent, that has not happened."

He paused for a second. "I am terminating parental rights as of today. You no longer have any rights or responsibilities to this child, although I see he is almost sixteen and has spent most of his life in foster homes. The child will continue to be a ward of the state and will remain in the foster home he is in, and is now available for adoption, although at his age I don't hold out much hope." He looked at her. "How do you feel about that?"

She sobbed, her head down and her long hair falling toward the floor.

"Please understand I have to look at the welfare of the child."

She nodded.

"I see he has a CASA assigned now. I've reviewed your report and hope that you continue to have a good relationship with this young man. He deserves nothing less." Juan nodded to the judge.

He pounded his gavel and said, "Next case."

We left the courtroom. Juan and I went down in the elevator together in silence. Finally, he said, "Will you adopt him?" That thought had niggled at me. Selfish as I was, I only wanted to get rid of him and have my house to myself. Well, maybe that was too harsh, but I certainly wasn't in this permanently.

"Come on, let's grab a bite," he said, apparently noticing I didn't have an answer. We went to the cafeteria and ordered sandwiches and sat.

"Tell me about being a CASA," I said. "I'm not sure what it entails. I saw the size of your report. That's a lot of work."

He then told me of this organization, Voices for Children, which trains and uses volunteers to be available to the foster kids for support and advocacy within the system. The social workers were overworked, the lawyers had so many cases they only go by the book, and having this person, not biased in any way other than what's best for the child, helped them do their jobs. The CASAs get exposed to the family that has taken the child in and moves with the child when they change foster care.

"Does that happen?"

"More often than you'd think. They move all the time for various reasons, none of which are the kid's fault," he said. "These poor guys are shoved around with no input as to where they want to go, which is, not surprisingly, with their own parents, bad as they are."

"What? They'd rather live with losers than in good homes?" I couldn't help it. My filters were again leaving me—in droves.

He swallowed, took a drink, and said, "Think about it. Mothers are mothers; there's a biological connection that no one else will ever have, no matter how much they may love the kid. A child always, always, always wants their mother. Fathers, too, but less so. It's the umbilical cord that does it, I think." He smiled, enjoying his own little joke. "Studies have shown that no matter how bad it is, kids do better with their own parents. Time after time."

"No matter what? Even if the bio parent is a murderer?"

"That's what they tell me."

I wanted to spit out the tuna salad in my mouth. Yes, I wanted my own mother back the day she deserted me, and I lived with Jen and her family, but I always had hope. I would much rather have been in the flophouses and motels with my mom than with the Palmers, with all they had. Not only was she my mom, she needed me. I was the one who took care of her, not the other way around.

"You sound familiar with the situation," I said.

"No, not like that, but yeah, maybe. My parents divorced and my dad remarried. I love my stepmom, but it's just . . . different. I have a real connection with my mom." He thought about it for a while. "I don't know that

I'd like to choose between them—thank God I was never asked to, because they both mean so much to me—but Mom . . . maybe it's the genetic component." He shook his head. "I don't know, but all I know is kids want to be with their parents, and sometimes the parents just shouldn't have the kids."

Brother, you just said a mouthful.

Chapter Thirty-Eight

"COME ON OVER. JEN IS FEELING MUCH BETTER AND WE'RE OUT ON THE patio enjoying the evening. She wants to see you." I hopped into the car without changing and headed over. Lenny worked on some homework and I yelled I'd bring dinner home. No answer.

I'd had a few drinks, but knew I was okay to drive. I was fine until I turned the corner at Jen's, hit a trash can in the street, overcorrected, and smashed into the back of Bruce's work truck. The sound blasted my eardrums and I think I blacked out a minute.

"Renee!" Bruce banged on the driver's side window and tugged on the door handle. "Renee!"

"'M'okay, 'm'okay." I saw blood on my hands where I held my head and started to panic.

Bruce had pulled the passenger side door open and now sat beside me, looking at the gash on my head. "You've been drinking."

"No." Why am I denying it?

"Okay, let's get you inside." He went back to the driver's side and managed to pry the door open with a loud creak. I stepped out and almost fell. "I got you." We waddled up the walkway where Jen stood, holding the door open with fire and fury in her eyes.

"You've been drinking." What happened to checking on me and the blood?

I entered the bungalow. Sticks and Stitches stared at me from the back of the hallway and would not come near me. I flopped onto the couch. "What the hell is wrong with you?" Jen stood over me. "Driving drunk? Are you insane?"

"I'm not drunk . . ."

"Don't deny it. What's wrong with you? Why are you acting this way?"

"Everything is bad," I said.

"What? Your brand-new business is not doing well? Your love life is the shits? Boo-fucking-hoo. Poor baby, nothing is going your way, is it?" Her hands were on her hips and her turban began to slip. If I had not been in such bad shape, I would have laughed. She turned to Bruce. "Does she need to go to the doctor?"

"I don't think so. There's a gash on her forehead, but I don't even think it needs stitches."

"Go into the bathroom and clean yourself up. I'll make you some coffee. At least you'll be a wide-awake drunk." I did as instructed. When I came out, a steaming cup of coffee sat on an end table. I perched. Bruce was nowhere to be found.

"So . . . how are you?" I asked.

"I'm not the issue right now, thank God. Renee, what is happening to you? You are not the same person I knew. You are responsible for a child and a business, not to mention yourself, and you act like none of it matters. Stop feeling sorry for yourself, get your shit together, and live your life. Don't destroy it. This kid needs you. I need you." Jen sat down. "As for your question, the new treatment seems to be working. I feel much better and I'm able to at least get out of bed. It's not a bad treatment. I'm going to get through this just fine, so don't worry about me."

She lit a joint. "Renee, I will get well, but it will go much faster if I'm not worried about you. And believe me, I am worried about you."

I thought about Sally and how she had missed so much of her life because of her drinking. I didn't want to be like that, and I needed to support Jen. I saw that very clearly. This was no longer about me.

"Okay, no more," I said. "Guess I'll go home and get myself together."

"Bruce will take you home." He came out of the kitchen and pointed to the door. I crawled into his truck and he took me home in silence.

"I'll call the insurance company and get your truck fixed," I mumbled as I crawled out of the truck. "And get the car towed. Tomorrow."

"Fine." He handed my keys to me. I walked in to find Lenny in the living room. "What happened to you?" he asked when he saw the gash on my forehead.

"Car accident."

"Uh-hunh." He went upstairs without another word.

I had forgotten to pick up dinner.

I had not had a drink in over a week, and I felt better and better every day. It still pulled me in a big way, but I resisted and kept myself busy. The Beast was there, but I knew better than to try to squell it with alcohol.

I called Margie for a phone session; she asked me questions about my drinking, and we talked about handling pain. She convinced me to begin meds for depression. Turns out alcohol is a depressant. Hunh.

My feelings were just under the surface—I knew I was stressed and not dealing with it very well, but I was handling it without a crutch. What began, I think, as a way to sort of wind down after a long career, had given me permission to do whatever I wanted, and it became a way to blot out old pain that was beginning to surface. And new pain was coming from every direction.

Both Elena and my mother used drugs to make things go away. I at least had Jen to set me straight, and Bruce, and Sally had Eddie to fall on, but those two women had nobody, and they had kids. It must have been a horrible box to be put in, and the only way out was to blot out the insecurities and fear of failure. No wonder they fell short of societal norms. They had to have their blanket of denial and would do anything to get it.

Sally, now that I think about it, pulled her blanket around her tightly, denying what she knew her husband was doing. As much as she said she was okay with it, that was a lie. It had to hurt, and for several decades. And it was my fault. All of this was going through my head in class. As I painted, I saw things pretty clearly and knew I had to make some movement.

"Are you free after class for . . .I was going to say a drink, but maybe dinner?" I need your help." Lenny was with Adam tonight, so I didn't worry about him. Her head reared back a bit ad her eyes pinpointed; I could see her collapse into herself. "Sure. Why not." She focused on the easel and didn't say another word. I smiled as I chipped away at my own defenses.

We walked across the street after class. "What's up?" Sally asked as we settled into a booth at the diner. I could tell she was on alert; not sure what it was I wanted, she had her defenses up. Couldn't blame her.

I sighed. "I could use a friend. I'm drinking too much. I had an accident a little while ago. It would not have happened if I had not been drinking."

She nodded. "Go on."

"I don't know. How do you know if you're an alcoholic?"

"When it starts to control you and you screw up your life." I waited. "Do you think you're an alcoholic?"

I shook my head. "No, but isn't that what every drunk says?"

"Do you crave it?"

"Not particularly."

"Do you want a drink now?"

"No. It would probably make me sick."

She leaned back in the booth. "Tell me why you drink."

"At first it was social, then I started adding some to my coffee and drinking by myself, which is something I've never done. It just never appealed to me. It seemed . . .I don't know, sad, I guess."

She nodded. "Then, what are you trying to forget?"

"My life."

She sat up straight. "Sounds like you need someone more than a recovering alcoholic to talk to."

I smiled. "No. Just a friend. Look . . . about Eddie . . ."

"Ed."

I nodded. "Ed. If that situation made you drink to cover the hurt and I'm responsible for it, I want to apologize."

She took a deep breath. "You give yourself way too much credit." I didn't know if that was a diss or not, but I let it go. "Listen, if I drank because of it, that's on me, not you. Ed was the one who cheated. He bears some responsibility, but I'm the one who drank. You were just a young kid who got swept up by a charming man who really did care for you. He got into it for his own reasons. We are discovering a lot through therapy now and we are working hard to mend what was torn years and years ago, but rest assured it is not on you."

"Well, thank you for that, but I do have some responsibility."

"That's for you to deal with, not me. I have my own problems." She smiled. "I didn't mean that the way it came out, but honestly, it's the truth."

"Can I ask you something?"

"Sure."

"When did you know about me? That it was me?"

"When I went home after class and told Ed I had met the former mayor of San Diego, his reaction made me think back a bit, and the pieces came together when I realized you were at Duke when Ed was there. You confirmed it when I came to your house for pizza."

"Really."

"Really."

"And now?"

She sighed and looked away. "Now I think we are all clear and ready to move on with our lives—our real lives, not ones we make up, but deep down, real honest-to-God commitment and unification. As for you, if you find yourself drawn to the bottle, going through the physical symptoms of detox, and getting out of control, get help. I suspect your dependency is more in your head. You just want to get rid of it all for a bit and not think about all the stuff that's going on—and I do realize you have a lot of stuff—but there are better ways to cope." She took a sip. "Love helps."

That one hurt.

Chapter Thirty-Nine

"Ms. Murphy? This is Ellen Drake, Lenny's math teacher."

"Yes?"

"I wondered if you have a few moments to chat."

"Yes, of course."

"I am concerned about Lenny's progress. He does not hand in any assignments and he failed the last test. I think he's just not trying." I didn't know what to say, so I waited.

"Is there anything going on at home that might be the problem?"

Is his foster situation a secret to the school?

"I am aware that you are his foster parent and that he has been in several homes, so I understand that this may be problematic for him, but I was wondering if there was something specific we can address."

She's just doing her job. "Well, there have been several developments that may make him pull back."

"I ask because you have not responded online to my inquiries and that of other teachers."

"What inquiries? Have you sent me emails?"

She sighed. "There is a website where we communicate directly with parents and students and this is where we let you know how he is doing. You will have other messages, I am sure, from his other teachers. I have checked with them, thinking maybe I was the problem, but apparently he's having trouble in all his classes."

"Really." God, how lame can a foster parent be? I think somebody told me about this website, but with all the stuff going on how was I supposed to remember? "Please give me the website address and I will get on it right away. I think I have been lax in following up on his schoolwork. This is all new to me." It sounded defensive, even to me.

We agreed to talk later after I checked out the website and absorbed everything they were saying.

Damn. Why can't this be easy?

Lenny came home right after school and headed upstairs.

"We need to talk," I said as he was halfway up. He turned around, clomped into the living room, dropped his backpack on the floor and slouched into the overstuffed chair.

"Yeah?" Crossed arms.

"Do we need to get you a tutor?"

"No."

"Then why am I getting calls from your teachers that you are failing?"

"Because I am."

"So, what are you going to do about it?"

He shrugged.

I am so inept at this. He needs to be with someone who can help him.

"Do you do your homework?"

"Sometimes."

"Do you need help?"

Shrug.

"Lenny, I know this can't be easy."

"You don't know shit." He got up and left.

Well, that was about as true a statement as anyone ever made.

I had gotten online and read the many, many messages left for me on the school website. Lenny was not doing well—he was not socializing, not joining any groups, kept to himself, and was not participating in class. But he was going, which was a point in his favor.

My responses to each teacher were the same—can we please all get together to discuss this at school? I was new to this process and needed all the help I could get. The responses were overwhelming—they banded together to find a date that worked for everyone and let me know where and what time to meet. I had no idea what to say, but I had a responsibility to see this through, and maybe I could get some help for him.

The school had worked out a date two weeks later. I put on a skirt and sweater combo, trying to look parental, grabbed my bag, and went into the kitchen to pluck the keys off the nail. They were gone. I went into the garage to find my car gone. I had not had a chance to get the car fixed, so he was driving a car that would stand out. It wouldn't be hard to find if I had someone put an APB out on it.

The doorbell rang and I ran to answer it, bag still in hand. A policeman stood with Lenny. "This yours?" he asked. He clearly recognized me, as he became more formal.

"Yes," I sighed. "Lenny, where were you, and where is my car?"

"The car is on Fuego Street, not far from here. I pulled him over for erratic driving and discovered he did not have a driver's license and could not produce the insurance or the registration." He must have seen the look on my face when I realized Lenny was headed back to juvvie, no questions asked. "I did not issue a citation. This was a joyride, not far from home. He was polite, cooperative, and kept apologizing. I believe he's sincere. He's a good guy. He made a mistake." He looked at Lenny. "We all do."

My relief was out of bounds, but I managed to say, "Thank you, officer, for bringing him home and your courtesy. Lenny, thank the officer." He mumbled his thanks and the officer left. I could see nosy neighbors looking out their windows at the cop car sitting in front of the house.

"Keys, please. Did you even go to school today?" I held out my hand. He fished in his pocket and dropped the keys in my hand as he nodded no, then turned to go upstairs.

"No. You're coming with me."

We walked quickly to the car three blocks away and I got in. I motioned for him to get in, he hesitated, then sat and slammed the door shut. I drove to the school. He followed me from the parking lot, through cheerleaders practicing, students painting posters, and cliques standing around with backpacks stuffed full. I followed instructions and made it to a conference room in the front of the administration building, to find seven people waiting in a circle.

"Hey, Lenny!" one of them said, "Come on in." A teacher looked at me quizzically and I shrugged. "Lenny needs to be a part of any conversation that has to do with his life," I said, and earned a good look from Lenny. They introduced themselves in turn, including the school counselor, who was there to offer any help we thought was necessary.

Lenny clammed up. After about fifteen minutes of teachers talking and not getting a reaction from him, and me being quiet, I called a halt to the meeting. "Lenny, come outside to the hallway for a minute." He followed me outside and leaned against the wall, hands in pockets.

"I know you are pissed at everything that's happening to you, and I'm as frustrated as you are, but this is your life we're talking about. Remember we talked when you were in jail and we agreed that you were in charge? Don't let them bully you. You are in charge of your own life, nobody else. No one can make you talk, study, or pass tests unless you want to. But for God's sake, just make a stand one way or the other. If you don't want to participate, then tell them that." He looked at me like I had lost my mind. "But be prepared for the consequences if that's your decision."

He nodded. "I'll be back in a minute," he said.

The teachers were mumbling but stopped when I entered the room again. I sat down. "He's taking a moment." They all nodded.

"I don't envy you your position, Ms. Murphy," said one of them. "He's a tough kid."

My blood pressure skyrocketed, and my voice grew stronger, as though I were giving a graduation speech. "Yes, he's tough; he's had to be, but he's strong, and he's smart, and he will do very well if only he can find the right people to guide him. He's been damaged beyond belief and everyone he has ever known has deserted him. I can't blame him for tuning out, honestly." I was amazed to realize tears were about to spring down my cheek. They all looked a little shocked except the counselor, who was looking over my head. "Did you hear all that?" he asked.

"Yes," Lenny said, and sat beside me and looked me in the eye. "Do you really believe that?"

"What? That you're going to do great things? Oh, yes." And I did. I realized it for the first time. I knew this kid, as little as we had really talked. I knew him because I *was* him. All I needed to do was reach that part of him that I knew someone needed to reach in me. I had the key.

The knowledge that I had the elusive key make me giddy, and I grinned like a fool. Why had it taken me so long?

We talked for another hour or so, going around the circle, each teacher giving Lenny their take on him and his talents/needs. They were, every single one of them, positive, upbeat, and supportive. The only negative that came out of it was he was not eligible for the wresting team until his grades came up.

I had been trying to do this alone. Here's a team.

After an hour of discussing Lenny's schoolwork, we ran home and got my painter's kit and drove to Canvas. Lenny was scheduled to work tonight, and we drove in silence, me grinning and him contemplating.

"Do you think I can catch up?"

"What I think doesn't matter. Do *you* think you can catch up?"

He smiled. "It's easy, except for math."

"Good. I agree. You're equipped to get it done, but if you want help, all you have to do is ask."

"I know."

Silence.

"Are you bummed bout the wrestling team?"

"No. Yes. No. I have to focus on school." He was quiet. "I don't deserve this."

"No, you don't," I said, thinking he was talking about his situation.

His head snapped around.

"What? Your mom, being in the system, and having no one to depend on is not your fault."

"No, I meant having all these people around me who want to help."

"See, Lenny, that's the thing. You do deserve it. Everyone does. We are all here to help each other. Everyone deserves a chance. Everyone."

"Even my mom."

"Yes, even your mom. The courts have given her, and will continue to give her, any help she wants. All she has to do is apply herself to that help. Her parental rights were terminated because it was very clear to the courts that she couldn't help you, and you were better off with someone who could. Although, why that's me, I have no idea."

"What about when Mom gets out?"

"That's up to you. If you want to see her, you make the call. But she no longer has the right to demand you visit her in jail or anywhere else."

He was silent for a while. "I worry about her."

"Of course, you do. She's your mom."

That didn't make either one of us feel any better.

Chapter Forty

*J*EN WAS NOT IN GOOD SHAPE. BRUCE HAD CALLED AN AMBULANCE AND she'd been admitted to the hospital. She hadn't eaten in days and was beginning to hallucinate. It was two days before I was allowed in, and by then she had been on all kinds of meds.

When I saw him, Bruce looked like he had been run over. "Go home," I said. "Go take a shower, eat something, take a nap. I'm taking over." Jen mumbled in her sleep. "Go!"

He looked over at Jen, hung his head and nodded. "I'll be back in a few hours." I nodded back. I wasn't going to keep him away. I sat next to Jen and wondered what I would do if she were no longer here. I couldn't help the tears that streamed down my face. This was all of a sudden real. I pulled out an old book of poetry I had kept that I knew Jen liked. I cleared my throat and began to read.

About half an hour later, a young man in a white coat came in. "And they're coming to take us away ha-haaa. They're coming to take us away ho-ho hee-hee ha-haaa," I said to her loud enough for him to hear. He smiled. Jen groaned. I introduced myself and he pulled out his tablet. Hunh. What happened to the metal clipboards?

"Are you family?"

"Yes, I'm her sister." The bald-faced lie was too much. "Well, not really, but we might as well be."

"Do you hold her healthcare directive?"

"No. I don't even know what that is."

"It's okay," we heard Jen whisper from the bed. "You can talk to her. I trust her judgment, as well as Bruce's."

216

"Fine. What's happening, Mrs. Conrad, is that the chemo has completely destroyed your bone marrow. You cannot tolerate any more treatment."

Jen nodded and I stopped breathing. Oh God.

"So, there's nothing to be done?" I asked, my voice loud and strong. This pissed me off, and when I get pissed off the whole world knows it.

"I didn't say that," he said. "There is stem cell treatment that seems to work well for some people. What we do is harvest some cells from around your waist, take the stem cells out, treat them, and put them back into your body through an IV drip. Takes about a day." He made it sound so easy.

"How does it work?" I asked, knowing Jen would want to know the mechanics of it.

"The stem cells are programmed to go find cancer cells and destroy them at their source. The platelets that come with them will reenergize your bone marrow and your cells should rebuild themselves. There is no risk of rejection since they are your very own cells. It's still experimental, but some people have had great success with it. My recommendation is that we do it now. I have a team standing by." He looked from me to Jen, who nodded.

"Go," she said, with a thumbs-up. He nodded to both of us and headed out the door, his white jacket flying in the breeze behind him.

"OK, so it's Pac-Man treatment," I said, trying to be cheerful. "Jesus, Jen, I'm so sorry. This must be horrible for you."

"It's not been a pick-a-nick," she whispered. "Hey," she said after closing her eyes for a minute.

"Yup. I'm here."

"Go do something."

"What?" I couldn't imagine. "Do you need something?"

"Yes. For you to have a life. You don't want to wind up here and wonder what could have been." The top of my head turned cold and the icy chill bled down my neck and arms. I started to shiver. I suddenly remembered Jen's sister. "Where is Maggie?"

"She just can't handle this. Dave took her to a," she used hand quotes, 'resort.'" I knew Maggie had had some recent mental illness issues and had spent some time in a facility. With her husband's illegal goings-on at his firm, her father dying, her mother dying, and now her sister being so seriously ill, she probably just couldn't take any more. For the first time, I felt sorry for Maggie; the woman with the strong-woman-attitude was really just a mush ball.

So that meant Jen had nobody but Bruce—and me. I made a silent promise to her that I would pay more attention and be better with Bruce.

She dropped off to sleep and I stepped out. My legs wouldn't support me. I sat and stared at the wall in front of me.

"I think you should prepare yourself for the worst," said a voice from above me. I looked up to see the man in the white jacket who was with Jen earlier.

"You don't know my sister," I said. "But thank you for your advice." I stood and left the building.

Chapter Forty-One

CAMILLE CALLED THE NEXT DAY, BUT I WAS READY FOR HER. "I RECEIVED A notice from the school that Lenny is failing all his classes."

"Yes, that's true, but we had a meeting yesterday with all his teachers and I believe we have a plan to get him back on track, and he's bought into it. We are making progress with him and I think we are beginning to have a connection."

"Also, we were notified that there was a traffic citation that Lenny was driving your car. He does not have a license that we have approved."

"You have to approve getting a driver's license?"

"Yes, any major change in the child's life goes through us until he's adopted out. I have to say, this raises some red flags. I'm hearing that he is uncooperative at school, anti-social, not joining in any extracurricular activities, and now he has stolen your car and gotten a ticket. This is not good progress."

"Now, hold on a second . . ."

"And my supervisor wants to come for a home visit and see how things are, and how he's feeling about things."

"You can imagine how he's feeling . . ."

"We will be out there at three o'clock this afternoon." No choice.

Well shit.

But that reminded me. I sat down and wrote a very strong letter of accommodation for the officer who had treated Lenny so well. I sent it to Ron and asked him to forward it to whomever needed to see it. That officer took a risk and I wanted everyone to know that it turned out well. I wanted Ron to know one of his recruits had behaved with compassion and sensibility.

Then I started to plan for the meeting with Chloe and her supervisor.

Lenny walked into the living room and stopped, seeing Camille and her supervisor, a very large black woman named Donna something. His face went pale and he dropped his backpack on the floor with a loud thump. "Am I being moved?" he asked quietly. I recognized the look of total defeat.

"Not if I can help it," I said. "Ladies, let's hear what you have to say."

"Lenny, you are not doing well in school." Camille said in a soft, easy voice. She began to say something else when her cohort interrupted.

"And you stole a car and got a ticket. What do you have to say for yourself?" Donna said. I wanted to interrupt but watched as Lenny sat up straight and looked them in the eye.

"I have plans to fix both problems," he said.

"And may I ask what those plans *are?*" Donna said with a hint of sarcasm. Camille looked over at her, surprised at her tone, apparently. I didn't appreciate it, either.

Lenny zipped open his backpack and pulled out a string of paper, three sheets taped together. He laid the paper on the table and I saw his classes listed, assignments posted, dates noted, and help-needed boxes all lined up like a military operation. Something I would have done. Three of the tasks had already been accomplished. I felt a little thrill.

"This is incredible," said Camille, and took a picture of it. "I know kids who could use this kind of organization." She smiled at him. Donna was not as easily impressed. I certainly was, and I grinned as I slapped Lenny on his back.

"I see you have a plan," Donna said. "Very impressive, but the proof will be in the pudding."

"I'm sorry?" Lenny said.

"It's an old saying, meaning 'make sure you do it,'" Camille said with a grin.

"Now, about the stolen car . . ." Donna was determined to make Lenny the bad guy.

"It was my car, not exactly stolen," I said, having none of it.

"Did you give him permission?"

"Well, no, but . . ."

"Then it was stolen."

"I got a job," Lenny said. "I work at Canvas at Heritage Art Park. I will pay back the repairs."

"Why did you do it?" Camille asked quietly, with a hand on his back.

He hung his head. "I wanted to get away—far, far away. My mom, my grades, not knowing how long I was going to be here, missing my old friends, not knowing anybody . . .I just needed to escape for a bit."

"By driving without a license?"

"It's better than alcohol or drugs," Lenny said, his eyes lasering through both of them, the intruders.

Camille stood and motioned for Donna to stand as well. "I think we're done here. We'll have to check back in in one month and see progress before we talk about moving him out. Let's see if he improves by then. We will talk again in one month."

For Camille to take charge like that meant the world to me. Donna had made up her mind that this kid was trouble. They left and, as much as I wanted to, I denied myself a drink, and decided to get him a mountain bike—a legal escape.

"Hey, Renee, something's wrong with the dog," Lenny said.

"What?" I came around the corner to find Lenny bending over Gunnar, who was on the floor, tongue hanging out, panting. His belly looked bloated.

"Gunnar, come here," I said. He lifted his head and lay it back down. I saw a puddle of drool under his head.

"Did you pick up poop this morning?" I asked Lenny.

"There was none to pick up, which I thought was weird."

"Go look at his bowl." Lenny clomped into the kitchen and returned.

"It's still full."

"From this morning. Okay, he's sick. Gunnar, get up, honey, come on." I put his leash on his collar and tried to get him up. He tried, God love him, but his legs just wouldn't support him.

"Oh, boy," I said and stood, hands on hips. "We'll have to carry him to the car."

I found an old blanket we could roll him onto and hopefully use it as a stretcher to get him in the car. By the time I got back to them, Lenny was on his feet with Gunnar in his arms. Lenny's face turned red and he grunted a little. I rushed to get the keys and we put the dog in the car and rushed to animal emergency.

As we sat waiting for X-rays and the doc to come out, I saw Lenny's leg bouncing again, just as he did that first day at Jen's and just as his mother did in court. He was nervous and scared. I wanted a drink.

"It's probably nothing. Maybe he's just constipated, and they can just give him something to make him poop."

"Maybe," he said, and sighed. He sounded so adult, older than his chronological age. *Please don't let Gunnar die. It's just one more person abandoning Lenny.*

We waited over an hour before we were escorted back to an exam room. The vet put up some X-rays and showed us this huge mass in his stomach. "That doesn't look good. It may be a tumor, and it may or may not be cancerous."

Lenny sat down on the hard plastic chair. Dizziness overwhelmed me for a second. "What's next?" I asked.

"We'll have to go in and take a look, maybe remove the mass if it's not interfering with anything vital. I have to warn you, though, if we find that we cannot remove it, my recommendation is to put him down. If there is nothing we can do for him, why make him suffer more?"

"But he was fine yesterday," Lenny said with weak little-boy voice, a change from a moment ago. "He's a good dog."

"I know, son, but sometimes we have to do what's best for the dog. But this is a warning to be prepared for the worst. If it can be removed, we will do our best. The best-case scenario is that it's removable and benign. Then we take it out, stitch him up, and he'll go on as before. I just want you to be prepared if it's not."

Lenny nodded and I shook.

We left Gunnar there to be prepped for emergency surgery. I gulped when presented with the estimate of what the operation would cost, but signed the consent forms anyway, including instructions to euthanize him if they found the worst.

Anything to get this dog out of danger. Lenny couldn't have another abandonment.

We went home, carrying Gunnar's collar and leash, feeling like we'd already lost him. I emptied his bowls, washed them, refreshed his water, fluffed his bed, and arranged his toys, ready for him to come home.

"He'll be fine," I said.

"Yup, he will."

This was repeated all night.

I called Adam to fill him in and tell him Lenny wouldn't be in to work, and I wouldn't be in class, and that was why. As much as Adam didn't like dogs, he sure sounded sorry that this had happened.

"Such a fine specimen," he said. "I hope all is well."

"Me, too."

Four hours later, we hadn't heard anything, but had fielded calls from Marjorie, Patrick, and Adam. They were all concerned, as Gunnar had come to class several times and, after greeting everyone, curled up in his corner while we worked. They all loved him. Jade from the shop next door, Pages, had heard as well, and we got a call from her.

Dogs are like family. I now understood those crazy people who love their dogs above all else. I just didn't know how our world was going to proceed without this goofy guy in it.

Finally, the landline rang, and I hit the speaker button. A female voice said, "Hold for Dr. Patterson, please." My heart was pounding, and I wanted to burst out crying. He took forever to pick up.

"Mrs. Murphy? Dr. Patterson here."

"Yes? What can you tell us? We've been worried sick."

He laughed. "It wasn't at all what I thought. This guy fooled me."

I felt a little better. Good news, perhaps? Before I could ask, he said, "Missing any socks lately?"

"What?"

He laughed out loud. "This guy managed to swallow a whole sock. It got twisted together in his intestine and I had a hell of a time extricating it, but finally we were able to untwist it without twisting up the intestine by cutting tiny pieces out and actually unraveling it row by row. Took forever, but we did it. He was under far longer than he should have been, so it will be a while before he's back to normal, but he's going to be okay."

Lenny fist pumped, I cried, and we thanked the doc, saying we would wait for his call to pick Gunnar up tomorrow. I pushed the button to hang up and danced around, so happy Gunnar was going to be okay.

"Stupid dog," Lenny said with a smile. "Who eats socks?"

"Well, I don't wear socks, so they must be yours. You have to remember to put them somewhere he can't get them so this doesn't happen again."

"And washcloths, probably."

We spent the night dog-proofing the house and laughing about what a young dog just might get into.

"You were really worried," he said.

"Was not."

"Yes, you were."

"You were too!"

"Wasn't." The grin through the dimples just about did me in.

"Yes, you were." We looked at each other, grabbed hands and danced around in a happy jig. We then phoned back everyone who had called, even though it was eleven at night. They were all very, very pleased. Dogs is good.

A small part of Lenny's world had been saved.

Chapter Forty-Two

LENNY AND I SAT IN THE LIVING ROOM. "WE HAVE BOTH SCREWED UP," I said. "It's time to make some changes. Take control. You've already started on the school part, but this is about the life part." He nodded, head down. I knew this very moment would be the one where I either won him or lost him. I had to make this work and still be authoritative. Knowing that he liked to be organized, just like I did, I had an old-fashioned flip chart on an easel along with colored felt pens. This was going to be a brainstorming session.

"I think we need a schedule. It would help both of us get some things accomplished, knowing what's on for the day."

"Okay . . ." I heard the skepticism and ignored it.

"So . . . let's make some house rules."

"Rules?" If his eyes had been guns, the bullets would have killed me.

"Okay, guidelines . . . no, rules," I said firmly. "If we say guidelines, we'll both let things slide. Rules sounds more permanent. For instance, what time should you get up for breakfast and make it to school on time?"

That's where we started. An hour later, we had agreed to timing of house things, some rules about when he would be home in general. I called it my "worry time" if a specific time passed. "Just know that I'm worried here, not mad, when I haven't heard from you." He seemed to appreciate that one. We agreed to have dinner every night, a home-cooked meal that would be eaten in the kitchen, not the dining room, and he would do his homework after dinner. We negotiated a long time on chores to be done around the house. Gunnar watched us carefully. I think he knew something serious was going on.

"Now. I'd really like to see you get involved in some extracurricular activity, not at the art park, with other kids, and I'm concerned that you aren't connecting. "

"Well, neither are you," he mumbled.

I froze.

Dammit, he's right. I'm not really involved in the shop, I don't have any hobbies to speak of, other than the occasional painting in class, and Jen is my only friend.

I nodded firmly. "You know what? You are right." I flipped the page to a new, crisp, clean one. "Give me some ideas."

"You could go swimming," he said. I wrote it down. "Join a gym." Wrote that one down. "Start jogging." Wrote it down and turned around.

"Do I detect a pattern here . . ." I worked hard to produce a grin.

"I don't want to tell you what to do." Lenny's face was clenched, scared.

"I tell you what to do. Go for it."

"Okay, don't hate me, but you should lose some weight. You're really pretty, but you could look better."

A chill ran down my body. No one had ever spoken to me like that. But, alas, it was true. I gave a guffaw. "You got big ones, I'll give ya that." I sighed. "But you are right. Okay, improvement project number one, lose weight." Now it was about me. But that was okay. If he saw me willing to make changes, he might buy into some for himself.

"But don't do one of those liquid things. Those are stupid."

"Right. No stupid liquid diets."

"Just veggies and protein and exercise."

"Veggies and protein and exercise. Got it." Wrote it down.

"Because, if you're going to adopt me, I need you to not leave me."

Boom. My heart just left me. Flew away. Gone.

I drew a huge heart, thinking of keeping my physical heart healthy, but it ended up a love heart.

"And you can start dating. Don't not see anyone because of me."

"Who would want a used-up, middle-aged politician?"

His eyebrows went up. "You're awesome. Any guy would want to be around you." Ohmygodohmygodohmygod. No one has ever said that to me, either.

"And . . . now, don't get mad, but stop drinking so much. It makes me nervous."

"Already done."

"Cool."

"Now you." I turned to yet another clean page.

I wrote down knitting, sock darning, and basket weaving, just to start the list. He added a few other sillies, and we got down to business. He didn't know what he actually wanted to do, so we just left it at "three extracurricular activities by year-end," starting with just one and moving on. The wrestling team tryouts and the school not letting him participate held him back, but there was no reason he couldn't join a club or something.

Then we attacked his education and evaluated his progress with the plan he had come up with. He admitted he needed some help, so we set aside some time to go over math issues, which I majored in for my bachelor's degree, and agreed to feel free to ask any of the teachers in our meeting for help. He promised to bring up his grades and, much as I hated to do it—I had criticized parents for doing this—we negotiated a cash reward for As and Bs. If it's what motivated him, then we'd try it.

"So, we've agreed to be better than we are now, right?"

"I guess."

"And we have a plan, right?"

"I guess."

"You guess?"

"Yes. We have a plan." He tried not to grin, but I saw it. *I saw it.*

"Okay, then, Operation RenLen starts tomorrow. We keep each other accountable."

He grinned for real.

Lenny had been working hard at making up his schoolwork. He rode his bike constantly and would disappear from time to time, but I now understood that was his nature—he just had to get out of his head and relax. His future wife would have to understand that.

With a start, I realized he was closing in on his sixteenth birthday.

What to do, what to do . . . a coupon to go somewhere? New clothes? Games? A sporting event? I was lost, but thankfully I had time.

I began to receive notes from all his teachers about how much he was trying and how hard he worked. They noted that he even had a few friends and were pleased with his attitude and inclusion into small groups. Summer was coming up, and Lenny put together a flyer to do small odd jobs for the art park—a runner, bank deposits, go to the post office, clean, sweep, move furniture . . . whatever the stores needed, he would be on call. He showed the flyer to me one night. "What do you think?"

"That's a great idea. I'm sure they'll use you. But you don't have to make it full time, you know. Go to the beach, have some fun. It's what summer's for."

"Yeah. I have to take some classes, too, so I can go into my junior year ready."

"Well, this business sounds like a good one, and the classes may be necessary, but I still think you need to have some fun. You've been working very hard. Take a break."

"Yeah . . .I will, but you too, right?"

"Me too, right."

What the hell was I going to do to have some fun?

Chapter Forty-Three

OVER THE NEXT WEEK, I TOOK THE TIME TO RELAX AND GET MY HOUSE IN order, figuratively. I set up a schedule to do something active every day, reactivated my membership in Rotary, and made a list of all the people I thought I'd like to have in my life socially, keeping the impact on Lenny at the forefront of my thoughts. We were both working hard to make changes.

This was no longer just about me.

After I lost ten pounds, I thought I would reward myself and solve the problem of what to do for Lenny's birthday at the same time. The car I bought from the City for a very small price was still dented but drivable after a mechanic took a few tools and rattled a few things under the hood. That cost me about a grand. I had received the check to get it cosmetically repaired but for some reason hadn't bothered to do it. I was tired of it. Time for something new.

I thought I would get a simple sedan, much like what I had been driving for the past nine years. The salesman kept showing me different models, but my eye kept going to a white sportscar across the showroom. He made me look into all the sedans, test their instrument panels, talk about mileage and engine size, satellite radio, automatic lighting, all the things that sell a car, but it was all kind of ho-hum, and they all looked the same, just different colors.

"If you were to buy today," he said, "which car and what color?"

I threw out what I thought was an unreasonable combination because, honestly, it was all the same to me. The salesman then pointed to the sports car that had grabbed me from the get-go.

The guy was a born salesman.

"Do you want to test-drive one? Just for fun? I know it's not what you want, but while I'm locating the car you want in the color you want, you might as well take it for a spin. There's one on the lot—a demo. It's red, maybe too much for you, but just take it out, run it on the freeway and come back. I'll see if I can find what you want on another lot." He dangled the keys to the red sportscar in front of me. "Go on. It'll be fun . . .I trust you. When you get back, we can talk turkey."

I had no choice, you see.

It drove like buttah, and I found myself grinning and laughing out loud as I maneuvered it around corners and up hills. It practically parked itself, and I loved the new-car smell. The sound system was incredible, and although the GPS in the dash was not needed, it was much appreciated. And I liked the red. I was in looooove, and caved.

The laughter coming from me and the sheer happiness I felt was new to me. Before I became mayor, I had bought only used cars; I had never had a new car in my life. Taking inventory, I had a new car, a new kid, a new life, several new friends, a new business, and getting a new body.

The shopping center was on my way home. I had a few new pieces before the day was out just a few to fit my new, smaller body. I'd buy more as I lost more. I needed to lose another twenty. I was one-third of the way to becoming a new person.

And Gunnar would fit nicely in the back of Red Rosie.

With Lenny's grades and how hard he was working, I enrolled him in a driver's ed class; he got his learner's permit over the summer, and we took the old car on drives around town. He was a natural. Red Rosie stayed in the garage.

I informed Camille that he had his learner's permit, rather than asking permission. She did not fight but asked for copies for the record. Points scored against the system.

I was at Jen's one day, joyfully gabbing over munchies and soft drinks. She was feeling much better; the stem cell treatment seemed to be working.

Her hair was growing back, her color was much better, and her sense of humor was back.

Bruce was in the kitchen cooking up something that smelled wonderful and we were happily ensconced on the couch, legs tucked up under us, laughing ourselves silly about something, when my phone trilled.

"Renee?" Sally's voice came over the phone. *Alert, Alert.*

"What's wrong." I watched Jen stand and stare at me.

"It's Lenny. Adam called 9-1-1; he had trouble breathing and then he just stopped."

"Stopped what?"

"Breathing."

"*What?*"

"Oh, good. The paramedics are here." Click.

Jen was on her feet standing over me. "What is it?"

"Lenny stopped breathing."

"Okay, you. Take a deep breath." Her hands were on my forearms. "Bruce?"

"Yup."

"Code blue. Take Renee to the hospital. Something's happened to Lenny."

"Right." Bruce was there, keys in hand, and grabbed my arm, pulling me out the door.

I collapsed into his car and began to bend over, rocking back and forth, back and forth. *What is wrong with me?* Beginning to come back to myself, I straightened up and began to assess. *Put on your seatbelt. Wipe your eyes. Think. Think. Pray.* My phone was still clutched in my hand.

I ran into the emergency room and waited behind two people before I could see the receptionist behind a glass cage.

Jesus. Any second now.

A volunteer came into the waiting room, took one look at me and said, "Come with me." I followed her through the door as she turned and asked, "Who are you here to see?"

"Lenny Rudolph. Fifteen years old. Stopped breathing."

She nodded and grabbed a nurse. "Number eight," the nurse said. She walked me quickly to a bed where Lenny lay. A nurse was with him, checking his IV and all the tubing running into him.

"What's going on?" I said, very loudly. I had to force my words out.

"He's had a severe asthma attack. Does he not have an inhaler?"

"Inhaler? I didn't even know he had asthma."

"Are you his mother?" As though he didn't believe a mother would not know this.

"Foster."

"Aha. Well, he does have severe asthma and needs treatment. We now have a tube into his lungs to get some oxygen directly and have given him a sedative to tolerate it better."

"So, he's breathing? He's alive?"

His eyebrows went up. "Yes . . ."

"I was told he stopped breathing."

"The paramedics gave him Albuterol, and I believe he stopped breathing only for bit, but we won't know if there was any damage until neurology sees him."

"Neurology?"

"Just to be sure there was no damage due to lack of oxygen. The doc will be here shortly." I must have rocked on my heels, because he said, "Uh oh. Let me get you a chair." He scooted a metal chair under me, and I collapsed into it.

He handed me a cup of water and I gulped it down. "Got anything stronger?"

He laughed. "I wish . . . the doc should be here shortly."

A young female cardio-pulmonary specialist eventually came and explained to me that Lenny's condition was clearly something he had had for some time and it should have been treated long ago. I took the lecture, not explaining that I was not responsible for what negligence had happened before he got to me. She handed me several prescriptions and booklets about asthma, and said once his lungs were performing well enough, they would take the tube out and let him recover. I should be able to take him home tomorrow. She highly recommended he see his pediatrician immediately. She further told me there was no need for me to be there, as they would put him in a room upstairs to recover and he would not even know I was there. Since he was a Medicaid patient, he would be in a large ward, and there was no room for an overnight.

I texted Camille about this new development and discovered his medical history was not complete, and that this was a surprise to her. She recommended a doctor and said she would make an appointment for him. I left it to her. I was too exhausted and upset to argue. I found Bruce in the waiting room and he drove me back to Jen's place, the only place I wanted to be.

Gunnar would be fine with a late dinner.

Chapter Forty-Four

*J*EN HAD WAITED UP FOR US AND ENVELOPED ME IN A HUGE HUG. "Everything all right now?"

"It will be, I think. Jesus, Jen. He almost died. He wasn't breathing."

She nodded her head. "I heard."

I fell apart. I just fell over and bawled my eyes out while she rubbed my shoulders. Bruce handed me a scotch, which I gulped down once I got my own breath back. The warmth going down the gullet braced me. "I cannot imagine life without him," I coughed out. "It's just so weird thinking he might be gone. Like a part of me would be gone. He's lying there all by himself." I kept crying.

"But he's okay, right?"

I blew my nose. "They say he's going to be okay; they want to bring in neurology to ensure there weren't any consequences due to oxygen deprivation, but they don't think it's an issue."

"Those paramedics are pretty special; they got on it right away, from what I hear."

"What? How . . .?"

"I called Adam and got the story. They were right there, less than a minute. They injected him with something right then. Adam was impressed."

A calm came over me. Adam, Sally, Bruce, Jen . . . they were all there, supporting and loving us; what more could I ask for?

Jen smiled over at me. "You're going to adopt him, aren't you?"

I nodded. "I don't have a choice, do I?" I smiled. "It's inevitable."

"Yes, it is. I never imagined you as a mother, but now I cannot see you as anything else."

"Funny, neither can I." I drove home to find Sally sitting in her car in front of my house. She shot out of the car as soon as I drove up. "Is he okay?"

A smile came to my lips. "Yes, he's going to be okay. It was a severe asthma attack. He had lost so much oxygen, he not only passed out, he stopped breathing, but the paramedics got to him in time."

"Thank God. I was so worried. I love that kid; he's special."

"Sally, I . . . thank you. Thank you for caring so much."

She looked me over. "I never thought I would say this to you, but . . . you're welcome, and I am so glad things are working out for you." She nodded to me and went back to her car.

Gunnar met me but looked behind me for his buddy Lenny.

Lenny was discharged and we got him to a doctor who reviewed everything and let us know that with consistent treatment and inhalers when needed, this was manageable. He continued to work at Heritage Park to make some money, biked every day, sometimes for hours, we did more driving together, and we received his year-end grades, which had improved significantly.

Jen offered to do a birthday celebration for his sixteenth at her house. She wasn't up to going out but wanted to be part of it. On the morning of his birthday, I surprised Lenny by making an appointment for him to take his driver's test. I was sure he'd pass but warned him anyway that nothing is certain; if he failed, we'd try again, it was no big deal. He frowned at me.

Probably shouldn't have said that.

He sailed through with a perfect score. His dimples showed when he and the instructor came through the door. They took his picture, and he was a legal driver.

Dinner at Jen's was fabulous: all Lenny's favorites, with a chocolate cake and ice cream. Bruce did all the cooking with Jen supervising from a kitchen chair. Jen, Bruce, Adam, Tricia, Lenny and I were the party. When it came time for gifts, he received their small gifts quietly and with much appreciation, but I knew he was ecstatic. I went last.

I handed over a jewelry box. He unwrapped it carefully, flipped open the velvet box, and gasped. "No way!"

"Way."

He dangled the keys to my old car and said, "Seriously? It's mine? I thought you traded it in for Red Rosie."

"You pay for the gas, I'll pay for the insurance."

"I..I..I . . . really?"

"Really." Laughter overtook the table.

He got up and hugged me. Actually hugged me. I hugged back.

"It's in the garage," Jen said, "so you can drive it home."

Lenny jumped up and ran out to the garage to make sure it was still there. I followed. Jen had had the dent fixed and the body re-painted. I looked at her, brows raised, and she shrugged.

"Awesome!" He sat in the driver's seat and fiddled with the knobs, his face pure pleasure.

We followed each other home, taking the rest of the cake with us, then sat at the kitchen table and each had another slice.

Now or never. "Lenny, were you serious earlier about me adopting you?"

My nerves were on edge, and I realized what I desperately wanted his answer to be.

"Why?" he asked.

Ummmm . . . "Because we both need someone. We are in this together, and I think we can both use the knowledge that this is something permanent, not just another home for you. It would also get rid of Camille and Donna, the evil twins."

As the words came out of my mouth, I realized how it sounded. I could have done this much better. "And I really want it," I added. "I've grown accustomed to having you around. I kind of like you."

He smiled. "Okay."

"Really?"

"Yeah, okay." He headed for the stairs, and I could just barely hear him say, "And I was jazzed about the car."

Chapter Forty-Five

I HAD PUT MY TOE INTO THE DATING POOL AND RESPONDED TO SOMEONE on the site with disastrous results. I ran to tell Jen about it. Horrible. Thank God it was only coffee.

She laughed herself silly, then demanded to see his profile. We opened up the dating site and found him. His picture was definitely not like him at all—I could see some resemblance, but clearly the picture was at least twenty years old.

"Good Lord!" said Jen. "Well, he looks nice."

"Oughta see him now," I mumbled. "If I didn't know better, I'd swear he was pregnant, or just had twins."

Jen laughed. "Ooh, let's see who your next victim is . . ." She scrolled through the pictures and, as I sat down, exclaimed, "Oh, here, this is priceless. You HAVE to go out with him, if just for the experience."

She turned the computer to me and I saw a picture of a very nice-looking man with white hair, clearly a fitness freak, with defined muscles and a trim body. That was evident because he'd neglected to put his shirt on. The hanging elderly flesh that no amount of exercise can eliminate almost wobbled in the picture, and his chest hair, what there was of it, was silver. He stated he was sixty-five.

"Ha. Ha."

"Seriously, Renee. You should check him out, just for the story . . ." She poised her finger above "poke", a very unfortunate click button to show you are interested in talking, and looked at me, eyebrows raised.

"Don't you dare."

"Or what? You gonna give me a time out?"

"I'll hate you forever."

"You can't hate me forever. You love me." And at that, she clicked the button.

I gasped.

"Hell, Renee, you don't have to accept his request. Just for fun, see what happens."

We met for lunch, at my suggestion.

I got there early, greeted the hostess named Sylvia, who offered to be my wingman, and she set me up at a beautiful table.

He was actually very attractive, clothed. Nice haircut, trimmed mustache, polished shoes, the whole nine yards. His manners were impeccable, he called me a lovely woman, an accomplished woman, a woman who knew her own worth and stood up for herself—he claimed he had admired me for years. Then he proceeded to tell me about his ex-girlfriend. Every single detail. For thirty minutes. I never opened my mouth, but my ears were tired.

At the end, after he insisted on paying the bill, he asked if I wanted to meet up again. I said, "I think your heart is still taken, so I'll say no for now, but I do encourage you to try to make up with her, since you seem to be still hung up on her." It was the only way I could graciously say, "No, I'm not really interested." He was too into himself. And Lenny would have a real problem with that.

He looked at me as though I were an alien from outer space. "She's a fucking bitch. I never want to see her again." So much for the gentleman. I smiled, turned, and left.

Instead of being depressing, this was actually fun. I thought I should write a book about men looking for women and how they come across—I'd frame it from a widow's viewpoint and call it "Widow's Pique."

I regaled Jen with the story of his attempt at dating, embellishing it even more to make her laugh. I kicked off my shoes in the middle of it when I realized she wasn't laughing.

"What's going on, Jen? You okay?"

"Yeah, just tired. I'm really not feeling as well as I did."

"Talk to me."

"I don't know what to say. Going to see the doc tomorrow. Nothing to report now except Bruce is hovering. His son is here, too. Nice guy; he's helping him stay sane, I guess."

"Can I do anything?"

"Not that I can think of. Keep dating, though. These are great stories." She forced out a laugh that I could tell was just not felt.

Bruce called me a few days later. "I'm worried. She's not eating. She hasn't gotten out of bed in two days."

"Let me know what the doc says."

"Of course."

"And Bruce? I'm here, you know."

"I know. This is brutal."

Bruce reported the next day that Jen had received some treatment that made her feel better, but they were withholding judgment on the stem cell progress. A few days later I spoke with her and discovered her spark had come back. She was much better, eating again, and getting out of bed. She admitted to having some limitations, but things were looking up.

I thanked God we had more time.

I had not looked at the dating site since the last fiasco. Honoring my promise to Lenny and to myself, I dove back in.

My nerves were dancing when I saw I had received an answer—a guy named Horace (Jesus). I took a deep breath and answered. We exchanged pleasantries through the website and agreed to meet for lunch.

I arrived earlier than he did, although he was not late, and purposely selected a table in the back. Sylvia my wingman was there again, my co-conspirator. Tall, thinning hair, ruddy face, dressed well enough, and a smile that wasn't quite sincere, Horace approached the table with his hand extended. We introduced ourselves and he sat, pulling his phone out of his pocket and pushing a button on it. He turned very serious. "Here are the rules. I allow thirty minutes to see if this works for me. If it doesn't, I'll just leave and no hard feelings, okay?"

I sat back in my chair. "What if I give it twenty?"

"Surely a relationship is worth more than that." I laughed and let it go. He didn't and continued to glower. The waitress appeared with a broad smile. Before she could pull out her pad, he said, "Honey, I'll have the chicken salad, no dressing, and an iced tea. You?" he pointed to me.

"Just a small house salad." I had lost my appetite. *I'm doing this for Lenny. I'm doing this for Lenny. I'm doing this for Lenny.*

"So . . . you were the mayor."

"Yes."

"Must have been interesting."

"Well . . ."

"I mean, all those crooked politicos in your midst." He shivered. I laughed and started to respond. He jumped in. "I've never taken to politics. I mean, who would enter into such a corrupt world?"

"Who do you think?" I asked, smiling.

"I mean . . ." and he went off, didn't stop talking for the next twenty minutes.

Lenny would hate him.

It turned out the button he pushed on his phone was a timer. When it rang, he took his napkin, wiped his face, put it over his unfinished salad, got up, gathered his phone, and left.

No good-bye, no nice-to-meet-you, nothing. And left me with the bill.

Chapter Forty-Six

IT WAS NOW OCTOBER OF LENNY'S JUNIOR YEAR. I WAS IN THE KITCHEN prepping for dinner when Lenny came home one early evening. He had been doing well; the summer had been successful, he had made some money, worked hard, but made his way to the beach from time to time. His mountain bike was well used and well cared for. He had lost some weight, gained some muscle, and had seemed to relax a bit. He also was showering every day, which was a vast improvement.

"How was your day, dear?" I asked like a harried housewife.

He laughed. "Um, Renee, this is Brittany. Brittany, this is my mom."

My mom.

Before I could get over that, I had another shock. She was so cute. Long blonde hair tied up into a ponytail, tanned legs, and strong arms. She was also a cheerleader, wearing the requisite sweater and pleated oh-so-short skirt.

"Guess what?" he said as he dove into the fridge, bringing out two sodas.

"What?"

"I got on the wrestling team." His grin was wide, and I could feel his pride.

"Oh, Lenny. That's so great!" I couldn't help it. I hugged him, and he hugged me back. We both backed away, embarrassed a little. I wanted to talk about the asthma, but with Cheerleader Barbie there, I didn't dare.

"He's good," Brittany said. "He'll do really good. I mean, well." She blushed.

They went into the living room and switched on the T.V. This was something I hadn't thought about. Girls. Privacy. Sex. Ugh.

Lenny came into the kitchen a few minutes later, dug into his pocket, and handed me a five-dollar bill with a grin.

"What's this for?"

"She was in the restaurant that night." He grinned.

I stayed in the kitchen and noticed it was awfully quiet in the living room. I peeked around the corner to find them both watching T.V. quietly, not touching, drinking their sodas and laughing at the funny parts. For now, things were okay. No reason to panic. Yet. I went back to following instructions for dinner.

"Good-bye, Mrs. Murphy." A cherry female voice came from the front door. "It was very nice meeting you."

"You, too, Brittany, and please call me Renee. We don't stand on ceremony around here."

"I'll try," she said, and blushed a bit. "I have to get home for dinner myself."

"Okay, see you . . . later." I didn't quite know what to say. She smiled and Lenny walked her out the door, and the opened the car door for her.

She was driving a cute little sportscar.

"So, she's cute. What's her deal?"

"Deal?"

"I mean, her family, and whatnot." I waved my hands around like an idiot.

"I don't know that much about her. She's in my Spanish class and she was at cheerleading in the gym during wrestling tryouts. We kind of got together afterwards and she gave me a ride home since I walked today."

"Well, she seems very nice."

"Here's all the notes and *whatnot*," he smiled, "for the wrestling team. I have to get some stuff and you have to sign off on these forms." He piled some forms on the kitchen counter and ran upstairs. I heard his phone ping with a text notice.

That didn't take long. She's probably home by now. Hope she isn't texting while driving.

Aside from my worries about Jen, things were going well. Lenny seemed, if not downright happy, at least comfortable and at ease. The new school year brought new activities and new friends, and my house had become a place to store soda and snacks that rapidly disappeared through osmosis. Gunnar was in the middle of teen boys and was apparently thrilled to have his buddy bring home others. My porch had pumpkins and haystacks for the first time ever. He had strung purple lights on the wrought iron fence and made a gravestone for the front yard.

We were having yet another casserole (my specialty, it seemed) one night when I broached the subject of how things were going.

"Anything you need? Anything missing?"

He shrugged.

"What."

"I dunno."

"What. Talk."

"I feel like this can't last. Nothing ever does."

"I can see why you would think that, but I have no plans to change it. Do you?"

"No, but something always comes up . . ."

"If it does, we'll deal with it. The paperwork is already in."

Once again, his experience and instincts were right.

I received a call from Camille saying that Lenny's grandparents, his mother's parents, had contacted her wanting to see Lenny. She passed on the info to me to see if I was willing to bring them in and allow them to see their grandson. Lenny was ambivalent—he had not seen either set of grandparents since he was little and had no contact.

"I was wondering what we would do for Thanksgiving. Why don't we invite them if they want to come? It might be nice to connect."

He shrugged.

I called them and had a short chat; they seemed very nice and accepted my invitation for Thanksgiving dinner. I would have to ask them why they had never been in touch with Lenny, their only grandson. Curious.

Evelyn and Charlie Meyer arrived on time with a fresh flower arrangement and an expensive bottle of wine. Lenny greeted them awkwardly and was a bit standoffish. He had put on a black button-down shirt with his jeans instead of a tee-shirt. Progress.

I had done a ton of research and consulted with Jen about getting a proper Thanksgiving dinner together with all the fixings, following directions to the letter, and Lenny helped. I learned he had never had a Thanksgiving he could remember, and I reflected back to the Putnam house where they always put on the dog with silverware, crystal, and mincemeat pies, everyone all dressed up.

We had some wine before dinner, but it was awkward and I rushed them to the table, having run out of easy topics, like where Lenny went to school, what his favorite subject was, etc., that no kid ever wants to answer. We got to the table, where they helped themselves to more wine and we ate in between more nonsense conversation. With dessert, Evelyn leaned back and asked, "So, Lenny, do you hear much from your other grandparents?"

Lenny's fork was coming to his mouth with his third piece of pumpkin pie and froze. "No . . . I've never met them, have I?" He looked at me and I shrugged. *How would I know?* "But it brings up an interesting question," Lenny said, his voice becoming very adult.

"Yes?" Evelyn's penciled-in eyebrows rose. My stomach turned over.

"Why haven't I ever heard from you?" His eyes laid into his grandmother, then over to Charlie.

"Well, son . . ." Charlie said.

"I am not your son." He said quietly, between his teeth. I let it go, proud of him.

Evelyn said, "We were estranged from your mother, Lenny. She had done such horrible things we were no longer speaking. We didn't even know you were born until you were six months old, and she wouldn't let us see you."

"I don't believe you." Lenny stared straight at her, not wavering.

"You don't believe me?" She sounded incredulous.

He took a deep breath and I could see the effort he took to keep calm. "My mother may have been a drug addict, but she was no liar. She told me that once you found out she was pregnant, you cut her off. You hurt her a lot; she tried several times to get to see you, but you refused. I watched her call you, using up all her minutes trying to get to you, to get help, but you refused her. I saw it."

"That's not how it happened."

"You could have sent cards, acknowledged my birthday, her birthday, Christmas, or even just the fact I was here, but I never heard from you. Not once. And you didn't help my mom. You could have. You could have gotten her into therapy, you could have . . ."

"Lenny, sometimes therapy doesn't work if someone doesn't want it," I said, trying to make peace.

"They should have tried. They didn't." He threw his napkin on the table and went upstairs.

"I'm so sorry; he's very angry." I was trying to keep civil.

They looked at each other, and Charlie said, "We want custody."

"What? I'm adopting him." My fork dropped onto the plate and I wanted to throw up.

"We'll see about that. Courts always defer to family members."

This was nonsense and I was having none of it. "If that's true, why didn't you respond to the social worker's approach when Lenny was first in the system? I know you were contacted. I read the transcript. You wanted nothing to do with him." Camille had given me the background earlier. They both stared at me.

I stood. "I think we're done here. Thank you for coming, but I will stand up for Lenny and his wishes."

Charles stood and threw his napkin on the table. "Then we will see you in court." Evelyn grabbed her purse, and, unbelievably, took the centerpiece she had brought with her. They left without another word. I began to take plates into the kitchen and clear up. Lenny followed behind me with more.

"Some family, hunh?" he mumbled.

"Did you hear?"

He nodded. "See, I told you it was too good to be true."

"I'll talk to Tricia and Lacey tomorrow. Don't worry."

"Yeah, right." He stomped back upstairs. Old Lenny was back.

Chapter Forty-Seven

I WAS IN THE FLOPHOUSE, TRYING TO RESCUE MY MOTHER. SHE WAS ON the ripped-up, filthy couch, her arms akimbo, her mouth open, her eyes glazed. I tried to get her up, but some guy came and pulled me away.

"Whacha think ya doin'?"

I wasn't afraid of these guys; I'd been around them too long and I was younger and faster. I had escaped them many times before, but this time I was not going away without my mom.

"Gimme forty bucks and she can go. I gave her a pouch out of the goodness of my heart, but now she owes me forty bucks."

"No. I'm taking her."

"No way, little girl." He pulled out a knife and waved it in front of me. "I want my money."

I could see I wasn't going to get anywhere. I left her there, drooling and unaware.

Jen's house was over two miles away, and I ran like I never had before.

"Quick, I need forty dollars."

"What for?"

"My mom. I have to get her." I was embarrassed, but I had to tell her. I had never lied to her, so I had to.

Her eyes bugged out. "Come with me." We went into her parents' bedroom where her mom's purse was sitting on her dresser. Jen pulled two twenties out of her wallet, handed them to me, and said, "Go. This never happened."

I ran back to where Mom was and found her alone. I grabbed her and threw her arm around my shoulder and began to take her out. Maybe I could put the forty dollars back and not steal from Mrs. Putnam.

A hand grabbed my hair and a knife came from behind me, nearly taking my ear off and leaving blood all over my tee-shirt. I drew the money from my pocket and threw it on the floor and kept going. When Mom woke up the next day and saw the blood and heavy cut, she tried to clean me up, but I wasn't having any of it. I was pissed and let her know it. It hurt like hell and I just kept sopping up the blood until it stopped. She at least got me some pain pills from her friend, and I took half of one out of desperation. When I went to get more, they were gone. I stayed home from school until I could act normal. My hair covered the wound and I was careful not to scratch it. I made it through with Jen's help. Jen and her family saved me.

I woke up, sweaty and hot, remembering that night and how I rescued my mother with stolen money. This was no nightmare; this was reality. This happened. With a start, I realized I was not going to be putting Lenny at that kind of risk. He was safe here with me and I was just as safe with him. We needed each other and I was going to do anything I had to do to keep him.

Chapter Forty-Eight

"LET ME DO SOME RESEARCH," TRICIA SAID. "IT SOUNDS LIKE THERE'S something behind this. Why would a couple of seventy-year-olds want a sixteen-year-old kid from a child they never liked? This doesn't make sense." She stopped. "How's Lenny?"

"Morose. Things were going so well, he predicted something would come up to spoil it, and he was right."

"Nothing's spoiled. The courts usually give an older kid a choice about who they want to live it if it gets that far, but I doubt it will." She sounded so confident; I wished I felt the same way.

The Meyers fulfilled their threat and filed a lawsuit alleging I was unfit, and a hearing was set for two weeks, just before Christmas. Tricia told me not to worry about a thing; she said Lacey had something up her sleeve. Jen was apoplectic and wanted to write to them immediately. Tricia talked her down, but she was trying hard to do something.

Lenny and I showed up in Family Court, the same one I had gone to for his hearings, and sat outside with all the foster kids and CASAs waiting to be heard. Our case was called, and we went in. We sat in the gallery, while Charlie sat with his expensive attorney. Lacey, Tricia's partner, sat at the other table.

"All rise."

Judge Sullivan came in, sat down, the rest of us sat, and he read through the case documents. He took off his glasses and announced that he was taking a fifteen-minute break. He stood, we stood, and he went back to his chambers. We sat quietly, waiting for God knows what, while my stomach rumbled and my hands shook, and Lenny's leg jackhammered.

The judge came back and announced he would have to recuse himself because he felt it was inappropriate for him to adjudicate this session. "Fortunately, another judge has just wrapped up a case and is available, so you can proceed without losing any time." He stood, we stood, he took his nameplate off the front of the bench and left. Five minutes later, a female judge, Kathleen O'Hara, with the expected bright red hair and fair complexion, floated in wearing her black robe and popped her own nameplate in, sat down, and we all sat again. She reviewed the file.

"This is highly unusual. The child has been petitioned to be adopted," she said, looking over at Charlie and his attorney. The attorney rose. "Yes, your honor, but we have evidence that he is not in a safe place and the grandparents are very concerned about his welfare."

"I see. Let's wait on that evidence, shall we? I see the 'child'," and she used air quotes, "is sixteen now. I'd like to hear from him first."

"But your honor . . ."

"Yes? You have an objection to how I'm running my court, counselor?" The judge glared over her half glasses.

"No, your honor." He sat back down. Lenny went to the witness stand, climbed the step and sat, his hands folded on his lap.

"Tell me about your life," the judge said quietly, with a kind smile.

Lenny proceeded to tell her about his mother, where he went to school, all his placements, what he was studying, how he lived his life, Canvas, friends, and his car.

"You have a car?" she asked.

"Yes, ma'am. Renee's old car. I pay for gas, she pays the insurance." He grinned. "Sometimes I have to walk." The judge smiled at that, and said, "Counselor, do you have any questions for Lenny?"

"Yes, your honor." He rose. "How many boyfriends does Ms. Murphy have?"

"What?!" Lacey interjected. "Your honor . . ."

"It's a reasonable question, given the allegation that she's unfit. I'll allow it, but you're on a very short leash, counselor."

"None that I know of," Lenny said.

"She's not dating?"

"Yes, I know she is, but that's because I asked her to."

"You asked her to."

"Yes, we're on a self-improvement program, Operation RenLen."

"Operation RenLen." The attorney was just repeating what Lenny said, trying to catch up.

"Get it? Renee and Lenny? RenLen?"

I laughed out loud, then covered my mouth. The judge suppressed a grin.

Lenny continued. "We encourage each other to lose weight, get exercise, and have fun. Renee has worked hard all her life and she needs to have some fun, like I do. We agreed."

"Have you ever heard or seen a man called Ed Holcomb?"

My heart went into overdrive. *Where do they get their information?*

"No . . ."

"Ron Walker?"

"He's the mayor, right? Took over Renee's job?"

"Yes, that's the one. Has he been to your house?"

Lenny looked confused and said "No..."

Lacey stood as the judge interrupted Lenny. "That's enough, counselor. You've gone far enough."

"Your honor, this goes to . . ."

"Yes, I know where it goes, but I don't want it to go any further. The questions were asked and answered. Lenny has no responsibility to report on Ms. Murphy's personal life, and it's inappropriate." She turned to Lacey. "Any questions for Lenny, counselor?"

"Yes, your honor." Lacey said. She approached the witness box. "Lenny, if you were to have a choice, where would you live?"

"I would say with my mom, but that's not possible, so with Renee. She's cool and I know I'm safe and I have made friends in school and know the neighborhood. I'm doing good . . . well with her, but . . ."

" . . . but you miss your mom."

"Yeah. But I know she can't take me. She's too messed up."

"Thank you, your honor," Lacey said.

The judge took a moment, smiled at Lenny, and said, "I'd like to hear from Mr. Miller now."

Charlie Miller stood and approached the witness stand.

"Tell me why you think Ms. Murphy is unfit, and keep in mind you'll have to prove your allegations."

"Yes, ma'am. I have proof that she's had a twenty-year affair with a married man and a dalliance with the chief of police while she was mayor."

The judge looked around the courtroom. "Does that mean she's unfit?"

"Yes, it does."

"Why?"

"Well, it's a moral issue, your honor, and I don't want my grandson around such a . . . loose woman." I guffawed. I hadn't had sex in ten years.

"I see . . . and you say you have proof?"

"I can get it."

The judge sighed. "Anything else, counselor?"

"No, your honor."

She looked over at Lacey. "Would you like to question Mr. Miller?"

"Yes. Yes, I would, your honor." She stood and approached him. "Mr. Miller, I appreciate your willingness to protect your grandson, and your concern about *moral* issues." He nodded. "Can you tell me, please, when was the last time you saw him? I mean before Thanksgiving, when Ms. Murphy and Lenny took the initiative to invite you?"

He looked down at his hands. "When he was three years old."

"And why is that?"

"Because his mother took him away and we couldn't find him."

Lenny said out loud, "That's not true!"

The judge shushed him, and said, "Continue."

"Let me change tacks, then. Are you familiar and have you met with his other grandparents, Lenny's father's parents?"

Charlie looked stricken. "Yes, we've met them."

"You are friends, correct? You've kept in contact all this time?"

"I wouldn't say so . . ."

"Really. You wouldn't say so. You went on a cruise with them last September, correct?"

He looked a little surprised. Lacey had done her own homework. "Well, yes . . ."

"So, you *are* friends."

He straightened up. "No longer."

"And why is that?"

"For personal reasons."

"I see. I understand that they are very wealthy, and that Mrs. Cahill is now a widow."

"That is true, sadly."

"And that she now has a terminal illness."

"I have heard that, yes."

"And that she intends to leave everything to Lenny." Lacey turned the knife deftly.

"They didn't contact Lenny either." He sounded defiant.

"And why is that? I'll tell you. That's because *you* told them that you couldn't find Lenny. I spoke to Mrs. Cahill. She is desperate to see him. In fact, she's standing by her telephone now if the judge will allow her telephonic testimony." She passed while he collected himself. "I know what you told them, but you knew where he was all the time, didn't you? This is why the friendship broke up, isn't it? You didn't want Lenny to be the benefactor since he is the child of your biggest disappointment."

Miller sat quietly, his mouth open.

"Mr. Miller, I have to believe the only reason you want Lenny is to get your hands on that money while he is still a minor."

"That's not true. We love Lenny."

Lacey walked back to the desk. "Really? You don't even know Lenny. Let me ask you: What's his birthdate?" Charlie was silent, head bowed. "Tell me—what's his favorite food? His interests? Where does he want to go to college? Did you know he has a severe case of asthma? Can you answer any of these questions as a loving grandparent?"

He was silent.

"I didn't think so." Lacey threw a file down on the table and dropped into her seat with a scowl.

We took Lacey to lunch to record the end of yet another chapter. I insisted Lacey send me a bill, no more pro bono work for us; that new firm of Putnam and Associates needed paying clients. Lacey suggested Lenny visit his paternal grandmother as soon as possible; she was in good shape at the moment but only had a few months to live. She wanted to see him.

Lenny nodded and said he'd like to go, that maybe someone in his family would value him after all.

Jesus.

Lenny's paternal grandmother lived up in Santa Barbara, so with great trepidation I gave Lenny directions to get to her house and told him to drive carefully. He laughed and held up his phone; the directions were already plugged in. "Silly Renee, it's all done!" I think he was more excited about driving the long distance by himself than he was meeting his grandmother.

Lenny spent four days with his grandmother in Santa Barbara. He had texted me when he got in, but then I never heard from him. I was a bit nervous, but let it go. I recognized this was an important time for him, and him spending four days was two days more than planned. I thought I would enjoy the time alone; instead I was in agony. Between that and Jen's health, my emotions were tangled. What if he wanted to live with her instead?

When he returned, I saw a huge change. He stood taller, walked with purpose, and when he spoke, he looked me in the eye. The first thing he did was hug me, which made all my fears disappear.

"How did it go?"

"She's really nice. She told me all about my father and gave me pictures of him when he was a kid. I think I look like him. She really loved him; they both did. She talked a lot about when he was a kid: he was a good student, played music, and read a lot, but apparently" (*not I guess*) "he got mixed up with a bunch of KKK people, got tattoos, and got militant about black people and minorities. When he killed a black kid and wasn't sorry about it, they disowned him."

"How horrible."

"Yeah. It killed them both. She cried telling me about it. They hired private detectives to find me, but Mom wasn't using her maiden name anymore, so they didn't know how to find us." He snickered. "Rudolph is a made-up name. She was scared of my dad's white supremacist tribe."

"I'm so sorry, Lenny."

He cocked his head. "No, it's okay. At least I know my history, and I know I have at least one grandparent who loves me." He waited a beat. "I think I'm learning that my mom really did nothing wrong. She got involved with this guy and got on drugs and couldn't get out. Nana said she liked Mom when she first met her, but then Mom sort of descended into a different person."

I nodded, thinking about my own mother.

"I'm learning in class about drugs and how powerful they are, and I believe it. Mom tried and tried, I know, but it just kept pulling her back and she couldn't resist. I'm not sure I believe it's a disease, but it's more powerful than she is." I nodded again, not sure what to say. "I promised I'd keep coming back and be with Nana when she dies."

"That seems like a lot to ask."

"She didn't ask, but when I offered, she seemed relieved to have someone with her."

"Do you want to live with her now and see her through this?"

"I asked that, but she said no. She'll tell me when. She doesn't want me to miss too much school and wants me to live my life as a teenager, not a caregiver."

"What a wonderful woman." I was sort of jealous, but happy for him.

He nodded. "I drove all through Santa Barbara and picked up a catalogue from UCSB. I think I want to go there when I graduate. It's not too far and I can still come home for weekends and stuff."

Home. I smiled. "Sounds like a plan."

"Oh, and she said she's leaving a trust for me so I can pay for it."

"Isn't that amazing . . ."

"I'm going to call Brittany now and see if she's interested in UCSB. That would be awesome!" He jumped up the stairs, two steps at a time.

He stopped and turned. "Wait. You're still adopting me, right? I mean, you don't want me to go live with my grandmother, do you?"

"Of course not!" I stopped. "I mean, I course I still want us to have the adoption, but if it's important for you to spend more time with your grandmother, we can put it off."

He stared. "But be sure to come back, because I need you." I had a little trouble getting those last words out. He nodded and went back up the stairs, one step, then back to bounding up two steps at a time.

Chapter Forty-Nine

LENNY STAYED HOME FROM SCHOOL THE DAY OF THE CEREMONY, December 22. We had breakfast together and got dressed without much fanfare. We headed out early to the special courthouse set up for adoptions.

We sat on a long bench in a very crowded waiting room waiting for our names to be called to the courtroom. We waited over an hour, with small children running around, some dressed up, some in tee-shirts, with adults of all ages waiting for the formal adoption of these hundreds of kids who were given up or surrendered by their biological parents. My heart broke just thinking about the situations they must have been in, but now they had found people who actually wanted them.

Life can be a real bitch.

I know Lenny was thinking the same thing as he watched them run around in their excitement. One little girl immediately crushed on him. She wore a tiara and kept leaning over the back of her chair, quietly mooning over him. He smiled at her and she shyly came over and crawled up into his lap, sucking her thumb.

"You look like her dad," a woman said. "Only younger." She smiled sadly at the little girl. "And he was a nice guy, just made some bad choices." The little girl rubbed her tiny finger over his forearm. "She's looking for tattoos," the woman said.

"Are you adopting her?" Lenny asked.

"Yes, we are a team, aren't we?" The woman now was kneeling beside Lenny's chair and looking into the little girl's face. They both smiled. The woman reached into her purse and pulled out her own matching tiara. She held out her arms, and the little one went to her.

"God, that's the sweetest thing I think I've ever seen," Lenny said. I couldn't speak.

They were called into the courtroom and ten minutes later they came out, both crying. "We are family," they both sang as they danced down the aisle between the long benches along the entire length of the building.

"Well, this certainly is something, isn't it?" Jen stood over us, looking awful, but her attitude was upbeat. It hurt me to see her using a cane. Bruce supported her on the other side. Lenny stood immediately and gave her his chair.

"I'm so glad you are here," I said.

She sat with a sigh. I could tell she was weak and not feeling well again. "I couldn't miss this for the world. It's a big day." She smiled at me and Lenny.

We were next. A much older judge in a wheelchair sat at the table below the judge's bench. We sat on the other side. Jen stood to the side and snapped pictures.

"Well, you're a little long in the tooth, aren't you?" The judge said, smiling. "That was a joke on me, get it?"

Lenny nodded.

"No other family?"

"No, it's just us," Lenny said. "What do we do?"

The judge tried to suppress his surprise by sliding documents over to us. We signed the necessary documents, the court reporter took notes and took a picture, we took an oath, and it was done. We walked out, down the aisle of excited people and out into the parking lot, where others had balloons and cakes on tables set up in one section of the parking lot.

Bruce and Jen grinned. Jen had tears in her eyes. "I can't believe you're a mom," she said.

"Shall we go to lunch?" I asked.

Bruce looked at Jen and turned to me. "I think maybe I better get her home, but you and Lenny go on." Jen didn't argue. It must have taken a Herculean effort to get there. For me. For us. And it made me sad. I was losing her. We went to a restaurant in silence. What should have been a happy experience had turned into a sad one. I tried to keep things upbeat, but failed.

"It's okay, she's your friend," Lenny said. He understood. "I'm a little sad, too. I just pretty much let go of my mom."

"Your mother will always be your mother. There's a bond there that no one will ever cut."

"I know, but if she gets clean and gets out, we won't be together." I loved that he could speak so openly, finally.

"You can always go visit her. You're on the list."

"I know, and I will, but . . ."

"Tell you what, if she gets out and needs a place to stay, she can stay with us. I'll turn my office into a room for her."

"You'd do that?"

"Sure. We are now sisters. I'm raising her child. But the rules would have to be very clear. One drink, one drug, one mistake, and she's gone. You can't have that around you. Agreed?"

"Agreed." We shook on it and smiled.

Who is this person I've become? Harboring a drug addict. My God. We got home in time to change clothes and grab my paint supplies before heading over to Canvas for the Tuesday night class. We rushed down to Heritage Art Park and ran up the stairs. We were late. The second we opened the door, a boom box or something blared out music.

We turned the corner into the parlor and found crepe paper, balloons, and a huge cake. "Congratulations!" they all yelled and began to hug us and shake hands. Marjorie stayed in the background smiling as she watched Suzanne, Sally, Fancy Dan, and others gather around and celebrate the ten-minute procedure we had waited over two hours for.

"Wow! What brought this on?" I asked.

"It was all Sally's idea," said Suzanne. "When she heard today was the day, she just told everyone what to do, and we did it. She made the cake!"

I stared at Sally across the room and said, "Thank you." My voice came out hoarse and crooked. My throat hurt.

"It's the least I could do for a friend."

I wanted to cry. I went over and hugged her very tightly. "Thank you, my friend," I whispered.

The world has turned upside down. I'm now hugging and making friends. Jesus.

The cake read simply "Family".

Everyone took pictures. "Oooh, Ronny will love this one," Suzanne said as she clicked and apparently sent one over to him. "Are you going to change your name to Murphy?" she asked Lenny. He stopped mid-movement. "Hadn't thought about it." He took a bite of cake, pointed his fork at Suzanne, and said, "Lenny Murphy sounds like a dork." The group laughed.

"You have a paid night off," said Adam. "Paint something." He handed Lenny a brand-new painter's kit, all his own, and a canvas.

"Cool. Thanks." Lenny sat on the stool, opened his kit, and set to work organizing things. The rest of us followed. As I painted, I thought a lot about how things had changed. I was now a mom, totally responsible for another human. Not to mention a dog who ate socks. I had friends, people who actually cared. And the beginnings of a real life.

But something was still missing.

Chapter Fifty

AT THE NEW YEAR, I HAD ANOTHER DATE. THIS ONE WAS WITH A GUY named Guy. Again, I was earlier than he, and I chose the same table that would be discreet and quiet. That was my first mistake.

"Oh, this just won't do at all," said a voice behind me. "What a shitty table." I turned to find a very large man, gut hanging over his belt, stained shirt, and two-day growth. "How could you let this happen?" he demanded, loudly.

The hostess appeared at his side. "I'm sorry, sir. If you did not make a reservation, this is the best we could do," she said, looking at me and smiling. She knew I had chosen the table and that it was a blind date. Thank God I had given her a heads up.

"Well," he sputtered, "what about all these EMPTY tables," he wove his arm out from his side and knocked over what would have been his water glass.

"I think I've made a mistake," I said as I stood and placed my napkin on the table.

"No, it wasn't you, it was them," he said, not bothering to acknowledge the glass on its side. He grasped my shoulder in a painful grip.

"Take your hand off me," I said loudly as I knocked his hand away. "It really was my mistake." I said with emphasis. "Trust me."

The hostess giggled as I walked out.

"Never again. Never, ever, ever again," I muttered as I walked quickly, my head down, trying to extricate my keys from my bag.

"Whoa, there . . ." I heard a male voice and looked up quickly enough to stop myself from ramming right into him on the narrow sidewalk. It was Judge Sullivan.

"Hello there!" I said with more zeal than I felt. "I'm hungry."

The look on his face was a mixture of amusement and concern. "Then, may I observe you are going the wrong direction?"

"You may."

We were stopped in the middle of the walkway and both burst out laughing. Well, his laugh was more of a guffaw. I turned around and followed him into the restaurant again. The hostess's eyebrows went up a solid inch when she saw I was with yet another man. "Your Honor, I have your table for you." She smiled at me and led us back to the corner table with not one, but two, windows.

I told him about the formal adoption. "That is the best news I've heard all year," and ordered two glasses of champagne. "With your permission, of course."

I accepted.

"So, may I ask why you were leaving the restaurant?"

I laughed. "Bad date—blind date gone wrong."

"Ahh . . .I haven't dipped into that pool. I cannot imagine being with someone other than Claudia, but life is somewhat lonely."

"Are you always so honest?"

"Yes." And he smiled such a bright smile that it made me happy.

"Is your date still here?" The judge looked around the restaurant and lit on the messy table that was being cleaned up.

"I left in a hurry. I cannot imagine he's gone yet. Must be in the loo," I said looking over the menu. "May I ask you a question?"

"Of course."

"Why did you recuse yourself from the family court case?"

"I didn't think it was appropriate. I was planning to ask you out; I'm terribly ethical you know," he said with a grin.

I laughed. "Tell me about Voices for Children. How does it help your work?" I did want to know, but this was a perfect way to deflect. *He was going to ask me out?*

He began to talk at length about Voices. I found him to be articulate, sympathetic, pragmatic, and well-versed in his job. He recommended several books to read as well as other resources. He was so enthusiastic about what

Voices did and said that the CASAs made his life much easier. He trusted their lengthy reports and read their reports first before the social workers' and the lawyers' reports; he said the CASA reports were concise, heartfelt, and their recommendations mostly right on.

We finished dinner and talked about local politics and books, and over coffee we compared our college experiences. Not only was he easy to talk to, he had the same reading tastes as I did, and we compared notes on our travels in Europe. He laughed easily and I found him attractive.

Was this a date?

A few weeks later, the judge had asked me out to dinner.

Another first. A real ask. I ran out to find a dress (God help me, I was becoming a girl) to wear along with pretty, not-too-high shoes. All my pantsuits were too big, and besides, I wanted something different. I put on makeup and even a pair of earrings. The firsts continued. Lenny approved.

Jim arrived with a bouquet of flowers, which made me a little giddy. I took him into the living room and pointed to the bar where I had a bottle of white wine chilling in a bucket of ice and told him to help himself. I heard ice clunking as I took the flowers into the kitchen to put them in water.

Do I arrange them and display them, or leave them in the sink? *Oh, hell, find a vase and display them.* I took my time making them perfect. When I returned with them, Lenny sat in the living room chatting with the judge. Apparently, he had told Lenny that he was the judge in his case and he was familiar with his bio mom.

"What's she like, in court, I mean?" Lenny said.

He took a deep breath, seemed to ponder a bit, then said, "Quiet. I think she knows she's overpowered."

"By the courts?"

He gave a slight smile. "No, son, by the drugs. It can be so controlling, you really have no power over it, especially if you've been at it, and I'm sorry to say this, as long as your mother has."

Lenny nodded, head down. "I know, but do you think there is any hope?"

"There's always hope, Lenny." He turned his head sideways a bit, which was sort of cute. "But I found the key is someone having trust in them. If they are left alone, they will just keep doing it. A drug addict needs someone to believe in them because I'm convinced they sure don't believe in themselves."

Lenny's eyes filled. Mine did, too. I stood in the space between the hallway and the living room, listening. As I entered and put the flowers on the coffee table, Lenny stood up and said, "It was nice to meet you. Have a nice dinner." He nodded to me and left.

"Nice kid," Jim said. "You're doing a great job."

"He came that way. He's less angry than he used to be, but I don't blame him for getting upset. I was also a child of a drug addict, but I didn't go into the system and wasn't shoved around, and I'm still plenty pissed off." I had not meant to give him my history on the first date, but it certainly was appropriate at that moment.

I avoided the scotch and poured a small glass of white wine, knowing my childhood was a trigger. I was not an alcoholic, but I knew that I did use it to squelch pain, and I didn't want to go there anymore. For some reason, I thought wine the lesser of two evils. We chatted about the Padres and how lousy they were doing, and the ideas for a new basketball team, all minor stuff, and finally left for the restaurant.

I was glad to be in my new duds—it was a fancy place, and I fit in perfectly. I allowed myself a real drink at the bar, then enjoyed talking during dinner. I learned that his daughter was also a drug addict and had given him parental rights to raise her daughter, Annie, who sounded like a nice young lady. His daughter, whose name was Lisa, was nowhere near ready to give up her party life and was just as happy to give up her daughter.

"Annie saved me after my wife died. Without having this person to be responsible for, I would have quit my job and become a beach bum," he said.

"I doubt that.".

He shook his head. "I was a mess. I think I really would have dropped out. She kept me sane. She loved her grandmother, so we cried together and shared our grief. We are very close."

"She's a lucky girl."

"No, I'm the lucky one. Really." We smiled at each other, realizing that some things work out, much as we may hate the reasons why. He took me home, I thanked him for a lovely dinner and the flowers, he kissed me on the cheek, and ambled on down the walkway, hands in pockets.

My home phone was ringing as I opened the door, and I ran to answer it.

"Renee? It's Bruce." His tone was terse and businesslike.

"Hi, Bruce . . ." I knew what he was going to say next was not going to be easy to hear.

"Hospice is here now. There is a hospital bed and round-the-clock pain management care." His voice cracked.

"Oh, Bruce. Should I come over?"

"Not tonight. It's still a bit of a circus, talking about medications and care. She's pretty much out of it most of the time, but I wanted you to know they are taking over now."

That means the end is near. Oh God.

I sat on my couch in my new dress and bawled my eyes out. I reached for a glass on the bar, stopped, then ran into my room, got out of my dress and into my running gear, and took off at eleven o'clock at night for a run, tears streaming down my face the entire time. I stopped and puked up a fabulous dinner into a shrub.

What am I going to do without her?

Chapter Fifty-One

CANVAS WAS DOING WELL; IN FACT, THE WHOLE ART PARK WAS DOING well. Stitches, Canvas, and Pages were open and now others were in development. Traffic was coming through consistently; we were getting a lot of publicity and good press. There was always something going on, parties were held here, and the synagogue, the first in San Diego, was now being used for services and celebrations. Wedding receptions were held every weekend on the large grassy area, and non-profits used it for free for gatherings and fundraisers.

I should have been ecstatic, but Jen's health stopped all enthusiasm. It colored everything, but I forced myself to go forward. The art park was exactly what I had envisioned, but I needed more. Now that Lenny was looking forward, it was time for me to do the same. Senator? No. That door was closed. Painting? No. I'm not that talented; it's fun, but not something I'm passionate about the way Adam is. Should I serve on boards again and get involved in community projects? Maybe, but I've done that. A job? God help me. I can't even think about any of that while Jen is so sick. I just can't. Left foot, right foot, left foot, right foot . . .

Lenny will be gone in less than two years; in fact he's already spending a lot of time away in Santa Barbara and with friends, spreading his wings, making them stronger. It's beginning—his independence. Shouldn't have given him that car. I laughed at myself as I realized how petty I was being and reached for the phone to laugh with Jen about it, then pulled back. I can't. She's probably resting.

What would Iris advise? *Iris, help me.*

Canvas was open and bustling, so I went in to pay more bills and check up on how we were doing, which was a chore for me. I'm just not admin material, but I did my best. We were slowly coming to being in the black, but far from it. Adam slid quietly into the office and sat in the visitor's chair.

"How are we doing, fair lady?"

"It looks like we are doing well. We have a way to go before my investment comes back, but we have not lost any money on classes. I haven't seen any sales of paintings, though. Are we doing enough to market them?"

"I have an idea I'm working on—lending some pieces to galleries in town. I'm curious to see if people are interested. I've invited some gallery owners to an evening soiree to see the talent."

"You have?" I was surprised to not be consulted.

He nodded. "It seemed a good idea at the time—why, do you disagree?"

"Not at all . . ."

"It was impertinent of me, I admit, but you seemed otherwise occupied and I decided to just, as they say, go for it."

I fiddled with my phone, turning it over and over, grappling with my feelings about this new development. Why wouldn't he take control? He was the manager. That was our deal. I felt upstaged; I was the owner, after all. But then I quickly realized I didn't much care . . . he was the expert and was much more involved than I.

"Of course," I finally said. "It's a great idea. When?" We chatted about the event and other business items until Adam left to go help a patron. Glued to the chair, I mentally walked through the shop/studio and felt no kinship, no pride, no ownership. I vowed to get more involved.

Once Lenny was gone, it would be everything I had. That and a goofy dog who ate socks.

I had received an invitation for the annual Gala for Voices for Children. The cost was exorbitant, but they needed funding and I wanted to support them. CASA Juan was a godsend, but they had programs that cost money. An engraved invitation had gone out to all societal, political, philanthropical, non-profit and fundraising contact lists across the land. It was to be a formal event held at the Hotel Del, a famous, elegant historical estate across the bay. Tickets were expensive for the VIP section, which included dinner and dancing following a cocktail hour and silent auction.

Fortunately, since Suzanne was on the board, she arranged for Heritage Art Park owners to be granted one ticket, and of course the mayor was comped. I was hesitant to ask someone to go with me, as that meant they'd have to fork over a large amount of money just to go, which felt . . . awkward. I had a vision of folded bills on the nightstand. Fifteen hundred dollars for the honor of spending the evening with me. Bah. I wasn't sure Ron would bring a date either for the same reason.

I turned into a teenage girl and shopped forever for the perfect dress, matching shoes and bag (which didn't make me nauseous, by the way). When I had the total look put together, I took my purchases over to Jen's for approval. She nodded and pointed to her closet.

"What?"

"Jewelry case." I found it and brought it to her. She extricated a strand of pearls studded with sapphires, the exact same shade of the dress, and threw it on top of the rich fabric. "Take them."

"No. I can't." My heart dropped. She meant to give them to me permanently, and I just couldn't deal. Tears sprung to my eyes.

"Take them," she said in a stronger voice. "I've worn them once and probably never will again. They suit you. Simple. Elegant." She stopped and closed her eyes, her face grim.

"Okay, that's enough," said Bruce from the doorway. "She's so weak, this is really tough on her." I began to walk toward Bruce. Tough on *her*???

"Bullshit." Jen's voice came from the bed. "Renee? Remember who you are. Strong. Independent. Fierce. Don't give in to anyone. Your instincts about people are right on. Trust them."

"I love you, Gigi." I forced the words through my thick throat.

"Love you too."

I turned to find Bruce conferring with the hospice nurse, nodding as she talked and held his hand. Bruce was crying quietly. "It won't be long now," the nurse said.

"Is she in any pain?" I asked her.

"No." She shook her head. "Her pain is being managed well, but it makes her weak and very sleepy. She'll slip into a coma and drop off quietly." Her compassion came through loud and clear, and her experience and strength made me feel as though this was the right path for Jen.

Jesus God. This is decimating. I'm losing her.

Chapter Fifty-Two

*J*EN HAD GIVEN TRICIA HER TICKET FOR THE VOICES FOR CHILDREN GALA, so Tricia and I decided to go together. Neither one of us was in the mood, but felt we had to go; it was something to do, and Jen would have a conniption fit if she knew we stayed home to worry about her. This was an event Jen would have gone to easily; this was her thing, and I missed her terribly.

Adam said he would be working at the studio and offered to take Lenny in until we returned. Lenny was happy to work with Adam and I was a bit relieved I didn't have to worry about him and Brittany being alone in the house. Totally a mom thing.

Tricia and I both looked fabulous, if I do say so myself. Tricia doesn't drink, so she offered to drive, and we arrived in style and valeted her car. We slowly ascended the steps, being careful of the long dresses and high heels, adjusted ourselves, and entered the reception room for the cocktail hour and silent auction.

What a sight. Brilliant, glistening chandeliers hung from the sixteen-foot ceilings. Greenery still framed the tops of the windows, and red poinsettias stood in groups in every corner. White nasturtiums scented the room from discreet vases on the tables, along with candlelight and gleaming stemware. But the big Christmas tree was the main attraction still displayed in the beautiful old lobby. This year it was laden with Victorian teddy bears. It would be gone tomorrow.

The silent auction contained a few pieces of art, jewelry, and knick-knacks strewn around the room—some pieces from Canvas, mostly donated by the artists who worked at the shop, but I recognized Lenny's piece that he had so ceremoniously crumpled up and dropped on the floor so long ago. Adam had rescued it, Gessoed it onto a canvas, framed it, and displayed it. People remarked how unusual and electrifying it was. I clicked a few shots on my phone and said to the woman admiring it, "My son did that." For the first time in my life, I had to turn away so no one would see the tears that came so quickly, even a stranger.

One of the most talked-about pieces was a portrait of Iris signed by Adam Pechek. Soft instrumental music came from another room, soft jazz that elevated my mood while I perused all the silent auction items.

Tricia disappeared and I was left alone in all my finery, clutching a small bag; my elbows held my matching wrap around my back. I touched the pearls at my neck and said a silent thank you to Jen.

"My God, Renee, is that you?" Ron's voice came from behind me.

You're on, kid.

"Ron. Hello." I didn't quite know what to say. "Where's Suzanne?" I said, looking around him.

"Suzanne? Why?" He actually looked mystified. Good.

"Oh, well I just assumed . . ."

"Can I get you a drink?"

"Yes, please. Wine would be lovely."

He cocked his eyebrow. "Lovely?"

"Yes. Lovely."

"Renee . . ."

"White wine, to be exact."

"O . . . kay." He went off.

One point for me. I used a word I had not used in his presence. Channeling Iris—or Jen. I drifted into the crowd and met with people I knew, most of whom did a double take. I suppose I did look different—thirty pounds lighter, in a dress, for God's sake, and heels, wearing makeup and real jewelry. A costume. As I chatted with people I knew, someone appeared at my side. Assuming it was Ron, I turned to get my drink and discovered it was Judge Jim.

"Renee! How nice to see you tonight. I would have picked you up if I knew you were coming . . ." Just then Ron showed up with my drink, and the judge disappeared with an "Excuse me."

"Who was that?" Ron asked.

"A family court judge, Jim Sullivan. Nice guy. Thank you," I said as I took my glass. "Are you staying for the dinner?"

"No, I have another event." He smiled. "But I'm here to support Voices for Children and am bidding on several items."

"Oh? Anything interesting?"

"Yes, a weekend in Borrego Springs, complete with massage for two," he said, leering.

"I'm sure Suzanne will enjoy that very much."

"Suzanne? Why do you keep referring to her?"

I took a sip. "Aren't you seeing her?"

"Suzanne?" He looked shocked. "No."

My blood stopped running through my veins for a nanosecond. "Oh, really."

"Really. What gave you that impression?"

"Every time I see you, she's hanging all over you, and she certainly has alluded to a relationship with you."

He looked over my shoulder and I could swear his jaw clenched for a bit. "The only time I've ever seen her is the few times you've seen us together, and that was months ago."

"Could have fooled me." I turned to walk away, then said, "She said you had breakfast together?" I couldn't stop myself. I had to let him know I knew the truth.

"Breakfast?"

"Yes, she said that at breakfast one morning you told her you were pleased to hear I had signed a lease to open the store."

He again looked over my shoulder, apparently going through his memory banks, then smiled. "Breakfast. Rotary Club. Remember? Our club meets for breakfast? You were once a member, Suzanne is a member, I am a member . . . did you forget?"

I felt like an idiot. "Well, she certainly wanted it to be known you were having a thing." I sipped.

"Is that what this has been about, the cold shoulder?"

"What cold shoulder?" I waited a beat. "Maybe. I thought we had something, figured I was wrong, so I let it go. We're friends."

"Could have fooled me," he threw back at me with a laugh.

"So, you're not seeing anyone?" I asked coquettishly. Good God.

"No. Haven't had a chance. Too busy. You know how it is." He shrugged and looked at his watch. "Look, I have to go, but can I call you? Friend?" He smiled.

"Of course." He kissed my hand, turned, and left. Score one for me.

Dinner was in the ballroom, elegantly lit up with festive decorations. The centerpieces were pieces of art; sumptuous floral arrangements that rose high enough to allow diners to see each other across the tables but still enjoy them. Tricia and I wandered through the silent auction items, chatted with people, and bid on some items. Jade was there, courtesy of Pages, wearing a long gown that was the perfect color for her, but the kicker was she wore a diamond tiara in honor of Iris. Because Iris had the reputation of telling tall tales, Jade was kidded quite a lot with questions like, "Is that the tiara Iris wore to Buckingham Palace or to JFK's inauguration ball?" with accompanying winks. Uncharacteristically, she played it up and vamped herself silly. Her date, Robert Graham, kept her close and I guessed they were now an item. Good for her. Iris would approve. A bit later, I chatted with her and Robert about the tiara. I couldn't help it. Jade smiled. "You know those stories Iris told that we never believed? Like she was at Queen Elizabeth's coronation and all those other stories?"

"Yes . . ."

"They were true. I found a treasure trove of pictures and documents. All true."

I put my hand on her shoulder. "You know what? That doesn't surprise me one bit. God, I miss her."

"Me too, Ms. Murphy."

"No. It's about time you called me Renee, don't you think?"

Robert kissed me on the cheek and guided Jade toward another, younger group. Clearly, they were there for Robert to cover the social column, but Jade looked very much at home among the hoi polloi. Iris had trained her well. How things change.

Tricia and I sat at our assigned table and waited for a missing couple to show up. I sipped my wine slowly and wondered how Jen was doing.

Stop it. Enjoy yourself.

Judge Jim stopped by, all decked out in a dinner jacket with black onyx studs, a red cummerbund, and patent leather shoes. Quite spiffy. Tricia excused herself, saying she was going for a drink, and disappeared.

"Did the mayor leave?" Jim asked.

"Yes, he had a date," I said. I knew it wasn't true but wanted the judge to know we were definitely not together. His eyebrows shot up and he smiled. "I really enjoyed our dinner. May I call you again?"

"I'd like that."

He ambled away and met up with what I assumed were friends at another table, mostly males, some I recognized. Tricia ambled up to me. "What's that grin for?"

"Me? Am I grinning?" She cocked her head at me.

"Sorry, I'm just sort of feeling . . .I don't know . . . happy."

"Is that unusual for you?"

"Yes, as a matter of fact. I've been looking for a man for years but have been occupied with other things. Turns out now I may have two men interested, and they are both very attractive, but maybe I don't need a man. Maybe all I need is Lenny and some nice dates."

"You need more than that, Renee," she said, smiling, "but I get what you are saying." Her eyes looked over my shoulder and opened wide; her face fell into a grin of her own. "Well, look who's here."

I turned to see Adam and Lenny entering the room, both in dinner jackets, hair washed and combed, looking awkward but pleased. "It appears we have dates."

Adam sat next to Tricia and Lenny slid next to me. "We thought we'd surprise you tonight. You both have been so supportive and helpful, we wanted to show you how appreciative we are of everything you've done for us, right mate?"

Lenny smile and nodded, then said, "For sure . . . wow, you look, like, really nice."

"Why, thank you, kind sir," I said.

I saw Jim Sullivan wave to Lenny; he waved back and grinned. "Nice guy," he said, and elbowed me with another grin. I blushed like a bride.

I changed the subject: "Did you see your picture at the auction table?"

"No. What picture?"

Adam cleared his throat. "Sorry, lad, I didn't tell you, but I took one of your more interesting paintings and donated it to the cause."

Lenny's pupils came to a pinpoint. "Which. One."

The rage coming on was familiar. "Let's go see it. I saw a few people looking at it earlier." I rose, and Lenny followed. He stood in front of the canvas and stared. "I did that?"

I laughed. "You sure did, and look, high bid is five hundred dollars!"

He shook his head. "I thought it was shit. Turns out not everything is." His smile returned. I took his elbow and we went back to the table. Lenny nodded to Adam in acknowledgement and Adam went back to nuzzling Tricia from two feet away.

We had our dinner and the dancing began. Lenny and I both stayed put, but Adam and Tricia made a fine couple on the dance floor, as did many others. A gentleman came to the table, sat down next to me, and introduced himself as Steven Kidd. He addressed me as "Your Honor."

"I understand you have taken a foster child and are using our services."

"Services?"

"Oh, I apologize. I am the Chairman of Voices for Children."

"Oh, yes, your organization is fantastic. May I introduce my son, Lenny Rudolph?" Lenny stretched his arm out and shook hands.

"My CASA Juan is great; I love having him come to my wrestling matches and we go and hang out, even though he doesn't have to anymore. He's really nice."

"I'm glad to hear it. We have some fabulous people working and volunteering for us." He turned to me. "You might consider joining us as well, if you have the time."

Have the time? "You mean as a CASA? I'm not sure that's my specialty, but if you need some administrative work done, I can surely volunteer my time in any way you need. It's the least I can do."

"I'll remember that," he said, and smiled. "You'll be hearing from me."

"It was nice to meet you," Lenny said. He waved at us and walked away.

Chapter Fifty-Three

ONE MORNING I HEADED INTO CANVAS BEFORE GOING TO A LUNCHEON to review invoices and check up on the shop. It was very quiet, almost ghostly, and I found Adam in the desk chair looking pensive.

"Penny for your thoughts . . ." I said.

"Sorry?"

"An American expression. What's on your mind?" I plopped down in the extra chair and put my coffee thermos on the desk.

"Just reviewing choices I've made," he said quietly. I waited.

"Do you regret any of your choices?"

He turned to stare at me, those blue eyes alive and sort of questioning. "I put people in danger, most especially my wife, and I do regret that, but as for the final outcome?" He nodded. "It was worth it." He continued to stare at me. I took it as permission to ask questions.

"Do you want to talk about it?"

"Not particularly. I know Tricia gave you the basics, but I'd like you to know that what I did was foolhardy. I put my wife in jeopardy and possibly this shop." My nerves tingled. "But," he said with a bright smile, "all is well now. There is no danger. I did what I felt I had to do, and it turned out well, but I should not have." I waited. "I was asked to do something to close the book. It took me some time to get where I needed to be to get the . . . outcome . . . we wanted. I was successful, but it was stressful for not only me but my wife, and I'm guessing, you." I nodded. He stood. "I did what I had to do to get it right." He sighed. "My last one. Now I can put it behind me."

I nodded, waiting for more. He surprised me. "Now that I can come out from under, how do you feel about selling Canvas to me?" His hiding during

275

the soft opening made sense now. He didn't want to be recognized. All this cloak and dagger stuff was making me tired.

"I don't know, Adam. I hadn't thought of it. How about a partnership?"

He nodded. "To be discussed . . ." I felt like I was finally, finally, getting to know him. Tricia was a lucky girl.

That evening, Sally and I had worked side by side at our easels talking about Elena, drugs, and addiction. Sally was quiet, listening to me when I went into my rant about how drug addicts are worthless and should all be locked up.

"Remember, sometimes they may not have a choice."

"That's bullshit," I whispered. "You always have a choice." Then I realized I was talking to an alcoholic and shut up. I thought it was different.

She shook her head. "Unless you've been there, you'll never understand."

"I guess not." We were past our hostilities, on the downside of that mountain, so I knew she didn't mean it unkindly, but it hurt a bit. Drug addicts lie, cheat, and steal. That's the truth of it, and I wasn't going to be seeing it any other way.

"Want to grab a bite?" Sally asked when we were packing up. We had not done anything since our reconciliation and I hated to turn her down, as sick as I was with worry about Jen.

I hesitated, and she jumped in. "Meet you across the street." And walked out. Guess no is out of the question. I walked in to the restaurant after stowing stuff in Red Rosie and found both Sally and Dapper Dan at a table. "This is a nice surprise," I said. They both smiled up at me.

Uh-oh.

Dan and Sally had iced tea in front of them, and much as I wanted a margarita, I ordered the same. We chatted a bit and I learned Dan was a freelance musician, writing and producing songs and jingles, whatever he could get.

"How did you get into that business? Did you play in an orchestra? Where you classically trained?"

He smirked. "Ever hear of Grunge Folly?"

"Of course, they had several number one hits in the nineties. Everyone knows them, even me." He stared at me and waited for something. Recognition? I turned to Sally, who smiled.

"Look harder."

"What am I missing?" I finally blurted. I hate these games. Dan pulled out his wallet and unfolded a piece of paper that apparently had seen much use. "I keep this for posterity." He handed it to me.

It was a mugshot of a man with long, stringy hair, thick aviator glasses, a scraggly beard, and purple bags under his glassy eyes. "Is this you?" He nodded. I looked again. "You're Danny Boy—the bass player." My astonishment showed in my high voice.

"I was."

I looked at every inch of his clean, shaved, healthy face, his dark brown eyes, and his expensive haircut, the perfect clothes and the calm demeanor. This was no heavy metal musician.

His music was not my cup of tea, but the group had behaved so badly everyone heard about them and their antics. Hotel rooms destroyed, public urination, and badmouthing politicians and other celebrities were the norm. They got their PR and sold plenty of music because of it.

"What happened?" I asked quietly. There had to be a story here.

He shrugged. "What usually happens when you are twenty years old, have too much money, too much fame, and too much time—drugs. They were everywhere, and free."

My scalp burned. A druggie. Wait. *Dan?*

"What happened?" I asked again, looking for the end story. I didn't want to hear the horror stories I knew he had. Not interested; I wanted this discussion over quickly and get home to check on Jen. But I had to hear it.

"We got busted with a huge amount of drugs—everything, and a lot of it. People kept giving it to us, our managers and the fans, and it was there for the taking. So, so much . . ." he wandered off, then came back with, "Cocaine was my drug of choice."

"Cocaine? Wow . . . isn't that dangerous?"

"Sure it is, but if you want it badly enough . . ."

I looked over at Sally. "Is this because of our conversation a little while ago?"

She nodded. "You need to understand the reality, the evil, of addiction. It's the same whether it's alcohol, nicotine, or hard drugs . . . even caffeine is an addiction."

"Wait. Caffeine?" They nodded.

"The withdrawal isn't as severe, but if you are a daily coffee drinker and go without it for one day, you get a hell of a headache, right? That's withdrawal," Dan said. "The human body can repair quite a lot of damage, but not everything . . ."

"Okay, I'll bite. Talk." I knew I wasn't going to get out of this, so I decided to listen. I wanted to order a margarita more than ever but decided it would be inappropriate. LOL.

"I started with cocaine. At the risk of making it sound appealing, it is pretty awesome. You feel like you can do anything, and all your issues go away. You can solve problems easily while on it, and it's a euphoria you want over and over. Your sober life is boring: pale, not interesting, but on cocaine anything is possible. Write songs, sing, dance, play forever . . . but then you crash."

He stopped and gulped down more tea. "Then I got into heroin, which put me out, and I mean out, of this world. I shot up once a day, then twice, then took whatever anyone gave me. My life spiraled out of control."

"Obviously you hit rock bottom. When did that happen?"

His eyes filled. "When I demanded my parents sell their house and give me the money. I believe my exact words were, 'You're going to die anyway, you might as well give it to me now.'" He lowered his gaze to the ground, his fingers intertwined between his knees. "They called the police to do a 5150 on me—that's when they call in a psychiatrist and put a seventy-two-hour hold on you in a psych ward. They visited me just before I was let go. I was desperate for a fix, I was in withdrawal and the pain was coming, I swore my stomach and head were going to burst out of my body like in that movie Alien."

I kept staring at the top of his head, then he raised his chin and met my eyes. "They told me that I was going to Betty Ford directly from the psych ward; they had paid for it and I was expected. He took a gulp. "I told them to go to hell. I didn't need help. My father gave me a copy of a letter to his lawyer instructing him to leave all his earthly goods and money to the Rotary Club and that I was not to receive a dime from his or Mother's estate. I was cut off permanently. They would never see me again. They turned and walked out, and I was alone for the first time in my life. Totally alone. The band had broken up, all my money was gone, I didn't even have a place to stay. I finally realized no one could fix this but me. No one was going to bail me out."

"What did you do?"

"I got my ass to Betty Ford and followed through. When I got out, the cops were waiting to go to court on the possession charges. My *volunteer* rehab at Betty Ford played in my favor and my appearance helped. I spent ninety days in prison, and when I came out my parents were there. They still have me tested every week," he laughed. "And I don't blame them. I lied to them constantly, took advantage, stole things from them, and forgot to respect them. It was all about me and how I could get more more more."

"You couldn't stop."

"No. It had such power over me. Still does. But I won't go through that again. I won't do that to my parents or anyone I love in my life, and I do finally have a life."

"Why are you telling me this?"

"Because people need to understand that even though we have choices, and we choose to take that first hit, that first shot, that first high, some of us lose that choice. We have to chase it down and destroy everything in our way to get it, no matter what. We destroy the people we love and don't even acknowledge it. We know we're shits intellectually, but the means justifies the end while you are possessed."

"So . . . my mother abandoned me when I was nine; she was a drug addict. Are you telling me that people leave their children in pursuit of this? Their *children?*"

Sally looked over at me. "Why else would any woman leave her child? Can you give me one good reason why any woman would leave her child alone, unprotected, and homeless? Can you see how powerful this is?"

"I thought she was just tired of me; she didn't want to be a mom anymore."

Sally shook her head. "You've never had a child so you don't know, but that is so contrary to any woman who has ever given birth to a child. There is nothing you won't do to protect your child—nothing—unless you are, as Dan says, 'possessed' by something." She turned her head to me and said, "Would you leave Lenny for any reason?" She knew what the answer was.

"Of course not! This is what I don't understand. How can you do that?"

"Where is your mom now?" Dan asked.

"Funny you should ask. I found her recently and received a letter from her saying she had started over, has been sober for many years, but doesn't want to see me."

"She's going to have to come to you at some point and apologize. It's part of the program of sobriety. I bet you will hear from her, asking for forgiveness. Maybe now, with this understanding, you can give it." Dan leaned back in his chair. "I hope that happens."

For one brief, shining moment, I hoped, so, too.

Chapter Fifty-Four

I KNEW IT WAS COMING, BUT WHEN JEN DIED, I STOPPED THE WORLD FOR a bit.

Bruce came to the house and I knew the second I opened the door. He was quiet, pale, and exhausted. He stared at me from the doorway and I opened the door further to let him in. I listened to the clock tick and wondered how he was going to cope.

"Talk to me," I finally said. My eyes stung and my throat hurt and my fingers itched.

He leaned back. "She just stopped breathing. It was peaceful." I nodded. "It had to be brutal, but she bore it." He downed his drink. "She's being cremated tomorrow; everything is set. No service." Jen had walked away from the Catholic church during adolescence when she felt God deserted her.

"And Maggie?"

"Tricia is handling Maggie. I don't envy her." He tried to laugh, but it came out a sob. He collected himself and we sat a bit more.

"What are you going to do now? Sandpaper?" Bruce had been half-heartedly working on getting a shop ready at the Art Center where he would make wooden rockers and toys.

He shook his head. "No. I just can't imagine it right now. My son says he will take the shop and get it going. Maybe I'll join him later, maybe I won't. I don't know." He sounded defeated. I didn't know what to say, so I shut up.

Lenny came home from school, took one look at the two of us, nodded, and went up to his room quietly.

Jen would not have wanted a huge deal like Iris's funeral, so she had made arrangements herself to keep it a quiet affair. I knew that Telophase was putting her ashes out into the bay in the morning, so I went to Mission

Bay and watched through my binoculars at the boat as they respectfully laid what I knew were biodegradable envelopes and flowers into the bay. I didn't know which one was Jen, but I cried as she went into the air and the water, back to the earth.

When I got home, I went to fix a cup of coffee and found a little box inside my coffee cup. Inside was an angel pin, her belly a pearl, holding a red heart in her tiny hands.

Chapter Fifty-Five

AT FOUR O'CLOCK ON A FRIDAY AFTERNOON, LENNY AND I WALKED into the conference room at Voices for Children. Lenny sat in one of the chairs on the side of the room and I stood as I was introduced as the new CEO. The angel pin sat on my shoulder. I had named her Jen, but only to myself, as I wasn't sure men in white coats wouldn't come and find me if I made that public.

It had been an easy process compared to the rough-and-tumble political fights I had endured for years. A few interviews, a few lunches, a few phone calls, and I was made, as they say, an offer I could not refuse. Lenny was ecstatic with unrealistic expectations about how much I could do for the kids in the system; he was my grounding wire for everything I was going to do. It's why I brought him with me.

Jim had taken me to dinner the night before and I was flying high because I had received so much information from the legal perspective along with some great ideas, not to mention a chaste kiss and quite a few laughs.

A dozen department heads sat around the conference room, some smiling, some not. I knew they had respected and admired the person I was replacing, and I had some hard work ahead of me to get them on the team, but I had been given my marching orders by the board. We were going to get creative, make some impact, and hopefully have some fun. I had already had a preliminary conversation with Ron about his homeless taskforce; maybe there was a way to tie the two together; a productive partnership for the good of the kids.

I sat in the chair at the head of the table and told them the story of my life: my mother, Jen and her family, her death, and meeting Lenny. I was honest about my reluctance at first, and his, but how we made it work.

I asked him to speak a bit about his experience. He spoke strongly, loudly, and with confidence (a driver's license turns one into an adult overnight, it seems). As he spoke, I realized how much I truly loved him and wanted everything for him. I realized there was nothing I wouldn't do for him and wondered how close that feeling came to the biological pull of a birth mother. I had never felt anything stronger and I held onto it, realizing I had found what I had been looking for all these years. I finally understood the phrase "take a bullet for him."

When he stopped talking, I couldn't help but grin. "Isn't he amazing?" I said to no one in particular. One person clapped, then another, then they were all clapping and smiling. We had won them over.

This was going to be good.

Acknowledgments

I'd like to take this opportunity to acknowledge every social worker, administrator, court reporter, attorney, and judge working long hours with very little appreciation to help these little people who have done nothing wrong but are moved around from foster parent to foster parent waiting to be adopted. You are angels on this earth.

There are 60,000 children in the foster care system in the state of California today. As part of the "Katie A" agreement that resulted from a lawsuit of a death of a child in the system, counties across the state of California must be in compliance with an optimal caseload average of 14 children per social worker, yet they are assigned anywhere from 24–50. They cannot comply with this regulation or children are ignored. Mental health issues are rising with the pressure put on the system.

There simply are not enough foster parents, social workers, or volunteers. I find this deeply depressing.

Author's Note

Voices for Children is an outstanding organization that helps the overworked and underpaid social workers in Health and Human Services to do their jobs by providing volunteers to work with the children who have been removed from the home.

Anyone can become a CASA (Court Appointed Special Advocate) for these children by looking into Voices for Children in your area and signing up. It takes some intensive training, then they match you with a child in the system who can use an anchor in their lives.

I have been involved in four cases involving seven children, and each of them have been very different and very rewarding. The courtroom experience in this book is very much like all of my cases (except for the interested judge!), and cases move very quickly. You can have an impact.

The scene with the young girl in the tiara came directly from my own experience sitting on a bench waiting to be called in to adoptive court.

I highly recommend this for anyone who wants to add value to a child's life who otherwise would not have anyone in their corner. It's an experience you won't soon forget, and very much needed.

Please research your local Voices For Children organization and find out how you can be part of the solution.

About the Author

Kathy Weyer

Kathy Weyer is an author, artist, and advocate. After retiring as a human resources professional in corporate America, she and her husband moved from San Diego to Palm Springs.

She devotes her time to literary advocacy with Palm Springs Library and the Palm Springs Writers Guild, along with other organizations that seek to help the vulnerable. She is past president of the Rotary club, a member of the Watercolor Society, and helps authors by offering her services as the Manuscript Muse.

She lives with her husband of 41 years and their rescued pets, and revels in the views of the San Jacinto and the Santa Rosa Mountains in the desert air.

She is the author of *Stitches*, the first book in the Heritage Art Park series, *Canvas*, the second, and the forthcoming *Pages*.

You can find her at www.kathyweyer.com.

Made in the USA
Middletown, DE
18 July 2021

44101409R00175